The Road
to Golden Days

The Road to Golden Days

***

by Melanie Lageschulte

The Road to Golden Days
© 2023
by Melanie Lageschulte
Fremont Creek Press

Kindle: 978-1-952066-27-6
Paperback: 978-1-952066-28-3
Hardcover: 978-1-952066-29-0
Large print paperback: 978-1-952066-30-6

Cover photo: MarkGomez/iStock.com
Author photo: © Bob Nandell

✻ 1 ✻

A smile spread across Kate Duncan's face as she admired the artfully arranged pumpkins at the Prosper farmers market.

"Now, this is why I came home," she told her friends. "Look at this! Fall in the country, in all its glory."

Orange orbs were stacked in careful pyramids on both sides of a nearby vendor's table, and more stood at attention in neat rows across the front. Clusters of smaller pumpkins perfect for baking beckoned from baskets on one end of the display. Specialty varieties, in shades of cream and green and hints of pale yellow, showed off their stripes and bumps from a charming little wagon parked off to the side.

The market's seasonal sights mirrored the charm of Prosper's four-block Main Street on this final Thursday afternoon in September. Pots bursting with hardy mums marked most of the buildings' entrances, and the trees in the city park had started to swap their summer-green shades for scarves of red and gold.

The sun was warm and the skies were bright, but a cool breeze carried a hint of what was to come.

"You're right, you can't miss the change of seasons around here," Karen Porter said around a bite of caramel apple. "This is my favorite time of year, especially since I spend so much time driving the back roads."

Karen was a veterinarian at Prosper's clinic, and she spent more time out of the office than in it. But Kate, a mail carrier in the neighboring town of Eagle River, suspected she might have Karen beat in the number of miles clocked every work day.

At least, when she drove a rural route. As the newest member of the team, Kate was assigned to whichever beat was vacant on any given day. She had returned to her hometown in the spring, after more than a decade away in Madison and Chicago, and her flexible work schedule had made it a little easier to get reacquainted with the area and its residents.

Melinda Foster stifled a yawn. "I love fall, too. But it's not all pretty mums and pumpkin pie and new sweaters."

Kate smirked. "It's not?"

Melinda had just wrapped up a crazy day at Prosper Hardware, her family's business, and was so tired she'd tried to beg off from the trio's plans to take in the farmers market. Kate and Karen had insisted a ramble among the vendors would clear Melinda's mind before she headed home, but her outlook was still a little dim.

"Some fall things aren't so great." Melinda wrinkled her nose. "Like the dust, for example. It's always worse this time of year. It's on everyone's cars, and their shoes. Aunt Miriam's fed up with trying to keep the floors swept at the store."

"She should give that up until it snows," Karen suggested. "Or at least, until harvest is over. Sounds like some of the farmers will be in the fields starting next week."

"They'll have to run all day and most of the night to get done." Kate stifled a yawn; she'd had a long day, too. "It's going to be crazy around here for a good month or so. Dad's just hoping the weather holds."

Karen's eyes lit up with interest. "Are you getting in the driver's seat this time around?"

"Oh, not a chance." Kate snorted and adjusted her strawberry-blonde ponytail against the breeze. Why hadn't she grabbed a hat? The sun was a little too warm on her scalp. "Traffic in Chicago is a nightmare, but that doesn't mean I'm comfortable driving a combine. I'll be the taxi, instead. Rides to the fields, ferrying food, that sort of thing."

Kate had no plans to tackle harvest at full throttle, but she couldn't wait to deck out her little acreage for the season. She'd moved into her brick farmhouse a few weeks ago, and its expansive front porch begged for pumpkins in varying shades. Maybe a few corn stalks tied to the outer columns. So far, the entrance was only flanked with flowers. And those weren't faring so well.

"I wish my mums were doing better." Kate frowned. "I put those pots out on the steps, you know. But the barn cats think they're supposed to dig in them. I must have chased Scout away twice last night alone."

"He's not taking orders from you, that's for sure," Melinda said.

"What cat ever does?" Karen tossed her apple's stick in the nearby trash bin. "At least, not when they're in their home environment. Your little farm is his turf, so those flowers belong to him."

"What does Charlie think?" Melinda wanted to know.

Kate laughed. "He's a city cat at heart. He's usually content to lounge near a window and watch the world go by. That includes the three kitties that have the rest of the place to themselves. All in all, though, their limited introductions have gone well. We've had a little sniffing and hissing from both sides of a window screen, but that's about it."

Karen gave one of the larger pumpkins an admiring pat. "I could see a generous stack of these on each side of your front steps. Maybe another arrangement right where the sidewalk makes that bend on the front corner of the house. It'd be visible all the way up the driveway."

Despite Karen's great ideas, Kate's enthusiasm was quickly deflated. "I can't believe it," she whispered to her friends. "Did you see the sign? It's taped down on the table. No wonder they don't have it where you can see it easily. They want you to be so in love with their loot that you can't say no."

Karen leaned over and gasped.

Melinda's jaw dropped. "You're not in Chicago, anymore." The woman running the booth was deep in conversation at the other end of the display, but Melinda still lowered her voice. "That's what I would have paid at a market in the Twin Cities, when I was up there. Surely someone else has ..."

The ladies looked around. Kate shook her head. "This is the only one? Are you kidding me? We're in the middle of farm country! You'd think there'd be pumpkins everywhere."

Apparently not. Kate knew the orbs were heavy, and many vendors probably didn't want the hassle of hauling them to the market every week and dragging home the leftovers. Which, given how tall this booth's stacks still were, would be a significant task.

Maybe the woman would offer a discount just before the market closed, but Kate couldn't be sure. And even at a reduced rate, these pumpkins would still bring a hefty price. Her vision of a charming front porch, decked out for the season, began to slip away.

Melinda laughed. "You know, I think I have the answer to your problem."

"You do?"

"Yeah. One that will make Mabel very happy."

As in most rural areas, everybody knew just about everyone. Mabel and Ed Bauer were Melinda's closest neighbors, in friendship as well as proximity. Mabel's brother, Harvey Watson, was a good friend of Kate's Grandpa Wayne.

Kate was intrigued. "Well, then, how can I help?"

Ed still planted pumpkins every year, a tradition from his childhood that he refused to give up. They now gave away as many as they kept, and Melinda was sure she could broker sweet deals for Kate and Karen, too. The pumpkins were just about free if you hauled them home.

"After all," Melinda said with a raised eyebrow, "where do you think I get all of mine?"

With their pumpkin plan in place, the women moved down the row. The boxes of late-season vegetables, buckets of fresh-cut flowers, and trays of homemade candles and soaps all raised Kate's spirits. With her pumpkin budget now slashed to nearly zero, she could afford to splurge on something else.

A woman with her gray hair twisted into braids waved to Melinda, and the ladies wandered in that direction. Adelaide Beaufort was another of Melinda's neighbors, and her selection of honey and old-fashioned cut flowers quickly caught Kate's eye.

"You have your own hives?" Kate was impressed. "That must be an awful lot of work. And dangerous."

"Oh, we have a nice little truce going. And I've found that if I stay calm, the bees do, too." Adelaide gave a thoughtful nod. "Kind of like a lot of things in life, right?"

"These are beautiful." Kate admired the bundles of asters and goldenrod. "Perfect for this time of year. I'd love two bunches, please, one of each." She turned to Melinda and Karen. "These will look perfect on my table, in that old stoneware jug I found in the basement."

But when she reached for her wallet, Adelaide laughed and shooed it away.

"Are you sure?" Kate wanted to play fair. "I can't ..."

"Yes, you can." Adelaide already had the stems wrapped in brown paper. "No reason the first flowers can't be on the house. See what you think. If you want more, I'm here every week. The market goes until the end of October."

Adelaide did, however, accept Kate's money for a small jar of golden honey. Kate tucked her treasures into her canvas tote bag, and the friends moved on to join a small crowd gathered at the north edge of the park, under the water tower.

Kate heard laughter and cheers, then saw a Belgian Malinois roll over on command. The dog then went into a "sit" and offered its paw for a shake.

"Look at that." Melinda shook her head in awe. "I can barely get Hobo to come when I call him."

"I wondered if they'd be here today." Karen pointed out a sign for the canine training facility that was just outside of Swanton, the county seat. "One of the staffers said they're making the rounds at fall events around the area."

The program prepared dogs to serve as companion animals in addition to being the first step toward law-enforcement certification. While they often worked with purebred canines, the organizers also welcomed shelter critters without perfect pedigrees.

In addition to the Belgian Malinois that had quickly won over the crowd, a few more canines and their handlers milled about on the other side of the table. The display was anchored by a can't-miss donation box surrounded by pamphlets and baskets of doggie toys branded with the facility's logo, but Kate quickly found herself looking for something else.

Or someone.

"I don't see her." Karen nudged Kate with a smile. "Too bad Hazel's not here. Maybe you should head over there some day and pay her a visit."

Kate had never been to the training facility, but she'd met Hazel one morning when the dog was kenneled at Prosper Veterinary Services for a minor medical issue. Kate had volunteered to give Hazel her morning walk, and the dog had treated her to a haphazard dash around town that had been full of surprises.

One of the trainers made a beeline toward Karen. "There you are!" Kate heard him say. "Beautiful afternoon, isn't it? Did you bring Kate with you?"

"Why do I feel like I've been set up on a blind date?" Kate murmured to Melinda as they hung back from the crowd. "Karen was so insistent that we meet up here today. I should have known she had something up her sleeve."

"I don't know anything about it." But Melinda wasn't very convincing. She studied the young man chatting with Karen. "Come to think of it, the dogs aren't the only cuties around here."

Kate had to laugh. "I'd guess he's maybe twenty-five. A seven-year age difference is a little more than I want to take on." But she had to admit, the trainer's deep blue eyes and wide smile were certainly attractive.

She had moved on from her life with Ben, in so many ways, but hadn't dated since their divorce. So much of her time and energy had been taken up with moving back to Eagle River, finding her farmhouse, settling in at the post office, spending as much time as possible with her family ...

Yeah, she had a million excuses. But several months had passed. Was it time to try, even a little?

Someone else came to mind, and she didn't automatically push the thought away. Searching brown eyes and a quick grin that always warmed her from head to toe. If only she saw more of Alex Walsh around Eagle River. But running his bar meant he was a night owl, while Kate lived an early-bird life due to her schedule at the post office.

She didn't know what Alex's deal was, anyway. And, given his enigmatic vibe, he wasn't likely to be very forthcoming with his personal life. Kate had to admit, though, that was part of his appeal.

"You must be Kate." The young trainer interrupted her thoughts. "Karen's told me all about you."

"Has she." But Kate couldn't help but smile.

Hazel had quickly won Kate over with her bright eyes and fluffy tail. The German Shepherd mix was smart and affectionate, but the trainers had decided she was a little too rambunctious to be a service dog.

"Come by sometime." He wasn't about to let it drop. "Hang out with Hazel for a while, see how it goes. Of course, we have a lengthy adoption process for all of our dogs. But if she's a good fit, I have a hunch your references will check out fine."

"I'll think about it." Kate meant it. "I just moved two weeks ago, from town out to a little acreage. I need to get settled, first."

"We've had some other people interested in her. But don't take that as pressure to make a decision," he added quickly. "You can't rush it. And we won't, either. We want to find her the right family."

✳ ✳ ✳

It was soon time to head home. Melinda had chores to do and Karen needed dinner and a quick nap, as it was her night to be on call. After-hours requests weren't plentiful, but they often were the kind that turned into a long night for the veterinarian on duty.

Kate hadn't been able to find a parking spot in the shade, so her car was unseasonably warm inside. She powered down the windows on her way out of town, welcomed the breeze, and sighed with contentment. Nothing earth-shattering had happened that day, other than a moment of mild shock regarding the current retail price of pumpkins. There had just been work, and then an hour or so with good friends. She had to feed the cats when she got home, make dinner, wash dishes. Then there would be a few hours to read or watch television.

Nothing special, really. But at the same time, she decided, every day held its own blessings. She'd delivered packages and letters to countless residents on today's route, and shared laughs with her co-workers in the post office's back room. And now, she had a sweet deal on some pumpkins for her porch. Free flowers to grace her new home with autumn's beauty, and the generosity of a potential new friend. The heartwarming sight of some special dogs and their handlers, working together to bring awareness to an important program.

Kate would normally follow the blacktop south and east to Eagle River. But something about the crisp fall air, the still-bright sunshine, and the new treasures in the back seat made her flip on her blinker as she rolled past the city-limit sign. This winding gravel road went the long way around, but she couldn't resist taking it on a day like today.

As she crossed the old iron bridge over the river, Kate admired the riot of colors flashed by the oaks and maples that lined its banks. A left turn, then a right that took her up a steep grade, and soon the historic Benniger homestead came into view. Or at least, its robust windbreak appeared, cloaked in shades of orange and gold. Because the thick stand of trees held its secrets close, and was too far off the road to give her a glimpse of the once-stately brick home.

Kate had been right to pass on the property, as something better had been just around the corner. And so the old mansion still waited, as it had for decades, for someone to bring it back to life.

It was the same sad story now at Milton Benniger's place, which was several miles to the north, and Kate's spirits dipped as she thought about his farmhouse sitting vacant through the cold months to come. She sometimes wiped away a tear when she drove past the always-empty mailbox when she filled in for Mae, but knew she'd done the right thing by taking in Milton's three cats. His place wouldn't always be empty and forlorn, she reminded herself. The acreage would go on the market in the spring, and a new family would arrive to call it their own.

Autumn was always a bittersweet time, she decided as the outskirts of Eagle River came into view. Last weekend, she'd taken a deep breath (or maybe ten) and tackled the still-unpacked cartons of stuff that had been stored at her parents' farm since she came back to Eagle River.

She'd tried to cull her possessions before she returned to Iowa, but there were so many things she hadn't been able to let go of. *What if I need this? What if this would look perfect in my new house, when I find one?*

Her apartment above Eagle River's Main Street had been in a building as old as it was charming, and closet space was nearly nonexistent. It had been a relief to unpack only the essentials there, and file away the rest of her Chicago life in her old bedroom.

But now, with plenty of space to spread out at her own farmhouse, Kate hadn't been able to put off the emotional task any longer.

Every carton had been a Pandora's Box of memories. Many of them were good ones, but not all of them. With a few laughs and some tears, she got through it. What she wanted to keep found a new home at her new house. The rest of it was trucked to a thrift store. As difficult as it had been, Kate had felt lighter with every item that was set aside.

Her three-bedroom home wasn't that big, but it was spacious compared to her little apartment. That had bothered her, at first. Would she feel lonely there, with only Charlie, given all the extra room? But she'd adjusted just fine, and now saw all the possibilities around her. Every empty space was a spot that would someday be filled with just the right thing, the perfect piece of her new life.

As she waited at Eagle River's lone stoplight, just south of the bridge, Kate faced the truth that there were other holes in her life, as well. And in her heart.

It had been weeks now since she'd heard from Ben and, as time rolled on, Kate found fewer and fewer excuses to even think about calling him. What was there to say? After ten years together (no kids, a cat that had always been more hers than his, a house that sold within weeks in a hot Chicago market), she couldn't think of much to talk about.

Was that good, or just sad? She wasn't sure.

But now that she was again at home in Eagle River, and settled in her new house, Kate decided it might be time to think about those other parts of her life. As she drove east out of town, and the tidy grid of houses was quickly replaced by rolling, golden fields, Kate wondered if she could find the courage to slow down, let go, and take inventory of the rest of her life.

Maybe, if she did, she'd find room for a dog like Hazel. And maybe, even more than that.

✳ 2 ✳

For not the first time, Kate marveled at her luck as she rolled the car's window down at her own mailbox. "I can't believe I live here. It's like something from a magazine!"

Her foursquare red-brick farmhouse was capped with a hip roof, and its wide front porch beckoned visitors to sit a spell in the swing. As the sun lowered in the west, it bathed the front of the house in a warm, golden glow. Oaks and maples showed off their fall shades around the yard, which was punctuated by a two-car garage just behind the house and three sheds along its outskirts.

If only the pasture were as picturesque as the lawn. No livestock had been there for several years, and the balance of her almost-two-acre property was a tangle of overgrown grass, weeds and, well, Kate didn't even know what the rest of it was. This time of year, it was all a dull shade of brown. Should she let it go to seed? Cut it down? But that might be more than her new lawn tractor could handle.

"It'll have to wait until spring." Kate gathered up her newfound treasures and locked the car. The closest neighbor was a quarter mile up the road, but she couldn't break the habit. "One thing at a time."

As she exited the garage's shade, Kate sensed she was being watched. A quick sweep of the yard confirmed a pair of golden eyes peeking out from below the burning bushes along the old well pump's shed. But the hint of gray coat and white paws visible through the bright foliage made her heart leap with joy.

"There you are," she cooed as she paused on her way toward the house, careful not to rustle the contents of her tote bag. "Such a pretty girl! I hope you like it here. And one day, I hope you love it. But I know that's going to take some time. I'm willing to wait."

Kate had said too much, apparently. Or stood in one spot for too long. The skittish cat inched backward to the safety of the shed's weathered wall.

"It's OK," Kate whispered before she moved away. "I'm not going to rush you. But you do need a name. I've been thinking; I like 'Maggie.'"

No response.

"Well, you noodle on that for a bit and let me know. Your brother, I think, will be Jerry. You know, the orange one. Scout's all settled. He had to have that name, for better or worse."

As if on cue, a stout, long-haired black cat appeared around the corner of the house. His white feet were accompanied by a snow-colored vest that ran up to just under his chin. Kate wondered if there were white patches on his stomach, too. She hadn't glimpsed any yet, and expected it would be some time before this proudly independent cat would let her examine his vulnerable side. Maybe never.

"How are my mums doing today?" Kate raised an eyebrow, and Scout looked away. She was almost sure he'd lifted his nose in defiance. Just a bit.

"Taking the fifth, I see. Well, I'll give them a look-over once I get settled." And then she sighed. "It doesn't matter. You know it, don't you? I'm gone all day, and you do as you please."

As she took the three steps into the house's enclosed back

porch, Kate added additional pumpkins to her growing tally.

A few more would look perfect at this entrance. They wouldn't be visible from the road, and hardly anyone else would ever see them. But why not? Autumn was here, she was starting to settle into her new home, and Kate wanted it to be as cozy as possible.

Kate smiled as her key settled into the lock. "I got lucky. This place is so charming, and comfortable, and in this crazy sellers' market …"

She stepped into the kitchen, and her grateful smile morphed into a smirk. "Oh, yeah. This is why I was able to afford it."

Worn cabinets smothered in a dark stain filled the kitchen, whose counters were cloaked in a white laminate veined with gold and bronze. Hunter-green paint covered the lower portion of the walls, and a fussy flower wallpaper border of green, mauve and gold made a lap around the room. At least the rest of the way to the ceiling was painted a shade of cream.

Cabbage roses covered the dining room's wallpaper, which at least had the decency to coordinate with the kitchen. Sculpted olive-green carpet stretched across the spacious dining room and rolled into the adjacent living room. But the craftsman woodwork in this home was spectacular, and its oak finish had somehow escaped the paintbrush over the decades of renovations that had been inflicted on this century-old home.

Kate hoped her grand plans would let the house's natural beauty really shine, but it was going to take heaps of cash, and months of work, to pull it off. "It's like a grandma's house." She dropped into the chair inside the back door and kicked off her sneakers. "It's a time machine. So for now, I'll stick with it."

A blur of cream fluff with sable feet and a sweet face burst through the doorway from the dining room.

"Charlie!" Kate deposited her purse and tote on the counter and crouched down to give her boy a gentle squeeze. "How are you? Did you get at least one nap in while I was at the farmers market?"

His purr assured Kate that all was well. Then his nose caught the scent of the flowers resting on the counter, and his blue eyes lit up with curiosity.

"Aren't they pretty? I have just the place to show them off." She dipped her head toward her wooden table, which was square and laughingly small in a dining room that had been built for multi-generation family dinners and ravenous threshing crews. "Let me get them settled, and then we'll hang out for a bit."

The mahogany-hued, earthenware jug was still on the shelf in the basement laundry room. As Kate washed it out in the deep kitchen sink, she took care around the nick in its handle. The flowers' stems filled the pottery perfectly after a quick trim.

Charlie ran ahead as Kate started up the stairs. She was glad he loved the house as-is, because she hadn't had time to do much of anything. She'd aired it out, and given everything a good scrubbing. And so far, that was it. No renovations, no new carpet, no fresh paint. Not even to cover the mauve-colored walls of her bedroom.

"I'm thinking robin-egg blue," she told Charlie, who'd already launched himself onto the bed. "Or something, anything, better than what we have now. Maybe in a few months, I'll get around to it."

While she wasn't fond of her bedroom's walls, Kate really wished she could wave a magic wand and fix the house's only bathroom. Salmon-tinted tiles ran halfway up the walls, their hue a near-perfect match to the porcelain tub. And that burgundy carpet!

"Who puts carpet in a bathroom?" Charlie didn't have an answer for that. "I don't care if the pile is short and it's soft and whatever. But then, if you're old and afraid of falling and rugs are your enemy, I guess that's one way around it."

Her bedroom closet, which likely had been added in the last fifty years, was the largest one in the house. Which was a good thing. Kate may have ruthlessly scaled back her other belongings, but her clothes had escaped scrutiny. So far.

Cute tops, pretty shoes. Flowy skirts and dark-washed jeans. All the things she used to wear when she wasn't in work gear or sweats. Why had she brought all these things back with her? What would she do with most of them now? Kate needed chore gear, and lots of it. The few things she'd always left at her parents' farm weren't plentiful enough now that she had her own home in the country.

But for now, a pair of older jeans and a sweatshirt would do. As a former farm girl, Kate had to admit that carrying buckets of kibble and water to her barn cats wasn't exactly a hard day's work.

Her outside kitties hadn't quite settled in at their new home, but they were quick to come running when breakfast and supper were served. As she rounded the back of the garage, Kate saw Jerry dash out of the garden and scoot through the kitty door recently added to one corner of the machine shed.

The afternoon's golden sunshine had disappeared into a blanket of heavy clouds, and the temperature had dropped noticeably in the past hour. Kate almost wished she'd worn gloves, as the iron handle on the machine shed's side door was cold to the touch. The creak of the hinges was answered by a trio of meows.

"The gang's all here!" Kate made sure the door was tightly fastened behind her to keep out the chill. "And how are you all enjoying your fancy castle so far?"

With Karen and Melinda's assistance, Kate had constructed a spacious kitty compound on one side of the shed. Its scrap-lumber frame was covered in chicken wire, and the ladies had added insulation and plywood sheeting to its two outside walls. An old screen door, outfitted with another cat-sized opening, gave Kate access to the space. Two of the shed's windows were incorporated into the design, and wooden perches provided the cats bird's-eye views of their new yard. Separate areas for food dishes and litter boxes were also part of the layout.

The cats spent their first ten days at Kate's farm inside this habitat, which gave them a little room to roam while they became acclimated to the machine shed's look and smell. While she'd given them the run of the farm a few days ago, Kate would always feed the cats inside the enclosure to reinforce that this was home base.

With meows of impatience, the cats let her know they could tell time. Thanks to her trip to the Prosper farmers market, Kate was running about twenty minutes behind schedule.

Scout was right under Kate's feet, as usual, demanding his supper. "Hey, back up for a second! I'll fill your dish as soon as you let me get near it."

The big black cat gave a quick flick of one front paw, a motion Kate had quickly learned was his go-to way to show disgust. She wasn't his boss, and they both knew it. But she did have some tasty chicken scraps tonight, and Scout temporarily deferred to Kate so he could get what he wanted.

After she fed the cats, Kate checked the machine shed's dark corners to be sure no wild critters had found their way through the cats' exterior entrance. She always closed its little plywood door at night. That kept the kitties inside until breakfast, and also protected them from whatever dangers might be lurking outside in the dark.

What those exact threats were, Kate couldn't be sure. Which was why she was keen to take as many precautions as possible. She'd grown up on a farm, so she knew country life could be unpredictable at times, for better or worse.

The same could be said for life in general, for that matter. And that was why Kate paused outside the shed's locked door and prepared for the second half of her evening routine.

Her phone was secure in one sweatshirt pocket, and the small flashlight she pulled from the other snapped on quickly as she aimed its beam toward the shadows gathering in the garden. A flick of the wrist showed the plot was otherwise empty, except for the last of the tomato vines she had yet to add to the compost pile, and Kate set off toward the pasture fence.

Was she afraid out here, living alone? Kate tried to tell herself she wasn't.

When she'd returned to Eagle River, Kate had been reminded of how driving down gravel roads and past wide-open fields had always soothed her soul. But every night, as the sun lowered toward the horizon and the darkness descended, she found herself making this same march around the perimeter of her yard.

Crime was nearly unheard-of in Hartland County; some people still didn't lock their doors at night, which Kate could hardly believe. And it would be very difficult for a strange vehicle to arrive at her property unnoticed. Now, someone on foot ...

Kate shivered, and not because of the gathering chill. She'd been blindsided once while walking her Chicago route, and Kate had vowed that would never happen again.

So she walked, and shined her flashlight's beam this way and that. Peered into the thick tangle of vegetation along the pasture fence, kept a close watch on the shadows gathering in the windbreak, checked the doors on all her outbuildings to be sure they were secure.

This farm's barn was torn down years ago, as its structural issues were more than the previous owner could afford to repair. The old pump shed was small, and too packed with junk to give anyone a decent place to hide. The machine shed was already locked down, and so was the garage. But the chicken house ...

Kate paused at its main door, and reminded herself to find a padlock to put on it. This old coop was more like a chicken palace, with a high ceiling that took full advantage of a second row of south-facing windows tucked up under the ridgepole.

While it had been out of use for several years, the building was in remarkably good shape. It had so much potential and, someday, Kate would put it back to work. But for now, all she cared about was that it was empty.

A flip of the switch for the single bulb high above, and Kate sighed with relief. It was.

"It's only been a few weeks," she reminded herself as she headed back to the fence. Her next stop was the cluster of apple and pear trees just beyond the garden. "I'll get over this. Living in the country again has been a big adjustment. At least I can see the lights of town from the front of the house. If this place was even one more mile out, I don't know how I'd feel."

Even in the fading light, Kate noticed more apples and pears were nearly ready to harvest. It was a good thing she liked to bake, as there would be more pies, muffins and tarts in her future before the season was over.

A rustle in the fallen leaves brought her up short. Something was roaming around under the fruit trees. Kate soon saw a ringed, bushy tail, and knew it was only a raccoon. The best kind of masked bandit.

"Just help yourself," she said as she strolled past. The raccoon barely gave her a look as it snatched up a wind-fallen apple in its paws. "If they come off the tree before I can pick them, they're community property. Tell your friends. It'll save me some work."

* * *

Charlie barely looked up from his plush bed when she went into the living room to see if he was around. The fireplace was his favorite feature of his new home, even more so than the window seat in the smallest upstairs bedroom.

He loved the hearth so much, in fact, that he wanted to be next to it even when it wasn't in use. Kate had given in to his whim, and put one of his beds as close to the fireplace as she dared.

"After dinner," Kate promised Charlie as she patted him on the head. "Let's eat, then I'll get a cozy fire going. That'll feel really good tonight."

As soon as Charlie was settled, Kate pulled her own supper out of the refrigerator. Between the retro vibe of her new home and the crisp fall weather, she'd been craving nostalgic comfort food. Last night's tater-tot casserole would hit the spot, several times over.

While the television murmured in the corner and Charlie dozed before the dancing flames, Kate took up her after-supper post on the couch and settled in with a book. Unpacked moving boxes still waited here and there, but Kate had a firm grip on her priorities. One of her first tasks had been to wipe down the built-in bookcases in the cased opening between the dining and living rooms.

It wasn't long before Kate thought she heard something outside. "What was that?"

Charlie only yawned and stretched his front paws in bliss.

"It sounded like a siren." She hurried to the picture window and parted the mauve, pinch-pleated draperies. They certainly weren't fashionable, but they sure came in handy as the temperatures fell at sundown.

Kate heard it again. Her jaw dropped when flashing emergency lights flew past the end of her lane. It was too hard to make out the vehicle in the darkness, but the lights' height made Kate suspect a fire truck.

As she stood at the window, her pulse pounding in her

neck, Kate wondered what was going on. Had an ambulance already gone past?

One of her coworkers, Jared Larsen, served on Eagle River's emergency crew. And her cousin Corey was part of the Prosper team. Because of this, Kate knew most of a rural department's calls were for vehicle accidents and medical emergencies; structure fires were rare.

She didn't even reach for a coat, just unlocked the front door and hurried out to the open porch. It faced west, back toward town, and the cold air nipped at her hands and her face the moment she stepped outside. The dying grass crunched under her shoes as she hurried toward the road, her flashlight forgotten in the house, and tried to get a better look at what was happening.

More lights coming her way from the blacktop. Soon, another fire truck barreled past. "There must be an actual fire, then."

She couldn't smell smoke. Or see flames anywhere near her farm. But Kate crossed her arms against the chill, and the fear that crept down her spine. "I wonder where it is?"

Kate didn't know her new neighbors very well. In fact, sad to say, she'd yet to meet any of them. Between getting herself, Charlie and Milton's cats settled at her new place, she hadn't found the time to drive around and make introductions. And with harvest starting within days, Kate understood why none of her neighbors had stopped by.

Back inside, her chilled cheeks flamed in the house's welcoming warmth.

"I don't know what to do," she told Charlie as she locked the door. He didn't budge from his cozy spot, but the inquisitive look on his face told Kate he sensed her unease.

"There's nothing to call in, since I can't see anything. And the fire department's already responded, so they know about, well, whatever is going on."

She should go back to her book, not linger at the window.

But Kate couldn't help it. Her first concern was for what was happening down the road, but something else kept wandering into her thoughts. While she considered herself at home again in Eagle River, she still felt like an outsider in her rural neighborhood.

At her parents' farm west of town, no one within three miles was a stranger. Everyone had been in the area for at least five years, or ten; some, like the Duncans, for decades before that. Kate occasionally drove her new neighborhood's mail route but, just two weeks in at this place, only a few last names were even vaguely familiar.

She should have made more of an effort to get to know people right away. Because then, she might at least have an idea where the fire could be, who might be affected. Could pick up her phone, know who to call, see if there was any way she could help.

Instead, here she stood, staring out into the darkness.

And then, two more fire trucks flew past. "It must be bad, then. Really bad. Oh, I wish I knew what was going on!"

Seconds later, her phone rang. Auggie Kleinsbach's number flashed on the screen.

"Kate! I heard it on the scanner. What's going on out there?"

Auggie was the proprietor of Prosper's co-op and Milton Benniger's cousin. But his oversized ego was sometimes matched by his kindness, and he'd promised a lifetime supply of free kibble when Kate adopted Milton's cats.

Kate's proximity to tonight's incident had been more than he could ignore, and she wasn't surprised that he'd reached out to her, eager for details.

The problem was, she didn't have any to share.

"I don't know what's going on, I wish I did. Several fire trucks have gone by in the past few minutes, though. What have you heard?"

A barn was on fire about two miles south of Kate's

acreage, Auggie said. Land owned by the Donegan family, but no one lived there anymore. Based on the dispatch chatter he'd heard online, the flames got a good start before the incident was reported. The barn was likely to be a total loss, and the main objective now was to keep the flames from spreading into the nearby fields.

Along with Eagle River's fire department, Prosper's crew had been called to the scene. Charles City, a larger town off to the north and east, had another team on the way.

"It's an all-hands sort of thing." Auggie was nearly breathless with excitement. "Not just the firefighters. Eagle River police, the sheriff's department, anyone and everyone who's available."

He thought for a moment. "Hey, you should head down there!"

Kate shook her head. "Seriously? Shouldn't I stay out of the way?"

"You can do both." Auggie rattled off the address. "Don't you want to know what the deal is?"

Kate hated to admit it, but she did. It wouldn't be right to stay long; she'd never want to be a distraction to the crews working so hard to put out the blaze. But it might bring peace of mind to verify what Auggie had told her, see for herself that the authorities had everything under control. And then, she'd be able to come home, pick up her novel, and carry on with her evening. Right?

"Charlie, I'm so sorry." Kate doused the fire in the hearth, and checked twice that it was out. One renegade blaze in the neighborhood was more than enough. "I can't believe I'm doing this. I'll be back in a little bit."

✳ 3 ✳

The darkness pressed in around Kate as she hurried out to the garage. She was glad she'd grabbed a stocking hat and gloves along with a warm jacket.

"What am I doing?" But despite her misgivings about this errand, Kate found herself leaning forward as she headed south on the gravel. "None of this is really my business. If I can't see it from my yard, it shouldn't be close enough to matter."

But it did. She lived here now, this rural neighborhood was her home. If something was happening, she wanted to know about it.

"Donegan. Hmm." Then she gave an exasperated sigh. "Never heard that name before, I'm sure of it." She tried to picture a mailbox in this area with that surname on its side, but couldn't come up with one.

While the other driveways on this stretch of road led to occupied farms, Kate vaguely recalled a place that only had a barn. If she remembered correctly, the old structure sat far back from the road, up a lane whose weeds threatened to engulf it at any moment. It seemed there was one of those telltale gaps among some trees where a house used to sit.

Auggie said no one lived there now, hadn't for years. Leave it to Auggie and his razor-sharp memory to recall people who didn't even live around Eagle River these days. Or maybe, they still did.

Donegan ... wait, is that the name of ...

"I'd better be watching for deer instead of mulling over this family's business." Kate sat up straighter and turned down the radio. The critters were especially active at night this time of year, which was their mating season, and tended to dart into the road with little warning. "Besides, someone down there will probably be able to tell me more."

Kate knew she wouldn't be able to get too close to the blaze, which suited her just fine. But an event this unusual surely would draw other neighbors to the scene.

One crossroads, then another. And soon, Kate spotted a wall of angry flames soaring into the night sky. It was on the right, the west side of the road, just as she'd suspected. While it wasn't visible from this distance, she could imagine the cloud of smoke that rose above the barn in the dark.

"Look at that!" she gasped. "Oh, it's terrifying. Thank goodness it isn't someone's house, at least. But if the fire spreads into the pasture ..."

Kate slowed and started to watch for the next field drive. She could probably get a little closer, as a cluster of headlights down the way marked whatever barricade the sheriff's department had set up on the road. But she suddenly felt shy and awkward. She had no business being down here, nor did anyone else who wasn't fighting the fire. Which, given the scores of flashing emergency lights up near the barn, was a significant number of responders.

"Here we go." A turnoff to the right appeared in the gloom. "I won't stay long."

Kate cut the engine, reached for the flashlight kept under the seat, and opened her door. The blaze was as awe-inspiring as it was terrifying and, even from a quarter of a mile away, she got a glancing scent of its smoke.

The acrid odor assaulted her nostrils, and her pulse

quickened in a hard-wired response to potential danger. Even so, Kate couldn't help but stare at the blaze in morbid fascination.

What had started the fire? Who spotted it first? If the place was vacant, it must have been someone driving by. Was there a working well on the property where crews could draw water? Unlike in town, there were no fire hydrants along the rural roads. Or did all the water have to be brought to the scene by tanker trucks?

Kate had been leaning against her car for only a few minutes, her eyes fixed on the mushroom cloud of flames as her mind reached for answers, when she spotted another flashlight bobbing toward her in the gloom.

She cringed. Exchanging greetings while someone else's barn turned to toast wasn't exactly the best way to introduce yourself to your new neighbors. It would be best to just be honest: she'd heard about the fire, couldn't help but come down to gawk. They were obviously here for the same reason. Because on a raw night like this one, there was no other good explanation for someone to lurk about in this pasture.

Of course, they might be the owners of this field. And no matter her excuse, Kate was somewhere she shouldn't be. She wasn't parked on the shoulder of the road; she'd turned into the field drive and drove in a ways, determined to not impede the emergency crews' path to the scene.

Trespassing was a relatively minor offense, but still. Kate closed her eyes for a second and tried to recall what the post office's handbook said about federal employees who'd been charged with crimes. She didn't remember, but it couldn't be good.

As the man came closer, Kate realized he looked familiar. Which could have been in her favor, except for the fact he was a law enforcement officer.

"Deputy Collins!" she gasped. "How are you? I mean, I'm sorry, I shouldn't be out here." She reached for her keys. "I'll head home now, I just had to see ..."

"You and half of the neighborhood." Even in the dark, Kate sensed his wry smile. Steve Collins had responded to Karen's call the day she and Kate ended up at Milton's farm, then had a hunch something wasn't right.

Steve and his wife lived in Prosper, so Kate shouldn't be surprised to run into him out here. With such a small staff, the Hartland County Sheriff's Department would have dispatched the deputy living closest to a call that was this important, regardless of whether they were on duty or not.

"We expected this, actually." Deputy Collins' calm demeanor put Kate at ease. "The gawkers," he explained quickly, "not the fire. At least you had the self-control to stay back this far. We now have the perimeter set a good way out from the property, but when I first got here, I had to shoo some folks back."

Steve watched the flames for a moment, and Kate sensed he was in awe of them, too.

"I understand, though, why they couldn't stay away," Steve said. "It's an impressive fire, to be honest. We don't see many of these around here, thank goodness."

"Fire's always a danger on a farm." Kate thought of her dad's constant warnings about sparks from overheated machinery, sheds with outdated electrical outlets, and barns packed with straw and hay. "Especially this time of year, with harvest about to start. I know it's early, but do you have any idea what happened?"

"Not yet, and there doesn't seem to be anyone handy to give us an explanation. That place is abandoned, has been for a long time."

Despite his easygoing manner, Deputy Collins now sounded weary and worried. Especially for so early in a night that was certain to be a long one. "The house was torn down years ago. No one's living there."

"I heard the Donegans own it," Kate offered.

"They do. It's been in their family for generations." Deputy Collins leaned back against Kate's car. She waited, and hoped he was about to tell her something she didn't know. He was.

"Chester was in charge of those eighty acres for, oh, twenty years or so. He and Jean live not far from here. Last corner you came past, they're about two miles to the east. But he signed it over to his son, Brody, this past spring."

"Oh?" Kate was all ears. "And what does Brody do?"

There was a pause. And then, an exasperated sigh. "Well, not much. Chester gave these fields to Brody so he could get a leg-up on farming. But I'm not sure he's game."

Steve didn't say more, and Kate didn't have to ask. Farming was a hard way to make a living, always had been. Between the weather and crop prices, so much was out of the farmers' control. These days, many younger people weren't interested in the risks that so often outweighed the rewards.

That shift in rural society meant it was increasingly common to find abandoned acreages along the back roads. Kate drove past so many of them when she was on her rural rounds, and the sight of their tumbledown houses and weed-choked yards made her sad. And curious about the people who had left these once-vibrant places behind.

It took more acres to break even these days, and the fields in any given area were increasingly snatched up by larger, corporation-style farms. While the land remained in production, the left-behind houses and outbuildings quickly fell into decay. Old barns and sheds might serve as storage or shelter for animals for at least a few more years, but a dilapidated house carried no value at all.

But even if a house was in terrible condition, it was still expensive to take it down. There was often a tangle of red tape with the county, as archaic plumbing systems and asbestos-filled building materials required special permits for disposal. And for some families, there was an emotional cost, as well.

No matter how terrible the house's condition became, they couldn't let go of their memories long enough to level it.

It didn't seem as if Deputy Collins had any additional gossip about the Donegans. Or at least, any he was willing to share. So Kate moved the conversation back to easier ground. "It's sad to see a barn go down, but especially in a way that poses a threat to the neighborhood and first responders. Someone worked hard long ago to build it, after all."

"I feel the same. I'm just glad there's nothing up there but maybe a few bales of straw, an old plow or two. No one was hurt, and no animals were caught in the fire." Then he sighed. "But that's sort of the problem, too. No one should have been on the property after dark. There's not even a yard light, anymore. And no electrical service coming up from the road."

A new spark of curiosity flared in Kate's mind. Deputy Collins was right. Even if anything of value had been stored in the old barn, who'd be foolish enough to swing by this time of night? The darkness down that lane would be so dense, you wouldn't be able to see your hand in front of your face.

She shivered as a gust of cold wind brushed her cheek. "You don't mean ..."

"I wish I didn't. It'll be daybreak before the fire marshal can start his investigation. But if I had to guess? It has to be arson."

The closest branch of the state fire office was in Mason City, about forty minutes away, the deputy said. And even after the investigator did his work, it would take weeks to get those samples back from the lab.

A new pair of headlights crept toward them from the north, and Steve chuckled. "More rubber-neckers, I bet. If you'd promise to head home soon, I'd appreciate it."

"Sure thing. How long do you have to stay? Until the fire is out?"

"I wish." Steve groaned. "That would normally be the case. But we might have a crime scene on our hands. So we have to guard it, keep it secure until the state's fire investigator says he's done."

In the faint glow of his flashlight, he could read the question on Kate's face. "That'll take up most of tomorrow, I'd guess."

She gasped. "But there's, what, only a handful of deputies? You can't be doing your usual work, all across the county, and babysit this at the same time!"

"We're bringing in help." Eagle River's police department would take turns, as well as deputies from a neighboring county. "But that's just it; this is going to inconvenience everyone."

Kate thought of Jared and Corey and the other firefighters, and how they all had day jobs and families that required their attention. A fire of this magnitude would steal countless hours of work, not to mention sleep, from dozens of people around Hartland County. As she watched another ball of fire rise above what was left of the barn, some of Kate's fear turned to frustration.

"Is there anything I can do to help? Coffee? Sandwiches? I'm just up the road, and it's going to be a long night."

Steve gave a gentle laugh. "Now, that's one thing we have covered. My wife's on her way over with snacks, some of the other spouses are mobilizing, too. So we'll stay hydrated, warm and fed."

Kate reached for her keys. "I'm glad to hear that, at least." Her only other question right now was: why? "This is a senseless waste of resources. Who would do such a thing? I mean, what's the point? Insurance money? I can't imagine that barn had much value."

Deputy Collins' initial silence told Kate he was likely thinking the same thing.

"Who knows, sometimes, why people do what they do?" he finally said. "And I've learned the hard way that the obvious answer often isn't the right one."

The radio clipped to his jacket lapel gurgled to life.

"Yeah. Good. OK, I'm on my way." He turned to Kate and, even in the gloom of his flashlight, she could see the concern on his face. "You've been living out here, what, just a few weeks?"

Kate nodded.

"Quite the 'welcome to the neighborhood,' then." Steve tried for a rueful laugh. "But seriously, if you think of anything you've noticed that's out of the ordinary, anything at all, don't hesitate to call it in."

"Will do. I was already trying to think back, if anything seemed amiss."

"Excellent. That's what we need most right now, observant neighbors." He paused for a moment. "I don't want to alarm you unnecessarily, but when you get home, go right inside. And make sure everything's locked, the windows as well as the doors."

Deputy Collins didn't have to say more; Kate had caught his warning.

Someone dangerous may be out and about tonight. Do what you must to keep yourself safe.

As she started back up the gravel, and the flashing lights disappeared from her rearview mirror, Kate's mind raced ahead to home.

How many steps, how many seconds was it from the garage to the house? She had a yard light, of course, but its glow didn't reach far into the shadows. There's no way she'd be able to spot someone lurking around her outbuildings.

"Maybe I haven't been overreacting with those nightly security walks." Kate took a deep breath as her farm came into view. "But I can't patrol the grounds all night long. I just have to hope that nothing bad happens tonight."

* 4 *

The skies cleared overnight, and the subsequent sunrise promised another beautiful autumn day. But the sight of a Hartland County sheriff's vehicle rolling past the end of her lane at such an early hour reminded Kate that trouble was afoot in her neighborhood.

A late-night text from Auggie confirmed the old barn's roof had finally given way, but everyone at the scene was able to move back to a safe distance before the structure collapsed. Kate was relieved, but she wanted to know more. In fact, she wanted to go down there and see it for herself, now that it was daylight.

But she didn't have time. And she needed to stay out of the way.

"We need to let the authorities handle things," she told the barn cats as she set out their breakfast. "Besides, I'm sure I'll get all the scoop as soon as I get to the post office."

A co-worker's arrival usually brought a round of nods and waves from the carriers already preparing to make their deliveries, but the back room's on-edge vibe told Kate this wasn't going to be an ordinary work day.

At the far end of one of the sorting tables, Jack O'Brien and Allison Carmichael were already deep in debate about the fire.

Or fighting about it, depending on how one looked at things.

"That's Brody Donegan's land." Jack pounded one palm on the metal counter for emphasis. "You can't tell me he doesn't know a damn thing about it."

"No one knows that," Allison insisted. She was young, in her mid-twenties, but refused to let Jack get the upper hand. "Chester went to school with my dad, we've known that family for a long time. Dad says Chester would never do something like that, and he'd never let his son get away with it, either."

Jack's dismissive grunt said it all. He was one of the senior carriers, and had a know-it-all attitude to match his years of experience.

"Arson is usually a felony in this state!" Allison's voice went up a notch. "The barn's a total loss. This isn't some kid playing with matches, and you know it. This is serious business."

"That's exactly what I'm saying!" Jack pointed at her for emphasis. "Dig yourself enough of a hole, money-wise, and you don't know what you might be down for. People do terrible things, sometimes, when they're desperate."

"And is Brody desperate?" Allison raised an eyebrow. "Tell me, Jack, if you know something I don't."

Aaron Thatcher came out of the break room and set his now-full thermos on the table. He was one of the younger carriers, and as dependable as he was laid back. Which told Kate he had the temperament for a long, successful career with the post office.

"It's terrible, sure," Aaron said with a shrug, "but people who really need money do things much worse than that. I mean, if that's the conversation we're having. It was an old barn, from what I hear. Half fallen down, as it was. It couldn't have been worth that much."

"People could have died last night." Above his navy fleece pullover, Jack's neck turned red with anger. "Or been injured, putting out that fire. It could have spread into the fields, burned all the way into town."

"I know that!" Aaron was indignant. "I'm just saying ..."

Roberta Schupp barged through the swinging door that opened into the post office's lobby. Her husband served on Eagle River's emergency crew and, given the worry lines etched on her face, it was clear Kate's boss hadn't slept well last night.

"Enough!" Roberta snapped at her charges. "Come on, people. We're all tired and stressed, but there's mail to sort and deliveries to make."

Her outburst over as quickly as it began, Roberta pushed her black-rimmed reading glasses up over her head and looked around the back room with bleary eyes.

"Randy's off today," she said, mostly to herself. "Where's Jared?"

Allison sighed and shook her head. "In the break room."

Their boss hurried around the corner as Kate followed, thermos in hand, to fuel up for the long day ahead. Jared was indeed sitting at the table. But given the way his upper half was stretched out across its surface, his cheek planted to the scuffed laminate, he was fast asleep. Or well on his way.

"Oh, dear," Roberta muttered to Kate. "He's all worn out, that's what he is."

Jared must have showered after he got home from fighting the fire, but the faint smell of smoke still clung to him despite a change of clothes.

Roberta stepped quietly across the linoleum and put a gentle hand on Jared's shoulder. "Wake up, now. We need to talk."

Jared groaned slightly and raised his head, his brown hair sticking out every which way. "Hey, boss," he mumbled.

He blinked when he saw Kate standing there, then swiveled to check the clock. "I must have dozed off. I'll just get my case."

"You're not going anywhere today." Like a mother hen shooing along one of her chicks, Roberta gently nudged Jared into an upright position. "Scratch that. You're going home. Straight home, and to bed."

Jared's mouth fell open. "I can't! I have to ..."

"I don't care." Roberta's tone was kind, but firm. "I'm not letting you get behind the wheel of a mail vehicle today. Out there alone, on those gravel roads?" She shook her head. "You'll doze off before you get three miles out, I'm sure of it."

Roberta turned to Kate. "I'll have you take Jared's route today." Before Kate could even nod her agreement, the postmaster changed her mind. "No, you stay with Randy's stuff, here in town. You can walk a route, just fine. I'll call Barney, instead."

"Barney Wilburn?" Jared was suddenly more alert. "Jeez, he's what? Seventy-eight? He's ..."

"A fine carrier, even though he's long-ago retired." Roberta cut Jared off at the pass. "His driver's license is current, and he still has his mind. I just saw his wife yesterday at the drug store, I know they're around."

She shook her head at Jared in a compassionate gesture.

"I know you want to do your route, but this is for your own good. Stand down, just for today."

"I'm sure Bill's going to work." Jared's cousin worked at Prosper Hardware and served on that town's emergency crew.

"He'll do no such thing," Roberta said. "I've known Miriam Lange most of my life, and she'd never let Bill come in after what he, and all the rest of you, went through last night." A shadow of worry crossed Roberta's face. "We're just so fortunate no one was hurt when that roof collapsed."

Kate made her way over to the coffeemaker, and filled her thermos to the brim. As she started a fresh pot, someone tapped her on the shoulder.

"How are you holding up?" It was Bev Stewart, who had joined the post office after retiring from teaching. "Honey, I almost called you last night. How scary for you, when you've only been at your new place for a few weeks. Did you get any sleep?"

Kate merely shrugged, too tired to go into the details. It had taken a long time to wind down enough to rest at all, and then twice she and Charlie had mobilized to investigate startling sounds. One was a tree branch scraping the side of the house. The other, as far as Kate could ascertain, had been a grumble of discontent from the old refrigerator.

"By the way," Bev was whispering now, "Jeff called me, first thing this morning. I'd told him you'd moved, see, and he wants you to let him know if you've noticed anything out of the ordinary lately."

Jeff Preston was Hartland County's longtime sheriff. He was also Bev's high-school boyfriend.

"I ran into Deputy Collins last night, down at the scene," Kate told her friend. "Or, well, as close as I dared to get without getting in the way. He said the same thing."

Bev put up a hand. "I don't blame you for heading over there. I would have done the same, I'm sure." She turned her gaze toward the break room table. "Oh, dear, is he ..."

The soft snoring told Kate all she needed to know. "Roberta sent him home. Or rather, she told him to go home. I guess he didn't make it far. She's going to call Barney."

"I've got a bad feeling about this," Bev said, then quickly made herself clear. "The fire, I mean, not Barney. He's an old badger, but he's about the best pinch-hitter we have."

Bev agreed with Aaron that the barn couldn't be worth much. It seemed like too big of a risk for such a small insurance payout. And she didn't know the Donegans well enough to pass judgment on Brody or his dad.

"I think that's what bothers me the most." Kate shook her head. "I don't know them at all, and they apparently live just a few miles from me. I guess I have no idea of what any of them are capable of."

Bev finished Kate's thought. "And that's what's most likely to keep us up at night. The fear of the unknown."

While Bev revived Jared for the second time, Kate went out to prep deliveries for the first half of Randy VanBuren's route. She had almost all the packages sorted by address when there was a halfhearted knock at the back door.

Jack frowned. "Who would knock?"

"Who would come around back in the first place?" Mae Fisher wondered as she started for the entryway.

A gust of cool air rolled in with their visitor. "Hey, mayor." Mae was surprised. "What brings you in today?"

Ward Benson was a retired seed-corn salesman and lifelong area resident. When he and his wife moved into town a decade ago, several residents encouraged him to take up public service. A seat on the city council turned into the top job a few years later. Kate knew it wasn't difficult to be elected mayor in a town this small, as too many people wanted to complain about things but weren't willing to make an effort to fix them.

Ward held up the sheet of paper in his hand. "This. This is why I'm stopping in."

"A public notice?" Jack glanced at the clock. "The lobby's open at nine today. You could have come by after that. No need to stop in at this early hour, especially after all the commotion from last night's ..."

"Incident." Allison glared at Jack.

"Criminal activity," he shot back.

"That is exactly why I'm here now," Ward said. "I can't believe this is happening. It's the worst timing ever."

Jack, who apparently couldn't stand one more second of suspense, snatched the flyer from the mayor's hand. His eyes widened in surprise. And then, he started to laugh.

"Oh, man! I don't envy you one bit." He caught the rest of the room in his now-merry gaze. "It's a notice for next week's council meeting. They're going to discuss that plan to stop people from burning leaves in town."

Even though she was exhausted, Kate joined in the other carriers' laughter. Or maybe, she laughed so hard because she was so tired.

Seeing he was outnumbered, Ward finally joined in. "There's no way I'm going to saunter up to the bulletin board and post that myself. Every person in the place would demand five minutes to argue their side of the situation."

Like many small towns, Eagle River allowed open burning during a limited period in the fall so residents could dispose of dead leaves and yard debris. But growing concerns about smoke pollution and fire safety had caused the council to consider banning the practice after this autumn.

The purists had dug in their heels. The aroma of burning leaves was a nostalgic part of fall, they said. Besides, who wanted to bag everything up and set it on the curb, or haul it to the county's waste center, which was twenty miles away?

"The official window opens in early October, like usual," Ward said. "But the council decided over the summer that it would be best to address it this fall, when this is at the top of people's minds. And then, no one can complain they didn't know about any possible changes long in advance of next year's disposal."

Bev gave the mayor a gentle jab with her elbow. "People are really fired up about this."

Chuckles echoed around the room. "It's a hot topic, for sure," Kate said.

"I think this'll make for a real barnburner of a meeting next week." But Jack then grimaced at his own joke. "Maybe that's too much, too soon?"

Ward sighed. "Don't get me wrong, last night's fire is a much more serious situation. Especially if what we're hearing turns out to be true. But now we have to work through this issue as a community at the same time?"

Mae shrugged. "Can you put it off?"

"Nope. We have to have the initial discussion at our next meeting, so we can allow for a few weeks of public feedback before the council votes." He rolled his eyes. "And some of the members want this wrapped up before the end of October, since their seats are on the ballot in the upcoming election."

Mae promised to add the flyer to the post office's bulletin board. Ward nodded his thanks and took a deep breath, as he was off to repeat his explanation at several other locations around town in the next hour.

"Sorry we gave you such a hard time about the burn ban," Jack said. "I mean, the *proposed* burn ban. But in all seriousness, when might we know more about last night's fire?"

Ward shrugged. "Fire marshal's out there now. Stuff needs to go to the lab for tests, and that'll take weeks, I hear."

"Weeks?" Bev was shocked. "I hope he gets what he needs right off the bat. Because if he doesn't, it's going to be really tough to get more evidence later. Every day that goes by, won't that get harder?"

"Yes. Nearly impossible, in fact. The weather alone will tamper with the scene." The mayor's shoulders slumped in defeat, and it wasn't even eight in the morning.

"I'll tell you what I'm telling everyone else: Arson cases are incredibly difficult to prove, if that's even what happened last night. It's easier to catch a murderer than an arsonist."

No one said a word. But worry and fear were all over their faces. Ward gave the carriers a halfhearted wave on his way out the door.

Allison rested her cheek in one hand. "So they aren't likely to catch this guy?"

Jack couldn't resist. "How sure are you that it's a man?"

"Stop it." Bev shot him a withering look. Then she glanced around the circle. "All we can do is get to work. People need their mail and packages today, regardless of what else is going on around here."

There were a few more sighs and shrugs, and the carriers went back to their pre-delivery tasks. As Kate organized items for Randy's route, her mind ran ahead to the barrage of questions, opinions and theories that were sure to come her way that day. It would be tempting to share her experiences, chat about what she saw last night, but Kate decided that wasn't a good idea.

Her observations would be spread far and wide if she did, and their accuracy was likely to vanish. No; she'd nod, listen, and file away any interesting tidbits she heard. Then decide if they were worth passing on to the sheriff's department.

Yesterday afternoon, her biggest concern had been how many pumpkins she wanted to decorate her front porch. And now ... how in the world was she supposed to feel at home, in her new home, after what happened last night?

She was spooked, Kate decided. There wasn't any other way to describe it. But unlike the spirit of some long-ago resident, whoever was behind last night's blaze was a real, tangible person.

"I'm tired," she muttered to herself as she started across the parking lot with her mail bag over her shoulder. "It has nothing to do with me. I should let it go."

* * *

Before noon, Brody Donegan had been tried for the crime of arson at least twenty times. Kate gave up trying to keep a tally, but the unofficial jury she encountered on Randy's in-town route leaned toward the conclusion Brody was to blame.

However, this demographic pool skewed to the older side. Younger adults were either at work at this time of day, or maybe sleeping in preparation for their night shifts at one of the region's factories. There weren't any within Eagle River's city limits, but Charles City and Swanton both had large employers that ran assembly lines around the clock.

"You know he did it," one elderly woman told Kate. "I

mean, who else would be stupid enough to do such a thing?"

Kate only raised her eyebrows in answer. Because according to the guy across the street, Eagle River was full of foolish teenagers who liked nothing more than to drive the back roads and party in whatever sorry-looking structure they could find.

Hiding in a dilapidated barn was an easy way to keep the good vibes rolling without having to worry about some nosy neighbor calling the sheriff. Or at least, that's what he'd always heard. Didn't know anything about that, himself.

"Setting a barn on fire!" Another woman snatched her letters out of Kate's hand with an angry flick of the wrist. "And with the dry weather we've been having, too. I don't care if Brody's smoked most of his life, you don't light up somewhere like that."

From the gravelly sound of her voice, this woman likely had first-hand experience with such a dilemma. "He's a darn fool, I tell you. Could have burned half the county down last night."

In this instance, apparently, the charge was *accidental* burning.

"So, you know him?" Exhausted as she was, Kate was still intrigued.

"Goodness, no." The woman rolled her eyes. "But my sister, she was a teacher. Had him for high-school math. He couldn't do much more than add two and two, and I doubt he's progressed much since then. His dad, now, he has a good head on his shoulders."

More praise for the father, despite what was said about the son. It was a theme Kate had heard a few times already.

"Well, it will be interesting to see what happens. Try not to worry too much about it." If only Kate could take her own advice.

The hours were ticking by, and Kate was eager to be on her way. It was common for some customers to seek a minute or two of idle chatter along with their mail, but a suspiciously large number of residents just happened to be hanging out on their porches today, or clearing out the flowerbeds by their mailboxes.

As she walked around the east side of Eagle River, Kate filed away everything she'd heard about Brody. Some of it was new, but other pieces dovetailed with what Deputy Collins told her last night.

Brody was in his early twenties. Used to work at the auto body shop in town and helped his dad farm but, well, something had happened and he was currently out of a day job. The old homestead south of Kate's place had once belonged to Chester's great-grandparents, it was part of that land parcel Chester had given Brody so he'd get all the profits off this year's corn crop. A little seed money that, if Brody was ambitious enough, he could use to bankroll buying more land.

But that seemed to be the problem, Kate was told. Brody lacked ambition.

He'd rather spend his afternoons down at Paul's Place, the local dive bar, bemoaning how bad the economy was and how he was going to head out to California as soon as he could get some cash together.

"You know he did it," one man grumbled to Kate as she set his parcel inside his front door.

The sentence had been handed down, but Kate wanted to hear more. "So, you think he lit it on purpose, then? For the insurance money?"

"Where else is he going to get the cash? The barn was old, sure, but there are lots of them around here in worse shape. It has more value than you'd think. And I couldn't believe it when Chester bulldozed the house. He should have kept it up and rented it out. Or sold it off to someone who would have taken care of it."

Kate made a mental note to pull up the county assessor's website when she got home. Listings were public record, after all. But this man's musings made her suspect nostalgia was getting in his way. She liked to see old houses and barns saved, too, but most people didn't have the money and time needed to keep them up.

But one late-afternoon stop netted Kate some interesting information from a reliable source. Randy's route clipped the east side of Main Street, and Roland Sherwood was eager to welcome one of his former tenants inside for a chat.

Sherwood's Furniture Store had been in this location for over fifty years, but the structure itself was much older than that. Like much of the historic downtown area, the red-brick building had been built in the late 1800s. There were just three apartments on the second floor, but Kate and Charlie had been lucky enough to snag a vacancy when she moved back to Eagle River.

Roland was tidying up the front showroom when Kate and her mailbag came through the door. Customers were often scarce this late on a weekday.

"Hey there!" He waved, dust cloth in hand. "How goes it out at the farm?"

"It's lovely. I mean, outside at least. The inside of the house needs work." She fished in her bag for Roland's bundle, and he motioned for her to drop it on the closest end table.

Then Kate sighed. "Come to think of it, maybe the outside's not so great. Not after what happened last night."

Roland nodded solemnly. "I know you're out that way. I told Carrie last night, when we heard about it, that it wasn't more than a few miles from your place."

"Not quite two." Kate frowned. "Not far enough, I have to say. I'm already locking everything down at night, but this ..." She shook her head. "Makes you wonder about people, you know? What they're capable of."

Roland glanced out the store's plate-glass windows. He seemed to be considering something before he spoke again.

"I don't know anything," he said quickly. "Really, I don't.

But Brody was in here last month, wanted some stuff. Big leather couch, a new stand for a wide-screen TV. I guess he'd given up his apartment, moved back in with his folks. Needed things for his man cave in their basement."

"Didn't he already have furniture?" Kate thought of how difficult it had been to downsize from the Chicago bungalow she'd shared with Ben to the apartment right above her head.

"He sure did." Roland raised an eyebrow. "Wanted to trade some things in for the back room." The store kept a robust stock of used pieces at a steep discount. "But that wouldn't cover it, of course."

Kate had long ago learned silence was a good way to glean interesting tidbits from people. Too many questions, too much curiosity make people feel like they were being put on the spot. Let them talk, though, and you'd find out all sorts of interesting things.

Roland lowered his voice, even though they were alone in the store. "I checked his credit. Let's just say, Brody had to make do with what he already had. I know you won't spread that around."

Kate gave a quick nod of promise. Roland seemed like an ethical business owner. Why would he share something with her that was usually off-limits to others? But he soon made himself clear.

"I wanted you to know what I know, because I thought it might ease your mind. Brody needs money. Whatever happened last night, I believe it was an isolated incident."

Kate sighed with relief. "I keep trying to tell myself that, too."

"One and done." Roland gave her a reassuring grin. "So I don't think you, or anyone else around here, has to worry. The country's a beautiful, peaceful place this time of year. I hope you can relax enough to enjoy it."

Then he laughed as he picked up his stack of mail. "Well, except when the combines rumble on and on, all hours of the day and night. But harvest is one of the most important times of year around here, we can put up with a few disruptions for a month or so."

Kate left the furniture store with a lighter heart, and a reminder about the pre-holiday sale that would start in late October. Roland had several new pieces on order, and if Kate needed anything specific for her new place ...

As she finished that afternoon's deliveries, Kate sifted through the gossip she'd collected. Roland was probably right about last night, and about Brody, but she'd promised not to spread that information around.

And while the other residents' musings were interesting, none of them seemed noteworthy enough to pass on to Sheriff Preston. But she resolved to stay alert until this case was closed.

✳ 5 ✳

It was the perfect fall day for baking, Kate decided as she slipped the second pie into the oven. Raindrops slid down the farmhouse's windows, but the kitchen was bright and warm and smelled wonderful.

"What do you think?" she asked Charlie, who had just wandered in for a cat-friendly snack. "I'm almost out of apples for today. But there are pears left. And some dough. Hmm."

Charlie looked up from his bowl long enough to take in the scents of cinnamon and cloves that drifted around the kitchen. Then he turned back to what was most important: his own food.

"I'll decide for the both of us." Kate wiped her face with the back of one hand, and ended up with a smudge of flour on her nose. "We'll use all the leftovers, but give them a fancy name: pear-apple-spice tart, I think."

Tuesday was Kate's weekday off this week, and she'd expected to spend it helping her family with harvest. But this rain had everything on hold. Instead, it was a good chance to bake some treats and take them around to a few of her closest neighbors. After all, the ones who farmed were sitting on the sidelines today, too.

Kate had long ago mastered the proportions for Grandma

Ida's pie crust, but never ended up with an exact amount in the end. While the final scraps would be baked on their own, with a sprinkle of sugar and cinnamon, there was just enough left for that tart. Kate gave her rolling pin another dusting of flour and got back to work.

With his snack finished, Charlie took more notice of what was going on around him. His blue eyes fixated on the closest stretch of counter, and Kate shook her head. "No. You know I don't like it when you jump up there."

She was happy to see him choose another perch, at least this time. The stepstool with the flip-down, padded seat had been hiding in the basement, and Kate had wiped it off and set it by the largest kitchen window.

It gave her a leg up into the upper cabinet shelves, of course, but Charlie had quickly requisitioned it for his kitchen throne.

"Oooh, way to go, Charlie!" Kate's chipper tone was met with only a squint of acknowledgement. The stool was his choice, his expression said, not one made to gain her approval. "I'll get this in the oven while you supervise, then gather up these peelings."

Her parents had a flock of chickens, and Kate always saved any appropriate scraps for them. Some other trimmings went into the compost pile next to the garden and, since her dated kitchen lacked a garbage disposal, the rest was stockpiled for the county's weekly garbage pickup.

There was an ancient iron incinerator behind the chicken house, but Kate had yet to find the courage to fire it up. And after what happened Thursday night, an open flame wasn't something she wanted to deal with right now.

Kate had just settled the tart dough on a cookie sheet when a loud *clunk-thump* echoed above her head.

"Hey!" a man's voice called down the stairs. "Can you run up here for a second?"

"Be right there!" She wiped her hands on a towel. "Watch

the pies," she told Charlie, but he was determined to follow her out of the kitchen.

"What now?" Kate muttered as she turned the stairwell's landing. "He's found two things already that need fixing."

Charlie ran ahead of Kate and into the bathroom, where Richard Everton was sprawled out on the worn carpet, wrench in hand. He operated a construction company with his adult sons, and came highly recommended. Which was a blessing, since this bathroom was in dire need of assistance.

"Don't panic." Richard tried for a smile. "It looks worse than it is."

"I hope so." The sink's ancient pipes were currently just a dirty jumble on an old towel. "What's the deal?"

"Well, these fittings are so worn, it's lucky you didn't spring a leak before now. I need to replace them, for sure."

"Oh, goodie!" Kate gave a wry smile. "How much is this going to cost?"

Richard gave her a number, and Kate sighed and nodded in defeat.

Kate wanted to turn the kitchen pantry into a powder room, but she'd also set aside what seemed like a reasonable budget to upgrade this bathroom. After all, she didn't want to do anything too crazy in here.

Just demo the pink tile that ran halfway up the bathroom walls and replace it with beadboard and trim. Maybe put some of those faux-wood planks on the floor. Update the fixtures on the sink, and in the tub and shower. She could live with the toilet, as long as it didn't leak.

The room was so tiny. How much trouble could it be? Turns out, more than she had expected.

"I can run over to Charles City right now, be back with the parts in an hour or so." Richard looked around and nodded. "This place is pretty solid. But it's like a time machine when it comes to finishes and fixtures."

"You know, these tiles are growing on me." Kate smiled. "I

hear pink is making a comeback. And given how my budget is draining away, I may need to keep them."

Richard shrugged. "Well, the beadboard won't be that expensive. But that is some serious demo." He got up from the floor and wiped his hands on a towel. "But yeah, you can always put all that off until another time. Have you thought more about the fixtures you want downstairs?"

"I hope to finalize them next week." It was a forty-minute drive in either direction to reach the big-box home improvement stores. She'd made the trip to Waterloo once to look at her options, took photos and measurements, and had even made newspaper templates to keep the shapes in perspective. The pantry was so tiny, and the stores so far away, that she had to get this right on the first try.

"When I get this sink back together, I'll start on that other project." Richard grinned. "I can't wait to see how that high-tech doggie door works. I've heard about them, but never seen one in action."

"Well, we won't know for sure until Hazel gets here, which won't be for a few more days."

After a trip to the canine training facility, Kate had decided to adopt Hazel. She was excited, and a little nervous, too. While her family had always had dogs, Kate had never had one of her own.

Hazel's background wasn't fully known, since she was a rescue, but word was she'd started life on a farm. She was smart, the trainers told Kate, and would be good at staying in her yard. Even so, Kate didn't want her new pooch to have twenty four-hour access to the outdoors. And then, there was Charlie inside, and the barn cats outside …

Karen suggested a doggie hatch for the kitchen door that opened only when it detected a fob that would hang on Hazel's collar.

The pup could come and go, but the cats and other critters couldn't. Kate saved some money by ordering a low-tech door for the back porch's entrance, and crossed her fingers this two-step system would work.

Richard was on board to install them both, and Kate was grateful. After all, her dad and brother were knee-deep in harvest. And she had her hands full getting Charlie prepared for what would be a major adjustment to his lifestyle.

Dogs weren't always comfortable with change, but cats hated it outright. Charlie was like a sundial, regular as could be, and chose his nap spots throughout the day as the light changed. Kate had already moved his food dishes to the top of the new credenza in the dining room, which was just a long, narrow table she'd picked up at a secondhand store. She hoped if Charlie didn't have to worry about Hazel sampling his snacks, he'd feel less territorial toward his new fur sister.

Kate had also put his favorite bed in the smallest upstairs room, the one with the window seat, added more food dishes, and made sure to scatter his most-loved toys on the carpet. When Hazel came home, Kate would block the entrance with a borrowed baby gate so Charlie would have a safe space Hazel couldn't reach.

"Things are going to change around here," she told Richard. "I just hope it's all for the best."

"You'll get through it." He gave Charlie a gentle pet, which Charlie graciously allowed. "And so will you, pal."

A buzzer sounded below. "Time to check the pies. They aren't ready yet, but I can't leave that old oven unattended for long. It runs hotter than it should."

Richard followed her to the stairwell. "There's a guy over in Swanton who carries refurbished models. He gets them at auctions, fixes them up."

"That's good to know. As long as it keeps going, I might be able to manage for a while. But I'll keep an eye on it."

She almost added, *we don't need any more fires*, but it wasn't necessary. Richard's concerned expression said it all. Both of his sons served with Eagle River's fire department.

"You know, Sam was in there when the roof started to collapse." He looked away for a moment as he pulled on his coat. "They couldn't save the barn, of course, but they had to keep the fire from spreading into the field. The guys outside said later that they saw the barn tremble, there was no other way to describe it."

Richard rubbed the gray stubble on his chin, then sighed. "Everyone got out, that's what matters. That's what I keep telling myself."

"Thankfully, no one was hurt. And as dangerous as it is, we need people like Sam and Jacob who are willing to run in when everyone else is running out."

"I don't know Brody, but I know his dad." Richard's voice turned hard with contempt. "I know Chester can't control his son. No parent can, once they're grown. But I hope the marshal got what he needed to press charges."

Richard hadn't told Kate anything new; she'd heard the same sentiment several times in the past few days. But it was clear Richard needed to talk, so she followed him out to his truck despite the drizzle.

"Chester's son may be lazy and a fool," he said as he opened the truck's door. "Even a criminal. But my son? He almost paid the ultimate price for serving his community the other night. Well, enough on that for now. Your fur family is expanding in a few days, and there's work to do. I'll be back as soon as I can."

Kate waved him off, then stood by the side of the driveway for a moment. If Brody didn't do it, she hoped officials would soon know who did. If it had been an accident, most folks would be able to accept that, too. But with every day that passed without some sort of resolution, the fear, frustration and suspicion would only get worse. Her hometown needed closure; and the sooner, the better.

A rustle in the leaf pile by her feet startled Kate out of her thoughts. Jerry, wearing a smug look, jumped out of the mound and pounced on Kate's sneakers with his big orange paws.

"OK, Jerry, you got me." Kate hesitated, then reached down to give the cat a gentle pet. He liked it so much, she tried for another. Jerry's progress was slow, but steady. Like everything else at her new place.

"I'm glad you're starting to like it here. Seems like Milton hadn't had a dog for a few years; I hope you'll warm up to Hazel when she arrives." Then she laughed. "Don't people say cats don't like water? What are you doing out here in the rain? Karen and Melinda and I built you a super-cool cat house; maybe now's a good time to go in and curl up where it's warm and dry."

* * *

Charlie supervised Richard while he reassembled the bathroom pipes and installed the dog doors. By the time Richard left for the day, the pies were cool enough to transport. Kate splashed some water on her face and changed into a different sweatshirt while Charlie studied this new addition to the kitchen's door.

He stared it down, pawed at it with a curious front foot, and sniffed it so carefully that he pressed his face to the still-unyielding flap.

"Can't get it open, huh?" Kate shook her head. "That's the point! I put the magic token away. But it's for your own good."

Charlie pinned back his ears and stalked off into the dining room. He obviously disagreed. This was his house, after all.

"Fine, go sulk. I'm going to head out and be social, for a change." Kate pulled out two cookie sheets and loaded the treats. The rain had finally stopped and, if she left right now, she might be able to catch some of her neighbors before they started evening chores.

She decided to go north first. The closest place had a steep-roofed farmhouse painted a cheerful shade of blue, and Kate guessed it to be older than her 1920s foursquare. Three horses grazed in the front pasture, their barn faded and old but in better shape than most. "Ashford" was on the mailbox.

Kate knew the surname by heart, as she passed this driveway at least a few times every day, but that was it. This road was part of Jack's usual route, but Kate had resisted the urge to press him for details about her new neighbors.

She was paying a friendly call, neighbor to neighbor. It wouldn't do to come into the conversation with any kind of leverage.

Of course, there were few secrets in a town as small as Eagle River. Word of her acreage's sale would have spread quickly, as well as the basics of who bought it. As she drove up the lane, it didn't take long for Kate to guess what the story might be.

It's some woman who works for the post office. Grew up around here, but I heard she was in Chicago for a long time before the divorce. No kids, I guess, but she has this fancy-looking cat. You know, one of those really fluffy ones with the brown face? Word is she's going to renovate that house from top to bottom.

Normally, Kate didn't worry too much about what others thought of her. In a place like Chicago, there were too many people around to pay anyone much mind. Outside of one's social circle, at least. But here? Community mattered. And your perceived place in that space, whether accurate or not, could make a difference.

Besides that, Kate was eager to make more connections in Eagle River. Most of her high-school friends had moved away, just as she did. But very few of them had come back. At least, not yet. Getting to know the people behind these mailboxes would go a long way toward making Kate feel at home here again.

And give her peace of mind about living in the country, alone.

A black-and-white Collie dog spotted Kate's car, and its barks had the horses nickering and twitching their ears in interest. The dog's fluffy tail whipped back and forth, but Kate sensed the pup was showing curiosity and excitement, not aggression. Like most mail carriers, she had a master's degree in Doggie Thoughts 101.

"Hey, there!" Kate let the dog sniff her hand before she got out of the car. Her greeting was warmly accepted, but the tempting aroma of the pies in the backseat quickly got the dog's interest. "No, sorry, I didn't bring you any treats." Bertha, Kate's mail car, was stocked with dog snacks, but her personal vehicle was lacking in that department.

A woman whose short brown hair was woven with streaks of silver came to the back porch door. Her smile was genuine, and Kate was instantly at ease. "Maisie, be nice! Don't knock her over."

"I'm OK." Kate laughed as she balanced a pie in one hand and her purse over the other shoulder. "I'm Kate Duncan. Moved into the next place to the south a few weeks ago."

"Gwen Ashford." She reached for the pie. "Oh, this looks lovely. The boys have been begging for pie since the weather turned, but I just haven't had time to bake one. Or get down there to meet you."

Kate followed Gwen into the kitchen, which was surprisingly sleek and modern given the age of the house. "Oh, I understand." Kate took the wooden kitchen chair that was offered, along with a cup of coffee. "I drive by every day, and keep meaning to stop in."

"Fall's always a busy time." Gwen added sugar and milk to her own mug. Then a shadow crossed her face. "But things sure are different here, this time around."

Gwen worked for an insurance office in Charles City. Her boys were ten and twelve, and were at soccer practice that afternoon. She and her husband had divorced in the spring, and he'd bought a house in Swanton. It was closer to his day job, she explained, and he'd grown tired of farming on the side. The fields were rented now and, for the first time in many years, there was no harvest season on Gwen's horizon.

"Well, my parents are pushing hard to get their crops in," Kate offered with a smile. "I guess if you get really bored, they might welcome an extra set of hands."

Gwen laughed. "I'll keep that in mind." Then she leaned across the table. "Minnie called me when she knew the sale was going to go through. She was so excited that 'a local girl,' as she called you, was going to buy her place."

That warmed Kate's heart. *A local girl.* Yes, that was her. Once again.

Kate shared her hopes and plans for the farmhouse, but told Gwen she wasn't quite sure what to do with the sheds and the pasture. "There's not much acreage out there, of course, but the grass is growing wild and so are the weeds."

Gwen raised an eyebrow. "More critters, maybe? They keep life interesting."

"I'm giving that some thought." Kate held up a hand. "But I've had to take a firm stance with people, at least for now. Offers of goats and sheep, in particular, keep coming my way."

Chickens might be a good place to start, Gwen suggested. Minnie's dad built that impressive coop several decades ago, and the family sold eggs to people for miles around. Kate was eager to hear more; what else did Gwen know about the acreage just down the road?

Gwen thought for a moment. "You know, speaking of the pasture, has anyone told you about that little pocket of prairie plants?"

"What? I had no idea!"

It wasn't a large area, Gwen said, just some wildflowers and grasses on the far side of the creek. The bank was fairly steep in that spot, so livestock had never been too eager to venture across the stream and snack on that patch of vegetation.

Kate was thrilled by this news. "I've walked back there a bit, but everything's brown this late in the season. It all looks the same."

"Well, now you know. Something to look forward to in the spring, right?" Then Gwen stared out the bank of windows to where Maisie chased a few stray leaves across the brown lawn, and let out a long sigh. "But it's hard to look ahead sometimes, given what happened last week."

She didn't have to say more.

"I'm just hoping they catch this person, and soon." Kate took another sip of her coffee as she pondered her options.

Would Gwen offer an opinion on Brody? Should Kate ask for one? Maybe not. She was here to make friends, not snoop for clues. Kate decided it was best to simply state her own feelings and let the conversation take its natural course.

"I'm new out here, as you know. I love my place, but it's been difficult enough at night, and now we've had that fire. Mayor Benson was in the post office the other day, and he said arson cases are very difficult to prosecute, if that is indeed what happened. So, I don't know where that leaves the rest of us."

"Scared and unsure, I'd say." Gwen stared into her mug, then raised her chin. "I know what people are saying, but I don't believe Brody did it. He's young, sure, and he's ... lost his way a little bit."

Kate was intrigued, but kept silent.

"But that doesn't mean he's a criminal. And he's not dumb. There's no way that barn was worth much, anyway." Then Gwen glanced at the kitchen clock, and smiled. "I'm so glad you stopped by. You know, even with the boys here, I've been on edge at night, too. So, I guess you're not alone in that."

"Neither are you. None of us are." Kate was warmed through, and not only by the coffee. "We just need to look out for each other."

Gwen had to pick up her boys; it was time to go. After another wave to her closest neighbor and a pat on the head for Maisie, Kate checked the last two pies were still secure in the back seat and started down the lane. While the rain had let up some time ago, the skies were still overcast and fog was beginning to seep over the fields.

At the gravel, Kate turned back south. She now had a full tank of enthusiasm for her errand, but was running short on treats. "I have to pick and choose carefully," she reminded herself as she considered her options. "Thank goodness my orchard is still going strong; maybe I can do this again sometime soon."

The other pie went to the Campbells, an older couple living southeast of Kate's new home. They had been close friends of the Findlays, and were eager to welcome Kate to the neighborhood. She backtracked to the corner and went west to visit the Becketts. But the yard was quiet, and the curious barn cats milling about would be all-too-eager to sample the tart, so Kate knew better than to leave it on the front steps with a note.

The Zimmermans, just up the road, were at home and thankful for Kate's offer of a fresh-baked dessert. Evening chores were about to start, so there wasn't much time to chat, but Kate exchanged phone numbers and promised to come by for supper some night once harvest was over.

Back at the crossroads, Kate intended to go left and go home. But she sat there for a second, then made a right. South, toward the scene of the fire.

She was at least a little bit ashamed of herself, but she couldn't help it. No one else was out and about on this sleepy afternoon, as the combines and tractors were all idle in their sheds due to the wet weather. She'd never turn up the lane; it wasn't right. But to drive by, really slow, and see what she could see ... the opportunity was too much to resist. Besides, she had a kitchen counter full of dirty dishes waiting for her at home, and no dishwasher at her disposal. What was the rush?

Kate considered Brody again as she rolled down the road. Richard was so certain Brody was guilty, and Gwen had been just as sure he wasn't. Both of them knew the Donegans; whose take was more accurate? Gwen surely felt a loyalty to the family, the kind that comes from being long-time neighbors. And Richard's perspective was understandably colored by the danger his sons had faced fighting the flames.

"Perception is everything." Here was the last corner before Brody's land; she could still turn around and go home. But Kate went on. "Of course, there's always the possibility the fire was accidental."

She gasped when what was left of the barn finally appeared on her right. "Oh, no, just look at that. Such a mess! That's going to be expensive to clean up, no matter what happened."

Only an enormous pile of blackened beams and scorched boards was now visible where the barn used to stand. As she rolled to a stop at the end of the lane, Kate thought she made out a dented metal cupola down on its side in front of the rubble.

Her initial wave of shock soon evolved into sadness and empathy. For both the once-proud barn, and for the young man who now shouldered the gargantuan task of removing its remains.

The trees far up this lane still held most of their leaves. Their fall colors were muted on this dreary afternoon, but soon, they'd give way as well. Nothing else remained at this former farm but the overgrown grasses that long ago swallowed up what she imagined was once a tidy yard punctuated by a generously sized garden and clusters of perennials.

Deep tire ruts scarred the lane. Kate recalled the organized chaos of Thursday night, and thought of all the pumper trucks and emergency vehicles that had made those still-fresh tracks. And the dozens of firefighters who'd toiled for hours to keep the blaze from spreading.

Her focus shifted as a flock of large, dark birds erupted out of the line of trees just behind the towering mound of rubble. Crows, most likely, although they were too far away for Kate to be sure. She wondered what had stirred them up, especially on a quiet afternoon like this one.

But there, parked just beyond the charred pile, she spotted one back corner of an old truck. Dents and rust threatened to take over the metal, but the truck's once-bright paint was still easy to see.

It was a unique shade of reddish-orange and, if Kate hadn't been so disheartened about the sad state of this former farm, she might have admired how it added a quaint pop of color to this muted autumn scene.

The birds stirred again, and Kate caught a flash of movement on the other side of the truck. Someone was up there, walking around. All she could make out was a man in a cap and sweatshirt, but that was more than enough. Kate's stomach lurched, and her cheeks burned with shame.

"That must be Brody! Ugh, this is so embarrassing." She turned away, popped the car into gear and stepped on the gas.

Had he seen her? Oh, she hoped not! Surely Brody was too distracted by the mess before him to have noticed her car at the end of his lane. At the next intersection, she set out to take the long way around toward home; she wasn't about to drive by twice!

"Now I'm glad I waited a little longer to try to meet the neighbors." Kate had to laugh at herself as she drove along.

She was sure she'd never met Brody before. Which meant he didn't know her, either. Or her vehicle.

"That might have just saved me from some serious embarrassment. Isn't this the very thing I rolled my eyes about, growing up? How people around here always seemed to find the time to stick their noses into everyone else's business? Maybe I'm settling in here better than I thought."

By the time she'd turned up her own driveway, Kate had vowed her surveillance of the burned barn was over. Scout lounged on the back steps, his pensive mood a match for the dreary afternoon, and Kate took a seat next to him.

"Well, I might as well confess to you what I did." To her amazement, the big cat climbed into her lap and settled in with a purr. "I just acted like a total local. I purposefully drove down there to gawk at something that wasn't any of my business."

Scout's meow lacked judgment, Kate was sure of it.

"No, this is important." She cuddled him close, and he leaned his head against her sweatshirt. "Because if I'm not careful, the next thing you know, I'll be driving all over the township, checking up on the crops and then throwing my opinions around at the post office and the drug store. I'll turn into the next Jack or, even worse, the next Auggie."

Kate couldn't let that happen. She was back in Eagle River, but could she find a way to be neighborly without being nosy? She decided she had to try.

* 6 *

The fall decorations really added something to the post office, Kate decided as she looked around the lobby. Her former shop in Chicago had strict rules about such things, and one pumpkin-shaped gourd by the pen caddy was about all that was on display this time of year.

But Roberta knew her customers well. This was a public building in a very small town, and a festive, seasonal appearance was expected. After all, the library and city hall sported baskets of mini pumpkins and had faux-leaf garlands draped over their windows.

More leaves of the real kind danced down Main Street on this crisp, clear October day. Driven by a brisk northwest wind, they gathered in clusters along the curbs and then scattered just as quickly. Kate's thoughts began to tumble, too, as she took in the charming scene outside.

She really needed to get back to mulching leaves at her little farm. The grass probably should be mowed one more time. Thanks to Ed and Mabel's abundance of pumpkins, Kate's front porch and sidewalk now nearly overflowed with fall cheer.

The farmhouse's old windows were beautiful, but drafty. Most, if not all, of them should be wrapped in clear plastic before the snow arrived. And Melinda had promised to help Kate build a smaller shelter within the barn cats' enclosure that would provide a safe space to run a heat lamp. Maybe this weekend ...

Kate was just about to text one friend when another came in from the back room.

"How's it going?" Bev leaned on the counter, then ran one hand through her short white hair. "Goodness, it's a wild one out there. Glad it's my break."

"It's been pretty quiet. It's nice to be up here for a change, not out in the wind." Kate yawned. "But if it doesn't get exciting soon, I'm afraid I might fall asleep."

"Busy day off, yesterday, huh? How's that old bathroom shaping up?"

Kate sighed. "Well, my budget's already in the toilet, if that tells you anything. I think I'll have to settle for fixing up the bathroom I have, for now. The new one downstairs will have to wait. But I did meet a few neighbors, so that was nice."

Kate filled Bev in on her afternoon jaunt around the neighborhood, but left out the part where she'd been snooping at the end of Brody Donegan's farm lane. Instead, she shared her excitement about the prairie plants in her pasture, as well as Hazel's much-anticipated arrival Sunday afternoon.

"If Charlie and Hazel have their own zones, at least for a little while, they'll adjust," Bev promised. "Not everyone fights like cats and dogs, you know. We've had so many furry friends over the years, it always works out."

She leaned over the counter to get a better look out the side window. "Potential customer, ten o'clock. Oh, it's Edna Chesterfield."

Bev's tone carried a sudden hint of wariness that made Kate snap to attention.

"Edna looks like she's on a mission," Bev muttered. "I

think we're going to quickly discover what it's about."

Edna blew in with a gust of wind, then patted down her gray curls. "My goodness, such a gale!"

"Hello there, Edna." Bev was all smiles. "Can we help you with something?"

Edna dumped her purse on the counter and started to rummage through it. "You sure can! Oh, where did I ... here." She unfolded an orange sheet of paper and held it up. "Well, what do you think?"

Kate thought that the next few weeks in Eagle River were going to be very long ones. She also decided she should choose her words carefully.

"Well, this is an important issue in our community," she told Edna with a smile. "It's really good of you to get involved."

Edna's flyer announced a "concerned citizens group" that would gather at the library next Wednesday to figure out a way to smother the city's proposed burn ban. Monday's city council meeting had run far beyond its usual hour, and the chambers had been packed with residents offering heated opinions on both sides of the issue.

Word around town was that while the council wouldn't vote on the measure for a few weeks yet, a majority of the members were willing to end this long-standing tradition. Gossip also noted there was a determined, if small, group of residents mobilizing to fight the proposal.

Kate didn't know Edna, but this grandma-in-glasses didn't fit her profile of a rabble-rouser. Apparently, she was wrong.

"We need everyone to turn out next week." Edna was flustered, and not just from the wind that had pushed her down the sidewalk. "This abomination cannot stand! I've lived in this town all of my seventy-six years, and we've always burned our leaves in the fall. Why change it now? I tell you why, because some of those council members are overly concerned about what the young people think."

She cut her eyes at Kate, who decided to take that as a compliment. At thirty-two, she didn't exactly feel young anymore. But with so many of Eagle River's residents middle-aged and beyond, the term was certainly relative.

Bev slipped through the half-door next to the counter and reached for the flyer.

"We'll just put this on the bulletin board, right where everyone can see it." Bev's tone was chipper and soothing, and Edna's shoulders relaxed. "This orange paper will really make it stand out."

"It's so important that people educate themselves on this issue." Edna's outrage had cooled by a few degrees. "All this talk about global warming and air pollution and whatnot. Here, in Eagle River? I don't see it. Burning a few leaves isn't going to harm anything."

Bev wasn't about to get into a fight about climate change. Instead, she took the sentimental route as she searched for an unused tack on the board.

"It's certainly a tradition in this town. People like things to stay the way they've always been."

"It's more than that." Edna was gathering steam again. "It's our right as landowners to do as we see fit with our yard waste. If the city wants to come around, house to house, and bag it up for us and take it to the recycling center, well, fine."

Bev nodded with understanding, but Kate saw a hint of amusement in her friend's eyes. "There's nothing that says 'fall' like that wonderful aroma, is there?"

"No doubt." Edna's lined face turned wistful. "When you get your leaf pile all situated, and the wind is just right, and you light that match and that little flame catches on." She sighed. "It's like magic, you know? Just beautiful to see."

Kate's heart lurched in her chest. Edna wasn't just on the march about freedom of ... whatever this might be. She was enamored with the entire burning process.

Kate didn't believe this tiny lady was up to any big trouble, but Edna's emotional response reminded her it was possible that someone other than Brody was behind last week's blaze. But what was the motive, then? Money? Revenge? A simple urge to create havoc and watch something burn?

Kate had no idea. But suddenly, she had plans for one week from tonight.

The calculating look on Bev's face told Kate she was thinking the same. "Thanks for bringing that in," she gushed to Edna. "Let me guess, you're posting notices all over town?"

"Oh, absolutely." Edna checked the depths of her tote. "I have some more in here. Monday's meeting was a total sham, they barely let the public talk at all."

She narrowed her eyes. "I smell a conspiracy. It's time for everyone who cares to come together." Her eyes lit up with an idea. "You know, it's not enough to put up these flyers. We need people talking about this, too, spreading the word, encouraging everyone to get involved."

She looked hopefully at Bev, and then Kate.

"Oh, I don't know," Kate said gently. "We, um, as public employees, we're supposed to stay out of any sort of controversy in our communities."

"That's right," Bev added quickly. "Sometimes, it's tough to work for the feds. All those restrictions." Edna's aggressive nod made it clear Bev had struck a nerve. "You should see our handbook. There's a rule for everything, these days. Why, we're allowed to vote, and I swear that's just about it."

Edna patted Bev on the arm. "You poor dears. I can't imagine what you're up against." She waved as she went out the door. "Well, ladies, I better get on with my rounds. Hope to see both of you next Wednesday!"

With a surprising show of strength, Edna fought the driving wind to escape out the post office's front door.

When the lobby was empty again, Bev turned to Kate and

raised an eyebrow. "I don't even know where to start."

"I do. Are you free next Wednesday night? Because I'd rather not go to this hoedown alone."

"I'll meet you there." Bev began to straighten the counter as she organized her thoughts. "Edna certainly loves to burn her leaves. I got goosebumps when she started waxing poetic like that. I can't imagine she had anything to do with Brody's barn, but ..."

Kate shrugged. "I agree. But pyromaniacs are drawn to fires. And this meeting? It's the next best thing."

"What are the odds the guilty party is going to show up?" Bev laughed. "Pretty good, I'd say. Like a moth to a flame, they won't be able to stay away."

✳ ✳ ✳

Kate glanced at the dashboard's clock and gripped the steering wheel tight in frustration. "Come on, everyone! A traffic jam in little Prosper? On a Thursday afternoon, no less. It's harvest season, but I still can't believe how bad this is."

The fields had dried out over the past two days, so harvest was back to full throttle. She'd been waiting for at least five minutes for her chance to turn into the co-op's drive. Once she made it onto the property, it was going to be another slow crawl until she could ease out of the queue of grain trucks and gravity wagons and park her car in the lot.

It had been a long day at the post office, and Kate was eager to get home. But she would wait her turn here at the co-op, and try to do it with a grateful heart. Because it was time to replenish the barn cats' supply of free food.

The line to unload grain was carefully choreographed by the handful of retired farmers Auggie hired during this busy season. Kate gestured toward the parking lot, and one grandfatherly gentleman paused the outgoing line long enough to motion her through.

"Thank you!" She inched her way down the closest row.

The roar from the harvest vehicles and grain dryers was nearly deafening when she got out of the car, and the dust kicked up in the gravel lot added to the sense of barely controlled chaos. It was nearly as crazy inside, with the aisles jammed with shoppers catching up on their gossip while they packed their carts with supplies.

Kate wound through the crowd toward the register, then waved at Dan, Auggie's assistant manager. Dan pointed toward the end of the counter and, as she slipped past the four-deep checkout line, Kate almost burst out laughing. For just a second, she felt like a VIP guest at an exclusive club in Chicago. The kind that had never let Kate and her friends through the door.

Just as promised, there was an economy-size bag of dry food in the corner. And a pouch of treats.

Pebbles, one of the shop cats, was curled up on a padded bed on the counter's bottom shelf. "Hey, girl." Kate rubbed the gray kitty's ears. "Tired of all the visitors? It sure is busy in here today."

Kate hoisted the gifts in her arms, then caught Dan's eye again. "Is he out back?"

Dan nodded. "Over by the grain bins, west side."

With the cat food and treats deposited in the car, Kate zigzagged through the queues of tractors and their gravity wagons until she spotted the man of the hour. Or really, of harvest season itself. There was Auggie, in a gray windbreaker and store-branded ball cap, holding court with two farmers next to a grain bin. He gently shooed them off as Kate approached, and they waved and went on their way.

"Thanks again for the cat food!" Kate had to almost shout to be heard. "You didn't have to throw in the treats, too."

"I sure did." Auggie called back, then he grinned. "Nothing is too good for the Three *Mouse*keteers." He pointed toward a nearby shed. "Let's mosey that way, so we can hear ourselves."

They were soon at the far western edge of the property. Just beyond the fence, a half-harvested cornfield stretched to the horizon. "There, that's better. So, what's the latest on the fire?"

No chit chat, no ramblings about the weather. But Kate didn't mind one bit. This was the topic she most wanted to discuss, and the afternoon was ticking away.

"Not much. Or at least, nothing solid." She almost mentioned Wednesday's meeting, but decided to let that slide. Auggie had surely heard about it, and Kate wasn't looking for projections about what might happen next week. She was eager for whatever gossip Auggie had collected up until now.

"There does seem to be a sizable contingency that thinks Brody lit up his own barn," she said. "But I'm not sure if that's the majority, though."

"Well," Auggie said slowly, "Brody Donegan's not the brightest or most industrious member of our society. I suppose he might be foolish enough to do something like that. Either way, he's an easy scapegoat. Even if he might not be the right one."

"I wouldn't know." Kate sighed. "I haven't met him yet, or any of his family, and they live only a few miles from my place. It feels strange to not know the people around me; it doesn't matter how far they are down the road. Who are they? What are they like?"

"And are they capable of committing a crime?" Auggie finished her thought, then sighed. "There are all kinds of folks in this world, even way out here."

A sharp gust of wind blew in from the northwest, and whispered among the dried leaves of the corn stalks that guarded the other side of the fence.

Auggie had turned unusually quiet, and Kate wondered why. Then she knew.

"You think it was someone else." She crossed her arms

against the chill. Would Auggie confide in her? She was willing to wait around and find out.

He looked over his shoulder at the men milling about on the lot, the endless parade of heavy machinery slowly advancing amid the din of roaring motors and shouted conversation. After a quick wave of acknowledgement to someone, he turned back around and stuffed his hands in his windbreaker's pockets.

"Don't repeat this," he finally said. "But I heard something two weeks ago that now has me wondering about this whole deal."

"Two weeks?" Kate frowned. "But that was before …"

"Exactly."

The owner of a pasture north of Swanton had discovered something strange in one of his cattle sheds. The cows would soon be brought home to spend the winter in his barn, so he was tidying up in the shed on that warm afternoon. He was dismayed to discover the lock on the storage room's door was busted, and that there was now more than his supply of straw bales tucked inside.

Evidence of another plant-based product, if you will.

"It was weed?" Kate gasped, then lowered her voice. "Are you serious?"

"Quite the stash. I don't know much about these things but, from what I heard, it was more than enough for someone's recreational use. But that wasn't all."

Not all the dried marijuana plants were in usable condition. A bundle in one corner looked as if it had been set aflame, and scorch marks ran up the wall.

"But there was no fire when he got there, obviously." Kate tried to piece it together. "It was all done and over with. When had he last been in the storage room?"

"Several weeks, from what I heard. He'd visited property recently, of course, but hadn't gone way back in the shed."

Kate couldn't help but laugh. "Well, they can't be too smart if they dropped a lit joint or a cigarette on their own stash. Probably some teenagers, or something. At least they got the fire out before it spread."

"Yeah," Auggie said slowly, "But the more I think about it, I'm not sure it was an accident."

The exact amount of weed in the storage room varied, of course, depending on who was telling the tale at the time. But given what Auggie had heard, there seemed to be a consensus it was enough for a profitable side hustle. Enough that someone might have deemed it a threat that needed to be destroyed. Although it wasn't talked about openly, Auggie told Kate, drugs were a problem in Hartland County. Not like in the urban areas, but still ...

"Well, that's all I know." Auggie sighed in defeat. "My point is, we rarely have any fires, for any reason. On the rare occasions when we do, it's a vehicle that's been in an accident, or a controlled vegetation burn that got away from somebody. But structure fires? I can't recall the last one, anywhere in the county. And now, we've had two in only a few weeks."

It was hard enough to consider the possibility that one of Kate's new neighbors had deliberately torched his barn. But while Brody had been branded as lazy, she hadn't heard any murmurs about drugs. Were the two incidents even related? Other than the fact that both structures were in rural areas of the county, there didn't seem to be a connection between the two.

"I don't know what to say." She shook her head. "None of this makes sense, at all."

Auggie let out a bark of a laugh. "Kind of like life in general, huh?" Then his tone turned gentle. "Sorry if I've upset you. You just moved out to your new place, you're out there by yourself. I don't know anything else, it's just a hunch that there might be a connection between the two. I could always be wrong."

Now Kate had to laugh. "You? Wrong about something? I'm impressed you'd admit it."

"I haven't yet! Don't get ahead of yourself."

Auggie had called Sheriff Preston and shared what he'd overheard. The sheriff seemed intrigued by this bit of gossip, but didn't tip his hat regarding what he already knew about the cattle shed. And definitely didn't hint whether he thought the incidents were related.

"And he won't," Kate told Auggie as they started back across the lot. "He's a one-way street, and for good reason."

It took several minutes for Kate's car to creep through the parking lot and reach the highway, but she didn't mind. Auggie's assessment of recent events had her head spinning with questions. The tidbits he'd gathered from a handful of farmers were detailed and, more importantly, they were fairly consistent. That made Kate think the fire at the cattle shed happened just as reported. But did it have any connection to the one on Brody's land?

"The plot thickens, and so does the traffic." Kate eyed the queue of grain wagons waiting to enter the co-op. As afternoon gave way to evening, the line would get even longer before it leveled off for the night. "Well, I'd better get home. Scout and his gang will be waiting for their supper."

✳ 7 ✳

Kate checked her reflection in the mirror. "I definitely have plenty of team spirit. But the question is, will I be warm enough without a coat?"

Charlie barely looked up from his favorite corner of the bed, where he was curled up between the headboard and the side of Kate's pillow.

"I'll throw it in the car, just in case." She gave Charlie a quick kiss on the top of his head. "I'm glad the Three Mouseketeers are snug in their shed."

It was a chilly night, and a brisk wind scuttled the dead leaves across the yard and rustled the shocks of dried field corn anchored to the front porch's posts. But a full moon shone high above Eagle River, and the prospect of an exciting night out had Kate in a hurry to get out the door.

The annual football game between Eagle River and Swanton started in less than an hour, and several of Kate's relatives would gather at the high school to cheer on their favorite teams. Which was in the plural, as Swanton had absorbed the Prosper school district years ago and loyalties ran deep on both sides of the game-toss coin.

Swanton was a much-larger school district than Eagle River; in fact, they played in a different conference for regular-season games. But Prosper and Eagle River had taken turns hosting this showdown for decades and, when Prosper merged with Swanton, area residents were eager to keep the tradition going.

With the school-district boundary just a mile west of her parents' farm, Kate had former neighbors as well as family members who'd attended Prosper and Swanton schools. She was partial to the Eagle River Wildcats, of course, as that school was her alma mater, and her new, royal-blue sweatshirt made her allegiance clear. With spirit gear available in the high-school office as well as at Eagle River's pharmacy, she'd decided it was time to retire the faded pullover that had spent the last decade stuffed in a drawer at her parents' place.

But her new fleece was just the top layer. There was also a tank top and a long-sleeve shirt, as well as leggings layered under her looser-fitting jeans. Wool socks, a thick stocking cap and scarf, and heavy gloves completed her ensemble.

She wasn't sure if she'd be warm enough, but she was certainly excited about the game. The word around town was that Swanton's varsity squad wasn't the powerhouse it had been in recent seasons. Several of its high-profile players graduated in May, and two of them were now making waves at the college level. Maybe, for the first time in several years, Eagle River had a chance at victory.

Kate locked the back door and the porch's entrance before she started for the garage. Her steps quickened as she scanned her property, as the areas away from the yard light had already filled in with shadows.

Even as she checked her surroundings, Kate chided herself for her concern. She shouldn't be nervous about being out here at night. There wasn't anyone around, after all, not another house for over a quarter mile.

But maybe, that was the problem. If something was amiss, if there was someone lurking around her buildings, there was no one around to help, to hear her scream ...

"Stop it," she admonished herself as she punched the garage remote with more force than necessary. "I highly doubt there's some creepy dude hiding in the windbreak, gas can and lighter in hand."

Eagle River's Main Street was even quieter than usual this Friday night, but the streets leading to the school campus on the southwest side of town teemed with traffic. Kate finally found a parking spot, then made her way through the throng of fans to where her parents, Curtis and Charlotte, waited by the east gate.

It had been a long day at work, and Kate was tired. But the sight of so many people coming together for this annual event made her spirits soar. She was glad she'd made the effort to get off the couch, suit up in her new spirit gear, and join her family for this fall tradition.

Her brother, Bryan, and his wife, Anna, were running late, as evening chores had been delayed by wayward cows and open gates and foot chases around the pasture, but many of their other relatives were already in the stands.

"Everyone's gathering on the left side of the south bleachers, one-third of the way up," Curtis said as they followed the crowd through the gate.

Charlotte adjusted her stocking cap. "Is that left when you're sitting down, or left when you're facing the stands?"

"Oh, sorry. I guess I assumed that was from the front."

"We'll find them," Kate assured her dad as she paid her admission and got her hand stamped. "Call Aunt Marie, she'll tell you exactly where they are."

Kate was enveloped by a wave of nostalgia as they inched their way toward the blazing lights that surrounded the field. A housing development had taken root near the secondary-school campus, which was built only five years ago on the far edge of town, but the football field's south boundary was still marked by a wire-panel fence fronting a field of unharvested corn.

Kate was all for progress, and wanted her hometown to thrive, but she also relished the opportunity to sit on a backless metal bench with her extended family, breathe in the crisp fall air, and enjoy a cup of steaming hot chocolate. As well as some good-natured teasing.

"Where'd you get that sweatshirt?" Aunt Marie called out to Kate. "Were the lights off in the store? Because I think you got the wrong color."

"Not a chance." Kate gave her aunt a hug. "You know, royal blue is always in style."

"Yeah, but purple is the color of royalty." Marie pointed to her Swanton sweatshirt. Uncle Edgar was wearing his as well. They lived on the outskirts of Prosper, and their loyalty was clearly with the other side.

"A wildcat can outrun anything, at any time." Kate braced for the initial shock of the cold bench as she took her seat. "You wait and see."

"OK, ladies, that's enough." But Edgar was laughing. "Let's try to keep this civil."

Bryan and Anna arrived, and they joined the cluster of Duncan relatives already in the stands. Just before the starting lineups were announced, Kate spotted two of her cousins, Stacy and Corey, making their way up the steps. While both siblings had gone off to college in Minneapolis, Stacy now taught creative writing and literature at Eagle River's middle school. Corey ran his own accounting firm in Swanton, and was an on-call Prosper first responder.

"Hey, where's your school spirit?" Kate asked Corey as she pointed at his olive-green windbreaker.

"Too cold for that." Her cousin gave a rundown of the statistics that mattered most to him that night, which focused on how far the temperatures and wind chill were expected to drop before the end of the game. "Besides, you know I try to keep a neutral stance. It's good for business."

"Smart."

"What a crowd, huh?" Corey gave Kate a friendly elbow. "Who needs a Friday night in downtown Chi-Town when you can be here?"

She laughed. "You know, these days, this is more my speed."

"Sorry." Corey shook his head. "Maybe I shouldn't have brought that up. I mean, since you and Ben ..."

"Don't worry about it. I don't so much, not anymore." And, Kate realized, she really meant it. Nostalgia was harmless, most of the time; but some things were best left in the past. She took a deep breath of the refreshing air, and stood up. "I ate dinner, but those nachos smelled so good when we came past the concession stand."

Corey reached for his wallet. "Bring me some?"

"Sure."

While Kate's bleacher section accounted for an unofficial Duncan family reunion, another relative was also at the game. Grandpa Wayne Burberry, Charlotte's dad, was hanging out along the wire-roped sideline with his cronies since Grandma Ida was home with a bad cold.

Grandpa Wayne didn't mind, as he had worked at the Eagle River post office before retiring from the head position at Prosper's shop, and there were familiar folks to chat with wherever he went.

Kate checked in with Grandpa Wayne, promised to join his usual breakfast crew at Peabody's restaurant before work tomorrow, then moved on to the concession stand. The lines were long, but the nachos were too tempting for Kate to turn back now.

The stand was run by the high school's sports boosters, which was nearly the same group of people as the alumni association. As she waited with the rest of the throng, Kate felt a stab of guilt over how hard the volunteers worked to keep up with the flood of requests.

Maybe she should volunteer to help. There were just a few

more home football games this season, but a long slate of
basketball and wrestling events throughout the winter. It
would be a way to connect with some new friends, and maybe
some former ones, too.

By the time Kate made it back to the stands, the first
quarter was well under way. She passed Corey his plastic bowl
and his change, settled into her seat, and loaded her first chip
with ooey, gooey cheese. It was fattening, and over-processed,
and wonderful.

"No cocoa?" Corey asked before he dug into his own
nachos.

"I'm pacing myself," Kate said around a mouthful of
chips. "Not sure the two would go together very well."

Just as Corey predicted, the air grew colder as the game
rolled on. But Kate didn't care. The packed bleachers offered
a bit of protection from the wind, and the score stayed
thrillingly close. Swanton might get the upper hand by the
end, but little Eagle River held its own. As the third quarter
ticked down, the game was still close enough to give the
Wildcats fans hope for a victory.

"If we can pull this off, it'll be the talk of the school on
Monday," Stacy said. "Maybe I can somehow work football
into the next assignment for the eighth-graders. It might be
my best hope of holding their attention."

"Or go with sports in general, at least," Kate suggested.
"Or any narrative about someone beating the odds to
succeed."

"Thanks for upping my lesson plans." Stacy was about to
make a few notes on her phone, then put it back in her
pocket. "Nope, I'm going to wait until tomorrow. I'm not
about to jinx this."

Somewhere nearby, a phone began to beep. Stacy checked
hers. "Huh, not me."

Then another, a few rows above them. And two more.

Corey's buzzed next. Kate studied her cousin's face while

he scrolled his screen, and the showdown on the field was quickly forgotten.

"What is it?" she asked as Corey jumped to his feet. "Oh, no! Is there an accident?"

"Structure fire. The old Peterson place."

His nachos fell through the bleachers, but Corey didn't even notice as he barged past their seat mates and toward the stairs.

Kate's heart nearly stopped. No, it couldn't be.

But then, why not? The night of the big rivalry would be the perfect time to make your next move. The local emergency crews were so small, they rarely had anyone hanging around at their stations. And the local high schools' games required a handful of in-uniform first responders to be at those sites in case of injuries.

From the number of people rushing for the exits, Kate suspected many of the rest of those on call were here in Eagle River, in the far northeastern corner of the county.

"Where is this house?" she asked her dad. The cheers of the crowd still echoed around them, but Kate now heard a few murmurs of worry as well.

"Just east of Prosper, about two miles." Curtis suddenly sounded very tired. "A few miles west of our place."

"Does anyone live there?"

"No, no. There hasn't been for at least twenty years." His mouth was set in a firm line. "It's abandoned."

Down on the field, the game went on. The Eagle River cheerleaders started a crowd-response chant along the sidelines, and many of the Wildcats fans joined in with hearty voices and enthusiastic applause.

But Kate's school spirit had been doused by worry. She was too concerned for her cousin and the other first responders on their way to fight yet-another blaze to focus on what was shaping up to be a historic night in Eagle River football history.

Two fires in as many weeks. And before that, the one Auggie told her about.

Kate's phone buzzed in her pocket. It was Bev. *You at the game?*

Yes. South bleachers.

Me too. Meet me under the SW corner?

The chilly air scoured Kate's face when she got to her feet. "I'm going to the bathroom," she told her mom, then slipped out of their row.

Behind the bleachers, the roar of the field was muffled by the rows of closely packed bodies above. Bev had her hands clasped tight when Kate found her huddled against a corner post, trying to keep out of the wind.

"I can't believe this." Bev was nearly in tears. "I've lived around here my whole life, and we've never had something like this happen. Ever."

It was no use to offer the hope that this fire was accidental. Kate was sure it had been deliberately set by someone determined to scare people, strain local emergency resources and create as much mayhem as possible.

"There's Auggie!" Bev pointed him out. "He'll know the latest."

The women hurried over to where Auggie was deep in discussion with Harvey Watson and two other men Kate didn't recognize.

"What did I tell you?" Auggie said to Kate. "This is one time that I wish I wasn't right. The only question is, who's sick enough in the head to light stuff up, just to watch it burn?"

"Serial arson." Harvey rubbed the side of his face. Kate had never seen him so distressed. "We used to live out that way, before we moved to town. If someone wanted a big show, the old Peterson place would be the one to light."

All the buildings were gone except the farmhouse, Harvey said, which had been a grand home back in the day, built by the well-to-do farmer whose family had also owned Prosper's first mercantile.

Two stories with a full attic and basement. Double parlors downstairs, five bedrooms upstairs, porches all the way around. The property had changed hands several times over the years, and was last lived in by a couple with eight kids.

The house was so large, and needed so much work, that they couldn't find a buyer for the acreage when they retired from farming twenty years ago. The homestead was instead sold off with the surrounding fields, and the house had been vacant ever since. A family by the name of Snyder owned the land these days.

"My brother used to be on the Eagle River fire department," one of the other men said. "An old house like that? It's a tinder box. There's a reason they stopped building stuff with balloon framing." He made a top-to-bottom gesture with his hands. "Those gaps along the outside walls just feed the flames."

Auggie's grim face glowed in the dim light of his phone's screen.

"There's more than one ignition site. Good Lord, they set fires in every corner of the first floor! Whoever did this, they're determined to bring this thing down."

Kate wanted to ask who was feeding Auggie these details, but suspected he'd never reveal his source.

"Can they even get it under control?" Harvey asked. "I know the guy who owns those fields, saw him just yesterday. They haven't even started harvesting over there yet."

"Well, they're trying." Auggie sighed. "Swanton's already there, with Prosper and Eagle River. Charles City is coming, but it may take even more manpower than that. All I hear at the co-op is how everyone's on edge since the Donegan barn burned, keeping watch over their properties. Scaring people, wasting local resources? I say, this is domestic terrorism."

A cheer went up from the bleachers behind them.

"And Eagle River is on top!" the announcer boomed into his microphone. "But it's a narrow lead. This game is a real nail-biter, folks, one for the record books!"

"For a second, I thought Reid was going to call it 'a real barn-burner,'" Harvey said through gritted teeth. "And then I was going to have to go up there and give him a talking-to."

Kate looked at Bev. "I was starting to wonder if we were overreacting about that meeting on Wednesday. Not anymore."

"I can't let this drop." Bev shook her head. "Not after what's happened tonight. Well, I better get back to the stands, Clyde will wonder where I ran off to."

Kate was too wired to sit down just now. She wandered over to the concession building, determined to get her hot chocolate and try to enjoy at least a little of what was left of this game. The crowd at the stand was thinner than before and, based on the snippets of conversation that drifted Kate's way, now more concerned about the Peterson fire than the outcome of tonight's matchup.

"Here you go." The woman at the counter handed Kate a steaming Styrofoam cup. "Great timing, we just made a new batch. It's the perfect night for football, isn't it?"

She smiled now, even though her voice had been laced with worry. Kate caught the hint: *We need to put up a brave front. We can't let this get us down.*

Kate grinned back. "It sure is."

* * *

The Eagle River Wildcats were victorious Friday night, but it was old news by Saturday morning as word spread about the fire west of town.

A thick fog blanketed the brown fields, further dampening Kate's already troubled mood as she drove into Eagle River. It was going to be a long day, after a harrowing night, but Kate was glad she'd promised to meet Grandpa Wayne and his friends at Peabody's for breakfast. Their companionship and perspective were as needed this morning as a stack of Henry Peabody's from-scratch pancakes.

Even so, Kate blinked and rubbed her eyes with one hand as she scouted Peabody's parking lot for a free space. Sleep hadn't come easy last night, despite Charlie's purrs of reassurance, and it was interrupted by a series of texts from friends and family that rolled on into the wee hours.

Each one had been more dire than the last, and Kate hoped some of the rumors would prove to be exaggerated in the light of day. But the sinking feeling in her stomach told her that wasn't likely.

Unstable floors. Wind is rising. You can smell the smoke a half-mile away.
Reinforcements coming at two to relieve the crews on site. Fire marshal will be there at first light.
Flames shooting out of the roof. All crews are retreating to the yard.
It came down so fast you could hear the beams snap over the roar of the fire.

Peabody's was always a packed house on Saturday mornings, but Kate was surprised to find a sea of weary men's faces rather than the usual mix of families and friends gathered around most of its tables. The guys sported shadows under their tired eyes, and even their gestures and conversations were muted as they shoveled in pancakes, waffles, bacon and sausage, and eggs cooked to order.

Many of them wore faded tee shirts and sweatshirts emblazoned with the names of emergency crews from around the area and, even though they had left their fire gear behind, the faintest tinge of smoke wafted through the room.

Grandpa Wayne waved to Kate from a table close to the kitchen, and she made her way through the crowd.

"Morning, my girl!" Grandpa tried for a cheerful greeting, but his weary eyes said he felt differently. "Glad you could join us oldsters before you start on your route."

Normally this dig at their ages would have Grandpa's friends mounting a laugh-filled protest, but the men only offered faint smiles and waves this morning.

Kate spotted Lena Wakefield and Joan Murray, the two ladies who often joined the group, hurrying in and out of the kitchen. Joan worked part-time at Peabody's, but Lena was also helping shuttle platters of hot food to the exhausted firefighters.

"This is the place to be, even more than usual," Kate said as she took her seat.

"Nowhere else to get a big breakfast within twenty miles." Harvey nodded with a bit of pride. "And these guys deserve to fill up, whether they are heading home or heading back out there."

Just as when Brody's barn burned, firefighters and law enforcement officers had to protect the scene until the fire marshal's office completed its evaluation. The investigator had arrived in the past hour, Grandpa reported, and his work was expected to run into the afternoon given the scope and complexity of the scene.

First responders from as far as an hour away were on hand to give the local crews a much-needed break. All the support was welcome, as many of the volunteers had other important roles to play this time of year.

"There's no good time for a fire." Harvey mopped up his egg yolks with a scrap of toast. "But harvest season has to be about the worst. If you're not a farmer and working in your own field, you're on the clock at a co-op, or behind the counter at some store keeping folks stocked with supplies."

"Or serving food." Lena set down Chris Everton's breakfast and reached for the notepad in the back pocket of her jeans. "Kate, what'll it be?"

"You're getting good at this," Grandpa told Lena. "Eloise is going to want to hire you for real."

Lena laughed. "She'll probably say the same about you guys, if you follow through on helping wash all these dishes."

Kate ordered pancakes, sausage and coffee, then raised an eyebrow at Grandpa after Lena moved on. "Wash dishes?"

"Yeah, we've been recruited." He leaned toward Kate. "Don't tell Grandma I volunteered, or she'll give me extra KP duty at home. It's the least we can do."

Eloise and Henry had insisted all the emergency responders get their meals for free this morning. Chris, Eagle River's pharmacist, admired the couple's generosity, but hoped they wouldn't have to repeat the gesture anytime soon.

"I have to say, I have a really bad feeling about this." Chris shook his head and took a bracing gulp of coffee. "Makes you wonder, what will happen next?"

"You think there'll be more?" Harvey twisted his fork between his fingers as he mulled over the situation. "I still have my reservations about that Donegan kid and his barn. If he lit it for the payout, that's one thing. But what motivation would he have to torch that house last night? None. I'd say it's a copycat, some stupid kids."

Kate thought this was an interesting angle. Roberta had two teenagers, and kids loved to gossip. Perhaps her boss would have some tidbits to share at the post office this morning.

Grandpa Wayne wasn't sure about that theory. "I don't know. Most of the teenagers in the county, especially those from around here, were at the game last night."

"True," Chris mused, "but it's more likely to be kids that don't follow the teams, that aren't social enough to want to hang out at the stadium. Whoever it is, they picked the right night to do it, with just about everyone at the game."

"Including so many of our paid-on-call crews." Harvey frowned. "They never had a chance, given how far along it was before enough guys could get out there. If I wasn't so old, I'd volunteer myself."

"Carmen would never allow it, with your heart the way it is," Chris said. Then he laughed. "Maybe you could be the water boy, hand out energy drinks and donuts."

"Donuts?" Kate added sugar to her coffee mug. "Isn't that a cop thing, not a firefighter thing?"

"Snacks in general, then." Chris tipped his head toward the door. "Hey, look, it's Ward."

Eagle River's mayor took in the bustling scene with weary eyes. Most of the volunteers were from out of town, and too tired and hungry to notice a newcomer, but a few offered Ward a wave. The mayor perked up when Grandpa gestured for him to join their table, and he gave a grateful nod as Harvey reached for an empty coffee cup and poured out a hearty measure.

"I wish I had something new to share," Ward said before anyone could ask. "But the news is just as bad as it was last night. That house was a real showplace back in the day, but now it's just a charred pile of rubble."

Ward turned to Kate. "Maybe you don't have to worry about your neighbor being an arsonist, after all. I think something else, or someone else, is afoot."

No one nearby looked in their direction, but Kate sensed several sets of ears were now tuned in to the conversation at this table.

"Not that I have anything solid to share," Ward added, a bit louder than necessary. He sighed and picked up his mug. "It's bad enough this is even happening. But the bureaucratic red tape is about to do us all in."

Ben Dvorak, who was the maintenance supervisor at the auction barn, served as Eagle River's fire chief. Kate didn't know him well, but he'd been a few years ahead of her in school. Ben was dependable, Ward said, and expertly handled the department's day-to-day operations as well as its interactions with other local emergency departments.

But Ward had spent the last week shouldering the emotional burden of his constituents' fears. Even rural residents stopped him everywhere he went, eager for updates on the Donegan fire or just assurances that the potential threat to other properties was being taken seriously by law enforcement.

Which really meant the Hartland County Sheriff's Office, not the Eagle River Police Department. Because both burn sites were in rural areas, Sheriff Preston was tasked with protecting the scenes and investigating the incidents.

Well, sort of. Preston's deputies could arrest someone on certain charges related to the fires, such as trespassing, burglary, or criminal mischief, but only the state fire marshal's office had the authority to investigate the actual blazes.

Which meant if someone was suspected of arson, the marshal from the Mason City office would have to file those charges.

"What a mess." Harvey shook his head. "I hadn't thought about any of that before, but you're right. Several local agencies are involved, and then the county, and the state. It's an all-hands sort of thing."

"We're trying our best to keep everyone in the loop, and not step on any toes as we go." Ward nodded his thanks when Lena brought him a steaming plate of pancakes and scrambled eggs. The mayor was a regular at Peabody's, and the staff knew what he liked. But then he gave Lena a quizzical look. "Where's my ticket?"

"Not today. Harry says it's on the house."

"But I can't ..."

"Nonsense. Eat up."

Kate's pancakes were up next, and she mulled over the situation as she ate. As much as she'd like to stay at Peabody's and help serve the firefighters, she had to be at the post office in half an hour. What else might she do to help? Because it was hard to sit there and do nothing.

Last night, she'd been scared, and worried about the crews fighting the blaze. Today, her emotions slid toward anger and frustration.

Why would someone do this in the first place? And then, on what turned out to be one of the biggest nights in the history of Eagle River football?

The team should have been the toast of the town today. But their victorious efforts had already been pushed aside by someone's ... well, Kate wasn't sure what exactly was at play. Bitterness? Boredom? Obsession with fire? Whatever it was, it was cruel, and evil.

Harvey let Ward get a good start on his breakfast, then turned back to the topic at hand. "We were talking about this last night at the game." He gave Kate and Grandpa Wayne a quick nod. "And Auggie brought up something interesting."

"Oh, he did, huh?" Ward's wary expression almost made Kate laugh. "What was it?"

"Domestic terrorism. Is that a possibility? Whoever this is, who knows what their motive is. But in the process, they're knowingly putting firefighters' lives at risk, as well as those of the residents living near these structures. Not to mention, destroying people's property."

"And you could make the case they're scaring the living daylights out of everyone," Grandpa added, "especially folks living in the country."

Ward considered that idea for a moment. "Well, Auggie leans toward the dramatic, in case none of you have noticed." That brought a chuckle around the table. "But you know, it's an interesting question."

Then he looked at Kate. "I know I was complaining earlier about everyone with their hand in the cookie jar these days. Local, county, the state. But I think we need to get the feds involved, too. At least, some *local* federal employees."

Despite her weariness, Kate caught his meaning. "Do I need to be deputized, or something?"

"I don't think that's necessary; couldn't do it myself, anyway. But seriously, please spread the word at the post office: we need everyone to be paying attention. And Wayne, can you put in a word with Glenn?"

Glenn Hanson was Prosper's current postmaster. "We'll get all the area's carriers on alert," Grandpa promised, "and maybe someone will come across something that'll crack these cases. You never know if the perp dropped something on the side of a road, or threw stuff in a ditch."

Then he sighed. "Here's the thing, though: If anyone finds something, who do they call?"

Ward rolled his eyes. "Well, the chain of command is all over the place these days. But I'd say the best bet is to contact the sheriff."

From what Ward had heard, the regional fire investigator was trustworthy and determined to dispense justice, but having to make two journeys to this out-of-the-way corner of northern Iowa in two weeks was testing his resources. He had dozens of counties under his field office's jurisdiction.

The marshal wanted Sheriff Preston to serve as his contact with the locals, and Ward thought that was a good idea. Because while local public-safety officials were in desperate need of the marshal office's expertise, some were hesitant to involve the state any more than what was necessary.

"Around here, we like to take care of our own problems." Ward's proclamation elicited murmurs of agreement around the table. "At least, as much as we can."

If Kate hadn't been so tired, she probably would have rolled her eyes. She wasn't surprised to hear such a sentiment in a town as small as Eagle River. People were proud and, even if they wouldn't admit it, sometimes suspicious of outsiders.

But this was too important to go it alone. If ever there was a time for local leaders to set aside their biases and accept help, this was it. And the best way to encourage that was to turn up a lead or two.

Here, at last, was something Kate could do. She reached for her purse, pulled out a twenty, and laid it on top of her bill.

"I need to get to the post office," she told Grandpa Wayne. "Tell Eloise to keep the change. And Ward, I can assure you the Eagle River carriers will keep watch."

❋ 8 ❋

Kate knew the post office's back room wouldn't be as crowded as Peabody's, but she expected the conversation to be just as animated.

She was wrong. Jack and Allison were the only ones clocked in so far, and they apparently weren't speaking to each other unless necessary. Both offered Kate a weary "good morning," then Jack snatched his thermos and disappeared into the break room.

"What's up?" Tension filled the air, and Kate hoped Allison would fill her in.

Allison plopped a stack of mail on the metal counter. "Well, remember when Jack was so sure Brody lit up his own barn? Now that we've had a second incident, it looks like that theory was wrong."

Kate smothered her laughter, as she was sure Jack was listening through the open door.

"My dad knows that family very well." Allison raised her voice enough to carry into the break room. "I never thought Brody would do something like that. Looks like I was right."

Roberta soon came in the back door, tired and haggard. "Jared's out, of course. He was one of the first rotation out there, then went home for a little sleep, and he's going back to help while the marshal does his work." She dropped into her office chair with a resigned sigh. "So we'll shuffle the deck here, I've already called in backup. Thank goodness tomorrow is Sunday and there's no delivery."

Roberta's husband was part of the shift that was on site when the house collapsed. Even though he came home exhausted and dirty, he'd spent several minutes trying to describe the scene.

Several fires had been set inside the house, just as Auggie had heard, and all were in rooms with exterior walls. The old-style framing allowed the flames to quickly shoot all the way to the attic, which meant the house's structure was quickly compromised. Just like with Brody's barn, the crews mostly tried to keep the fire contained.

When it collapsed, the old house groaned and howled in a way that, according to Roberta's husband, was so eerie it made the hair on the back of your neck stand up.

"But the house is toast, at least." Roberta caught her own gaffe, and laughed. "Pardon my choice of words. The chiefs were sort-of relieved when they could tell it would be a total loss."

"I can understand that," Allison said. "There's no need to risk a heroic effort when you know it's a lost cause. That house was abandoned long ago; the safety of the firefighters is more important."

"That's true, but there's more to it than that." Roberta wandered over to the counter and began to sort the day's pile of packages. It was a routine task, but provided something productive to do. "I hadn't thought of this, but Oliver said if the house hadn't been destroyed, there was a real possibility the arsonist might come back and try to finish the job."

Allison and Kate stared at each other.

"They'd do it again, at the same place?" Kate asked as a chill ran down her spine. "One fire isn't enough?"

Jack came back into the room, his oversized thermos now full of fresh coffee. "Apparently, that's a hallmark of arsonists.

My neighbor's on our crew. He says, total destruction is usually the goal. That, and trying to hang around to watch the thing burn."

Sheriff's deputies and members of the county's police departments continued to man the barricades that had been set up on the gravel road, Jack shared, as well as watch the property's perimeter. That kept any gawkers out of the firefighters' way, but it also let law enforcement keep an eye out for anyone who seemed overly interested in the blaze.

Kate thought again of Wednesday night's meeting, and why she and Bev were so eager to attend. It wouldn't be right to fan the flames of gossip by sharing her theories right now. However, this was the perfect time to share Mayor Benson's plea for assistance.

"My area's out east, the opposite way from the scene." But the light of interest in Jack's eyes said he was eager to help. "We don't know who did this, where they live, or where they went after the fire. Could have been anywhere. I'll keep an eye on the shoulders and ditches."

As the other carriers filed in, Roberta made several switches to her Saturday lineup. Kate found herself with the vacationing Mae's northwest route. Jared's regular south-southwest run was light on mail that day, which made it a better fit for Marge Koenig, who'd been called in to pinch hit and was running a little late.

That meant Marge had the area that included the Peterson place. But while Kate was curious to get a look, especially now that it was daylight, she was glad to stay away today. There would be roadblocks and detours to contend with, and the residents so close to the scene would be understandably on edge.

She yawned as she filled her coffee thermos, then her water bottles. Bev was on her way in, but there wasn't time to waste in the office. Unlike the southern loop, Mae's route was loaded with packages and letters today. Besides, right now,

Kate didn't know what else there was to discuss with her friend.

She wanted to know why this was happening, who was behind it and, most of all, was it over? If not, when would it stop? And Bev didn't have those answers. No one did.

But the questions that burned bright in Kate's mind were voiced by the customers she encountered that busy harvest Saturday. Not everyone receiving a package was home, but most that were seemed to be stationed close to their front porches, whether they were baking in their kitchens or raking leaves on their lawns.

Everyone wanted to chat, even for just a minute. It was as if by discussing the situation, they might be able to make some sense of it. And as Kate traveled the gravel, with billows of dust following Bertha, another trail of thought surfaced.

All around her, harvest went on as usual; a chance of rain was forecast for tomorrow, and there was a sense of urgency in the crisp air. As always, she returned the half-waves of those behind the wheels of the combines and trucks she met down every road, smiled into the windshield of every vehicle she met.

But now she gave those people a second look, weighed the possibility that any of them might be involved in what was going on in her community.

Of course, an outsider could be the culprit. But something told Kate the arsonist was a local. The destruction at the Peterson place was so complete, so carefully executed, that it almost had to be the work of someone familiar with the goings-on in Hartland County as well as which old houses down which gravel roads held the most potential for their goals ... whatever those might be.

Which brought her thoughts back to Brody.

If anything good had come from last night, Kate decided as she slowed for the next creek bridge, it was that Brody Donegan might be able to breathe easy again. He'd been dissected and blamed by so many; including, although she now cringed to think of it, Kate herself. Maybe this was a bit of justice for him, at least.

It made Kate want to bake him a pie, turn up on his parents' doorstep with a peace offering.

Sorry I thought you were a criminal. Sorry I hadn't gotten to know you and your family well enough to give you the benefit of the doubt.

* * *

By the time Kate finished her route, the sun was hiding behind a bank of heavy clouds. She was bone-tired and emotionally weary, but decided to drop in at The Daily Grind for some caffeine.

She had java at home, of course, but nothing matched those specialty drinks Austin Freitag and his staff brewed up at Eagle River's only coffee shop. And while Kate was done with her post-office run, her day's work was far from over. Beyond the usual chores, there were some last-minute things to do around the house before Kate brought Hazel home tomorrow.

The shop's plate-glass windows glowed with light and warmth, a beacon in the gloomy late afternoon, and Kate's flagging spirits raised the moment she came through the door. The business was housed in an old storefront, and featured exposed brick side walls as well as high ceilings. Fans swooped above, spreading the invigorating aroma of fresh-pressed coffee beans.

Austin's crew had outdone themselves with the autumn decor, but Kate loved the seasonal spark it gave to the place. Faux-leaf garlands not only outlined each oversized window, but they were woven with strings of tiny, clear lights. Leaf cutouts danced down some of the panes, and throw pillows encased in autumn prints bookended the wooden bench under the community bulletin board, just inside the door.

Stacks of small pumpkins and baskets of gourds were tastefully arranged around the shop, and the menu reflected the changing weather outside. Apples, pumpkin and warm spices were sprinkled everywhere, from the baked goods behind the glass case to the lattes and ciders served at the counter. Austin had gone to school with Bryan, and he gave her a big wave as he came out of the kitchen.

"The place is packed!" Kate leaned on the counter, suddenly more tired than she'd realized. "I'm glad to see it so busy, even during harvest."

"Everyone who's not in the fields is looking for a distraction." Austin pushed up his glasses and logged into the second register, as his weekend part-timers were busy filling orders at the other end of the counter. "After last night, there's a lot to discuss. I just wish it all could focus on the big game."

"Go Wildcats," Kate said with a sigh. "You know, any other time, that would've been the talk of the town for weeks." She placed her order, and Austin shook his head as he punched it into the system.

"We don't have this kind of crime in Eagle River. Or any crime, as you know. Oh, sure, some houses get wrapped in toilet paper during homecoming. But that's about it. Even on Halloween, it's pretty tame around here."

While some communities in the region long ago moved trick-or-treating to October 30 and christened it Beggars' Night, Eagle River stood firm on its Halloween traditions. Besides, it gave the local children a chance to make their rounds in other towns the night before, and brought visitors to Eagle River on the official holiday to enjoy the festive open houses at the downtown businesses.

Austin was the current chair of the small-but-mighty chamber of commerce, and he'd expanded the event in the past few years to include a scavenger hunt with prizes, as well as a costume contest for the kids.

Not only was it something for Kate to look forward to, but it was also the perfect antidote to last night's trouble.

"Well, I have good news on that front," she reported. "I'm working on Roberta about those ideas for the downtown trick-or-treat night. I think you can expect the post office to be open beyond regular hours this year, so we can take part."

"Excellent. Do you think she'll wear a costume?"

Kate laughed. "Other than her federally approved postal shirt? Probably not. But she's warming up to the idea of hosting an apple-bobbing activity in the lobby."

"That's a cool idea," Austin said over his shoulder as he worked on Kate's order. "Old-school easy."

"That's what I told her. I think it'll be fun! And we certainly could use some of that around here."

The Daily Grind staff had taken pots of hot drinks and trays of pastries out to the old Peterson place first thing that morning, Austin said, and a second round had left the coffee house not an hour ago.

Crews were about to wrap up their efforts at the site, but someone else's work was far from over.

Austin leaned in and lowered his voice. "We have a special visitor this afternoon. Care to guess who it is?"

Kate frowned as she scanned the busy bistro. Some customers were flying solo, taking in the autumn gloom outside or staring at their laptops. Most were in small groups, laughing and chatting as they devoured their drinks and snacks.

"I have no idea." She shrugged. "Care to give me a hint?"

Austin tipped his head toward one back corner. "Second table from the merch display."

Kate glanced over her shoulder and spotted a man of about forty, wearing jeans and a fleece pullover. The glow of his laptop screen was the best source of light in that shadowy corner, and his coffee was seemingly forgotten as his fingers flew over the keyboard.

"Him?" Kate blinked. "I don't recognize him. Could be anybody, I guess."

"But he's not. That's the state's investigator."

Her mouth dropped open in surprise, and she quickly filled it with a bracing gulp of her latte. "Really? Why isn't he down at the fire station?"

And then, it all made sense. It was just like Mayor Benson had said: local, county, state ... too many cooks in the kitchen. The Daily Grind was a bit noisy, but its hustle and bustle offered the perfect place for an outsider to fade into the background.

"He's been here, oh, about an hour, I'd say." Austin wiped the counter as they talked. "I ran into him at the scene this morning, mentioned we have free wi-fi."

Given Ward's assessment of the situation, and the weight of the job itself, Kate had assumed the regional fire investigator was older. But then, given how weary he looked, it sort-of made sense. It took endurance and energy to log so many miles around so many counties, day and night. Then to suit up in protective gear and spend hours combing through burned-out buildings and vehicles, searching for the kind of evidence that would hold up in court and lead to convictions.

This guy certainly had a lot on his plate. Kate had so many questions, but she wasn't about to disturb him. Much less draw attention to someone who apparently wanted to be left alone.

Austin, however, was eager to share what little he'd heard so far.

"I don't know much," he told Kate, "other than what you already know. It's pretty obvious accelerants were used; the place was set up to burn down fast." Then he shook his head in wonder. "Did you know they have special canine officers that can sniff out arson cases?"

"Really? I've heard of drug dogs, of course. How fascinating."

"Yeah. Well, there's only a few around the state, I guess. They call on them when they have to." He held up a hand. "Now, don't get too excited. Word is there's enough evidence to prove it was arson, so it's not likely one of those teams would show up here. I don't think there's any doubt that what happened last night was intentional."

Kate didn't know how she felt about that. On one hand, this news confirmed what she suspected. On the other, it snuffed out that tiny spark of hope the fire had somehow been an accident.

"Now we wait." Austin handed Kate her change, but she put all of it in the tip jar. "The evidence has to go to a lab to be confirmed. All that's left to do now, I guess, is to figure out who did it."

Kate sighed as she lifted her purse from the counter. "And that, I think, is going to take the effort of everyone in this county."

✳ 9 ✳

Kate took the leash in her hand and smiled down at the dog.

Her dog. It was Sunday afternoon, and Hazel was coming home.

"It's going to be fine." The outreach coordinator handed Kate a stack of paperwork. "She's a great dog; she deserves a fresh start."

The packet included Hazel's vaccination certificates, coupons for her favorite food, and an information card that made it clear questions would be promptly answered, day or night. Kate hoped she wouldn't need to reach out, but was relieved support was always available.

The woman knelt before Hazel and gave her a gentle pet. "You be a good girl, OK?" She looked up at Kate and grinned. "It may take her a few days to settle in, of course. I hear you have a cat?"

"Charlie." Kate took another deep breath. She had no doubt that she and Hazel would bond quickly. But when it came to the other member of their immediate family ...

"He has all his safe spaces set up, and his food's out of Hazel's reach." Then she frowned. "But I have three outdoor kitties, too. I'm not sure how that's going to go, either."

A fat brown tabby cat jumped up on the desk and meowed. Hazel barely gave it a glance.

"We have a few resident felines here, as you can see." The woman scratched the cat's back. "Hazel's been socializing with them, as well as the other dogs, from the day she arrived. It's part of the training, so they're able to assimilate into a family with other pets, kids, hectic schedules, you name it. Hazel's ready to go."

Kate was over the moon that her adoption application had been chosen out of what was apparently a sizable stack. But she was still nervous about the next few days. She and Hazel had an instant connection when they met at Prosper Veterinary Services over the summer, but Kate had never had a "house dog" before.

Her family loved animals, and there had always been a dog at her parents' farm, but those still-pampered pooches didn't live in the house. Waylon, their black Lab, had an insulated doghouse, easy access to a snug barn, cows to chase and room to roam.

"I hope I'm ready," Kate told the coordinator. "This is going to be a big change. But I'm excited to get started."

"You'll do just fine." The woman walked Kate and Hazel to the door. "Give both of you a little time to settle in, and I think you'll be glad you took the plunge." She patted Kate on the arm. "However, if for any reason it's not working out, just let us know. We won't have any trouble placing her with someone else."

Kate looked down at Hazel, who already watched her closely with those trusting brown eyes, and swallowed the lump in her throat. So many changes in a handful of months, so much upheaval for a sweet dog who just needed a home.

Hazel had her own family for the first three years of her life, from what the agency's staff knew, but they'd given the dog up when they moved from a farm to a large city out of state. Hazel had ended up at a shelter in Waterloo, and one of the training facility's volunteers had spotted her online. She was tagged as a potential candidate for the companion-dog program, and arrived at the campus in the spring. Hazel was patient, tolerant of change, and very loving, but her lack of interest in following commands meant she wasn't cut out for a life of service.

Kate was still getting to know Hazel, but she sensed the dog's hopeful attitude as they walked out into the cool autumn breeze. Her tail wagged with curiosity, and maybe a bit of excitement, as they made their way to Kate's car. It was as if she knew exactly what was going on.

Of course she did, Kate reminded herself as she unlocked the car and put the paperwork and her purse in the back seat. Hazel was very smart. And, apparently, comfortable riding in a vehicle. Shotgun.

"You all settled?" Hazel gave a happy whimper as Kate secured her harness to the seat. "OK, let's go!"

It was almost a half-hour drive from the facility to Kate's farm. While both were in the northern section of Hartland County, they were about as far apart as they could get. Kate took one blacktop south to Swanton, then turned east toward Prosper. When they were just a few miles west of that town, Kate tipped her head toward the south.

"My friend Melinda lives down that road," she told Hazel. "She has a dog, too. His name is Hobo, isn't that cute? I think once you get settled in, we'll try for a playdate. I hope you won't miss your doggie friends too much."

Karen also had a dog, a rust-and-cream Collie appropriately named Pumpkin. Both of Kate's friends were enthusiastic about Hazel's adoption, as were her parents. Kate had all the support and advice she could ever need, and the farmhouse was ready for Hazel's arrival.

All that was left to do was jump in, paws first, and start this new journey together.

By the time they reached Eagle River, Kate already felt better. Hazel had impeccable manners in the car. No barking, no jumping. She didn't even react when, as they paused at

Eagle River's lone traffic light, a Husky in a passing truck popped its head out a halfway-down window and offered Hazel a greeting or a challenge. It wasn't clear which, but Hazel didn't mind one bit.

"And I hear you like cats." Kate gripped the steering wheel tight as she slowed for her driveway. The biggest test was just ahead. "I have four for you to meet. But maybe not all of them today. We should take it slow."

The barn kitties had other ideas. All three of them were sprawled on the front porch steps, flanked by festive piles of pumpkins. At first glance they appeared to be sunning themselves, dozing in the crisp air of a perfect fall Sunday afternoon. But as the car came up the lane, Kate noticed Scout had set all pretense aside and was now up on his haunches, his laser-like gaze trained on Hazel. Jerry and Maggie soon did the same.

"There's the welcoming committee." Kate shook her head and smiled. "Can't get anything past them, they always know when something's up. Especially Scout."

All three cats started to saunter around the corner of the house before Kate made it to the garage. By the time Hazel dismounted from the car, the kitties had reassembled on the sidewalk between the garage and the back porch.

"Oh, I see!" Kate called to the cats. "No passage unless you get to meet Hazel, is that it?"

Hazel wriggled with curiosity but didn't bark, thank goodness. She pulled hard on the leash, eager to meet these furry residents. Kate had expected the dog to gaze around the farm yard, sniff the new air and study the trees and outbuildings and house, but all Hazel wanted to do was interact with the cats.

"Hazel, be nice."

Each kitty got a good sniff, but their reactions varied. Scout leaned forward and bravely touched noses, like he did this sort of thing every day. Jerry seemed more bored than anything. He allowed Hazel to study him from top to bottom, then wandered off to the bushes along the back porch. Maggie narrowed her eyes and pulled back at Hazel's greeting, then let out a ladylike growl of annoyance but stood her ground.

"I'd say you're maybe two for three." If this was as tough as it would get, Kate was happy to accept those odds. "Not bad for your first try. Give them some time, and I think they'll all come around."

Scout accompanied Hazel and Kate to the back porch steps. As Kate fumbled in her purse for her keys, the big tuxedo cat stepped over and rubbed against Hazel's lush coat.

"Well, look at that!" Kate laughed with relief. "Hazel, you've either been accepted or, more likely, claimed as Scout's personal property. I hope you understand where you fit in the pecking order around here."

Despite Scout's bravado, it was Charlie who reigned at this farm. And all the barn cats knew it. For his part, Charlie now merely blinked at his loyal subjects with an air of dignified generosity.

Kate unlocked the kitchen door, held tight to Hazel's lead, and ushered the dog inside.

"Charlie, there's someone I'd like you to meet."

He was already on his way down from upstairs, she could hear his claws clicking on the bare treads. He hurried through the short hallway to the kitchen, then his tail drooped as he skidded to a stop.

Hazel politely wagged her tail and lowered her head.

Greetings, King Charles, her posture said.

Charlie lifted one brown front paw, then the other, then took a few tentative steps forward. His blue eyes then focused on Kate. *What's going on?*

"This is Hazel, your new sister." Kate tried to keep her voice light and easy. "Charlie, you're still in charge, OK? And you're going to have your safe room all to yourself until I'm sure the two of you have become friends."

Hazel whimpered and tugged on the leash, eager to say hello, but Kate held her back. "Let him come to you. Hazel, stay." To Kate's relief, she listened. "Good girl."

Charlie proceeded cautiously. Kate sensed he wasn't scared, at least, just curious. And Hazel had an air of calm deference that was amazing to witness. Maybe she wasn't quite cut out for a life of public or private service, but she'd learned how to approach new and unfamiliar situations with a calm and patient attitude. "Maybe this won't be so hard."

Charlie touched his nose to Hazel's, and Kate held her breath.

Slap!

"Oh, Charlie, don't do that!" Kate checked Hazel's snout. No blood, not even a scratch. Just Charlie making it clear who was boss.

Hazel was caught off guard for only a moment, but then wagged her tail again. Charlie took a page from Jerry's playbook and strutted off into the dining room, where he promptly made a graceful leap to his special food table. Before he tucked into his kibble, he gave Hazel one more withering look.

Kate decided to keep Hazel on her lead until Charlie finished his snack and decamped upstairs. She gave him a few minutes, then tied the dog's leash to one of the table legs and tiptoed off to find her fluffy boy. He was settled in his special room, staring out into the golden light as the sun dipped lower over the fields.

When Kate let herself through the gate and approached his window seat, Charlie turned her way.

"I know this is going to be hard, for a bit." Kate petted his back, and he didn't protest. Well, that was promising.

"Hazel's a really sweet dog, and she needed a home. It's a good thing, though, that we have three bedrooms in this farmhouse. Everyone can have their own, I guess."

With Charlie in his safe space, Kate let Hazel off her lead

and gave her a tour of the house. The dog's food and water dishes were already prominently displayed in the kitchen, and Hazel seized the opportunity to test the couch's cushions for comfort as they went through the living room. Everything needed a sniff; some items got a gentle nudge of the snout. When they went upstairs, Hazel quickly realized she couldn't get over, or through, Charlie's special gate. The smirk on his face said it all, and Kate was relieved to see his haunches relax before he stretched out again on his padded window seat.

"He's laughing at you, I think," she told Hazel. "But it's better than hissing or clawing or fighting."

Kate wasn't sure what the sleeping arrangements would be, at least for a while. Charlie always slept on the bed with her. She'd bought two extra-nice pet beds for Hazel. One was in the second spare bedroom, and the other in a corner of the living room that was far away from Charlie's hearthside pillow.

With the house tour complete, Kate changed into her chore clothes. It had been an unforgettable afternoon, and she was suddenly exhausted. All the excitement and uncertainty about adopting Hazel had snowballed on her in just a few hours. Those first tense moments were over and, while things weren't as harmonious as they could be, it was a good start.

But even though Charlie had a safe zone, she wasn't sure it was a good idea to let him and Hazel have the run of the house together. Maybe this was a good time for some bonding and fresh air.

The fancy new dog door was still locked, and would remain so for at least a few days. Kate had decided to not show Hazel how it worked until she was free to roam. So with the leash in her other hand, Kate picked up the barn cats' food bucket and took Hazel out for a walk around the farm.

Scout's crew was too focused on supper's arrival to pay Hazel much mind. And when Kate commanded the dog to "sit" and "stay" outside the main door of the machine shed, Hazel did just that. Even though the yearning in her brown eyes said she really wanted to go inside with Kate and explore.

With the cats settled for the night, Kate left the empty food bucket outside the shed and gave Hazel a big smile. "Now, let's go for a little walk. I'm going to show you around." She checked the horizon. "We have some time yet before the sun begins to set. Which means the raccoons won't be out yet to raid the kitties' bucket."

She only made that mistake once, leaving the plastic container sitting outside the shed. It had held remnants of canned food that night, and she'd come out in the morning to find the bucket over by the garden. Or what was left of it. In their haste to get every last glob of goodness, the varmints had torn the container into pieces.

Kate and Hazel started behind the machine shed, on the edge of the windbreak, and headed north toward where the barn used to be.

Even though her fears had eased, Kate was usually still a bit on edge when she made this nightly trek. But with Hazel at her side, she saw everything with new eyes.

The dog was fascinated by every fallen leaf, every dip in the yellowed grass that might hint at an animal burrow to be investigated. When Hazel turned her fuzzy snout into the wind, Kate stood back and waited.

"What is it, girl?" Hazel only blinked and looked to her left, then to the right. "So much to see, so much to smell. It will take you a while to feel at home here, but I think we're off to a good start."

Down the lane they went. Kate wanted Hazel to get the feel of the whole place, the entire yard and then some, hoping maybe she'd be content to stay closer to the house once she did have her freedom. It was getting a little late, as their walk had been halted several times for exploration, and Kate didn't think there was good-enough light to take Hazel down to the creek bridge a quarter-mile away.

Or out into the pasture, either. Kate was eager to further examine the vegetation along the creek bed, see if she could identify any of the native species even though many of them had already gone to seed, but this wasn't the right time.

As Hazel inspected an apparently fascinating spot in the front yard, Kate stared up the slight grade toward her house and took a deep breath. She was home. Finally. And looking at it from this vantage point, seeing it in the way Hazel possibly saw it, made her proud and content.

The brick farmhouse was solid and comforting. Most of the first floor's lights were on, and the warm glow spilled out the wide windows. Her front porch was decked out in its fall finery, and the now-sleeping garden beyond held the promise of fresh produce for next year. Red and gold leaves, which still clung stubbornly to some of the trees, glowed in the waning light.

The garden was Hazel's favorite stop on the tour. Her twitching nose tracked several mysterious trails through the cold dirt before Kate decided it was time to head inside. Supper was fixed for everyone and eaten, then Kate cleaned up the kitchen with both ears attuned to any potential skirmishes in the dining or living rooms.

All was silent, and she wasn't sure what she'd find when she finally draped the dishcloth over the sink faucet and turned off the overhead light.

Had Charlie boxed Hazel's ears and sent her off to cower in a corner? Did Hazel chase Charlie until he slid under the couch? Were the two of them in a stare-down on the rug?

Kate held her breath as she came into the living room and found ... nothing much going on.

Charlie was on his padded throne next to the hearth, his back comfortably turned to the rest of the room. Hazel had sprawled out on her own bed, where her favorite fleece blanket from the rescue had been tossed over the mattress. A new toy, a plush in the shape of a teddy bear, had been selected from the pile Kate left next to the couch and was now tucked inside Hazel's paws. She looked up when Kate entered, and gave a polite wag of her tail.

"Everyone getting along?" With no need to referee, Kate settled into her usual spot on the couch. "I have my blankie, too," she told Hazel as she reached for the throw folded over the arm of the sofa. "Charlie, how goes it over there?"

The only answer was a quick flip of the tail. But her cat's relaxed posture told Kate he wasn't as put out as he pretended to be.

They all rested in companionable silence the rest of the evening. Kate streamed episodes of one of her favorite shows, while Charlie snoozed by the hearth. Hazel spent most of her time on her bed, but padded out of the room a few times to get a snack in the kitchen and, according to the clicking of her paws across the hardwood floors, give the downstairs' corners some extra examination.

The occasional headlights that swept down the gravel road were apparently too far away to pose much of a threat, but Hazel still padded to the picture window to give most of them a good look.

She didn't bark, as Kate had worried she might, but each instance brought a turn of the head and a questioning look.

"It's OK," Kate always said in a carefree voice. "Just people going here and there. We don't need to worry about them."

It was long past dark now and, while Kate felt more at ease thanks to Hazel's watchful presence, there was one more task she and her new dog had to complete that night. Until Kate was comfortable letting Hazel come and go as she pleased, bathroom breaks had to be scheduled. Including one just before bedtime.

Before now, Kate tried to stay inside after she fed the barn cats and walked the perimeter of her farm. Any late-night arrivals home had merited a quick glance around the yard when Kate exited the garage, and then a dash for the farmhouse's back steps and its left-on porch light.

But Hazel's needs were more important than Kate's insecurities, and Kate pulled on her chore coat and reached for a leash. Hazel understood what was about to happen, and offered a happy wag of her tail.

"We've had a good first day, huh?" Beyond the range of the yard light, the land was cloaked in darkness. Kate went down the back steps, Hazel at her side, and noticed for the first time that her little farm had a unique beauty at this late hour.

"You're not the only one with lessons to learn," she told Hazel as they lingered by the garage. "Let's just enjoy this peaceful night for a few minutes."

* 10 *

Morning brought a hint of frost along with loads of sunshine, and the brittle, brown grass crunched under Kate's farm boots when she headed out to give the cats their breakfast.

It promised to be another beautiful day, and the combines were already humming across the fields at this early hour. As Kate doled out affection and kibble topped with chicken gravy, she weighed her options with Hazel.

Kate normally didn't come home on her lunch break, but that would be necessary until she was comfortable giving Hazel unsupervised access to the yard. The night had passed peacefully, as Hazel had chosen the pup bed in "her" room and Charlie had staked out his usual spot on Kate's bed, but Kate wasn't about to let them have a free-for-all when she wasn't home.

She could kennel Hazel in the dog's unofficial room, with her toys, bed and dishes. But was there a better way? As she started toward the house, Kate had an idea. Once she was back in the kitchen, she texted Roberta.

"Let's see if this works," she told Hazel. "If I can manage it, you're not just going to get a short walk before I leave."

Hazel's arrival at the post office elicited a mix of gasps, shocked faces and plenty of laughter.

"I hear we have a new recruit." Mae hurried over to offer a

hand for Hazel to sniff. "Roberta said it's just for a day or two, but who knows? Hi, sweetie, I'm so glad to meet you."

Hazel gave her trademark happy whimper and butt wiggle, and hearts melted around the room. Even Jack couldn't resist the dog's considerable charms.

"Why wouldn't I like her?" He gave Kate a look of mock surprise when she challenged him on it. "She has impeccable manners. And you know we have two pooches at home."

"Yeah, but it's not exactly following regulations. And I *hope* she has impeccable manners while I'm on my route today. The squirrels in my yard can attest to the fact that even though she's had extensive obedience training, Hazel's still a regular dog at heart." Kate jangled the leash. "And I have the sore arms to prove it."

Hazel must have been settling in at the farm, because that morning's otherwise-routine potty break had been interrupted by a frantic sprint across the yard when she spotted a fat squirrel feasting on the leftovers under the bird feeder.

Randy was next in line to greet the newest member of the team. He'd farmed for decades before moving to town and getting on at the post office, and he claimed the hours of walking kept him fit and lean even though he was in his sixties.

"This shop has had a dog or two ride along before," he told his co-workers. "Oh, it's been a long while, way back before my time on the force. But when we were first married, out on the farm, our regular carrier was old Mac Feldman, and he had this big lab mix that came along with him most days. When you saw that blue pickup coming down the road, more often than not, Shep was riding shotgun."

Kate was fascinated by this bit of local lore. "Where did Mac put the mail case, then, if Shep was along?" While Hazel had the other front seat on the ride to town, she would need to be in the back when Kate started her route.

Jack and Marge shared an amused glance. As the two longest-serving members of the current force, they'd seen a lot in their time.

"Well, wherever he wanted to, I guess." Marge laughed. "I suspect he just put it on the floorboards. The stack of upcoming deliveries was probably at his elbow, and he just hoped Shep wouldn't sit on them."

"People weren't so fussy, like they are now." Jack took a sip of his coffee. "A bent envelope corner or a little smudge didn't matter. They were just so excited to get some mail." He gestured at Jared with his mug. "It may be hard for you youngsters to believe this, but before emails and texts, mail was a real lifeline for people."

Randy gave Hazel another pat on the head. "Especially for friends and family who were far away. Phone calls were for local folks only, unless it was a true emergency or on special occasions. Long distance was expensive."

Roberta came in the back door, and her eyes lit up when she saw Hazel. "There she is! What a pretty girl." Hazel made an excited noise at being fussed over, but reined in her impulse to rush toward this potential new friend. She looked to Kate for permission, and Kate gave it with a nod.

"Look at that!" Roberta was impressed as Hazel trotted her way. "So well-behaved, you can tell she's had extensive obedience training."

"She's a pro at riding in the car." Hazel's last move might have been a fluke, but Kate was still proud. "Which makes sense, given the facility's program. Thanks for letting me bring her along, at least for a day or two."

"It'll be good bonding time for you both." Roberta ruffled Hazel's thick coat. "You're so sweet! If you get tired of riding a route, you can hang out here in the office with me."

When Kate told Hazel to make herself comfy in the corner, away from the two long counters, the dog happily complied. She settled on the floor, stretched out, and watched with curious eyes as the carriers finished sorting the letters and packages for the day's deliveries.

As Kate loaded Bertha, she was careful to set her few parcels to one side of the back seat before she added her mail case to the front. With her coffee thermos and water bottles ready, it was time for a potty break for Hazel before they hit the road.

"You have to stay in the car," Kate told Hazel as they lingered on the patch of brown lawn next to the post office. "We have procedures for when a dog bites a carrier, but not for when a dog bites another dog. You'll be on their turf, so we have to be careful."

Kate had always been alone while on a route, whether in Chicago or back here at home. Her only companions when she traveled the country roads were the tunes on the radio, the purr of Bertha's engine, and the rumble of the gravel under the tires. But before they even left town, it was clear having Hazel as a partner would make this day special.

Several people along Main Street burst into smiles as they pointed or waved at Hazel, and Kate waved back on the dog's behalf. There was something about animals, dogs in particular, that made people happy and relaxed. And while Hazel hadn't made the cut as a service dog, she had beauty and charm to spare. Jared was off that day, and Kate had his route southwest of town. Her parents lived in the area, and Kate knew these roads well.

While she occasionally rested on the seat, Hazel spent most of the miles up on her haunches, taking in the scenery and studying the farms and front yards whenever Bertha stopped for a drop. Many rural properties were home to at least one dog, and the sight of Hazel in the back of the mail car brought several canine residents on the run to get a close-up look at the new carrier.

Kate's human customers were also fascinated with Hazel. Their tired faces lit up in her presence, at least momentarily, and Kate was glad her dog could spread some much-needed love and distraction on this busy harvest-season day. There were plenty of comments and concerns shared about Friday night's fire, but Hazel had a knack for quickly turning residents' attention to her bright eyes and soft coat.

The air was still cool in the afternoon but the sky was bright, and Kate's spirits soared as she and Hazel made their rounds. Her worries about the arson cases drifted away as she drove along. There wasn't much, if anything, she could do about the situation, other than pass along a tidbit of relevant information if it came her way. Maybe she should just set it aside, at least for now.

After all, like everyone else, she had plenty on her plate these days.

It was fun to have Hazel along for the ride, at least for a while, but that wouldn't work for the days Kate had to walk a route in town. The two of them needed to ease into some sort of manageable routine. Or really, the three of them, with Charlie ...

And every spare minute she had, which didn't happen often enough, Kate felt she should be helping her family with harvest or getting her own little place ready for winter.

"There's never enough hours in the day." Kate glanced in the rearview mirror to find Hazel nearly asleep. It was almost two now, and it pleased Kate to reflect on how well Hazel had responded to so many new people and places in their first full day together.

"We have over an hour to go yet, but I think one of our next stops is going to make you very happy."

The county nature preserve was one of Kate's favorite places in Valley Township. The site's timber and grasslands were especially beautiful this time of year, but that wasn't all it had to offer. The main building there was unlocked all year around, and it was the only public bathroom on this entire route.

This was the perfect place for both of them to get out of the car and take a break. And when Kate saw one of the county conservation department's trucks parked next to the concrete-block shed, she couldn't believe her good fortune.

"Look at that!" She pulled Bertha in next to the truck. "I hope they're around close, as we can't stay long. But if they are, I can ask them about those prairie plants in my pasture."

Ever since she'd learned about the native vegetation on her property, Kate had been fascinated by its potential. There wasn't much to see, not this time of the year, but her thoughts hurried ahead to what spring might bring.

It was a small prairie plot; it would never qualify for one of those conservation signs Kate occasionally spotted along the back roads. But she wanted to care for whatever was there as best as she could.

The preserve had a designated "pet exercise" area, which was just a corner of the grass where a poop-bag dispenser waited next to a trash can.

But what to do with Hazel while Kate was in the restroom? She didn't want to leave her in the car, even with the windows rolled down. So, laughing all the way, she guided the dog into the women's restroom and knotted the leash around one of the stalls' metal legs.

"Just a minute, and we'll go back out," she promised Hazel, who found this new place worthy of several sniffs. "Oh, won't this make a fun story to tell everyone when we get back to the post office!"

As they lingered in the grass just off the parking lot, Kate spotted a flash of orange bobbing along the nearby trail. It was moving her way.

Excellent! Most hikers and walkers didn't bother with blaze-orange safety gear until peasant-hunting season started later in October, but the county crews' jackets were always decked out with the telltale color. She could corner this guy for a minute, ask some questions, and be on her way.

As soon as he was close enough, Kate smiled and waved. The man returned the greeting and stepped up his pace. When he came into the clearing, Kate saw his trash bag and grabber stick.

Trail cleanup wasn't a glamorous task, but local residents were proud of this nature preserve and staff did their best to keep it tidy. Because along with providing peaceful views and serenity, its programs brought in much-needed money for the conservation department's shoestring budget.

"Lovely afternoon, isn't it?" The conservation officer waved again when he met up with Kate and Hazel. He looked to be in his forties, with sandy-blond hair that showed flecks of gray under his county-issued ball cap. "I don't know how many more of these we'll get this fall."

"It's beautiful out, for sure. But you're right, we're always on borrowed time when October rolls around." She extended one hand in greeting as she kept the other on Hazel's lead. "I'm Kate Duncan, Eagle River post office."

"Everett Whitcomb, Hartland County Conservation." He shook her hand, then leaned over and let Hazel give him a sniff. "And who is this? A fresh recruit?" He rumpled Hazel's thick coat, and she didn't mind one bit. "Are you the newest public employee around here? Welcome to the team."

"She's a temp. Just for a few days until we get settled."

Everett didn't seem to be in a hurry to go back to picking up trash, so Kate filled him in on Hazel's journey. He nodded his approval.

"A cousin of mine's a veteran, he has a dog from there. Great place, an amazing program. It's made a world of difference for Joe."

"Well, I'm biased, but I'm glad Hazel didn't make the cut. By the way, I'm glad you happen to be here this afternoon."

She explained about the patch of prairie plantings on her land, and Everett's blue eyes lit up with interest. "That's wonderful! You know there has to be more little parcels like that, all around the county, but we don't always hear about them."

"I'm sure many people are like me; they don't know what they have unless someone points it out. I'm so glad my new neighbor passed that information along. Anything I need to do to keep it going?"

Everett asked some detailed questions about what she had in the pasture, and Kate was glad she'd taken a few photos the other day.

While Hazel sniffed around, Kate pulled out her phone. Everett's knowledge of the various species was impressive, and he was able to identify most of what he saw despite the fact that the growing season was now over.

"That's fascinating!" Kate couldn't believe her luck in running into Everett this way. If she had arrived at the park only a few minutes sooner or later, they never would have crossed paths. "It means even more, now that I have a better idea of what's actually out there."

"You know, this might be more than you'd want to take on, but we're working on a new program we hope to roll out in the spring."

Milton Benniger's generosity meant a big boost for this nature preserve, which in turn would free up more money for the county's other parks and programs. County staff hoped to offer native-species seeds and plants at a reduced cost, or maybe even for free, to landowners willing to offer them a home. It would be a way to reestablish historically significant varieties, as well as offering food and habitat for bees and butterflies.

"That's a great idea!" Kate and Hazel needed to get back on the road, but Kate was eager to hear more. "I could add to what's already there."

Everett grinned. "That is exactly the reaction we want to see from people. If everyone is as enthusiastic as you are, it's sure to be a success."

The conservationists hoped to firm up their plans after the holidays, but didn't expect to hand out plants and seeds until late April or even May. "You know how unpredictable the weather is around here."

"Don't I ever. Well, it was nice to meet you. And thanks for your help!"

Kate groaned when Bertha's dashboard clock told her the truth: Her break had gone on far longer than expected. She'd need to hustle the rest of the afternoon, but it was worth it.

"We're already bending the rules today," Kate told Hazel as they left the nature preserve in their rearview mirror. "Might as well spare a few minutes for a good cause."

11

The tall, ornate windows of Eagle River's historic library gave off a warm glow in the deepening dusk. It was one of Kate's favorite buildings, for its design as well as all the books and services it offered. But tonight, she wasn't sure she wanted to push her way through its heavy oak doors.

"What am I doing here?" she muttered as she started across the parking lot, which was fuller than usual for a Wednesday evening. "This is probably a wild goose chase. I could be at home, relaxing on the couch."

Bev's text said she was already in the lobby. All Kate had to do was go in, sit with her friend, and … what? Try to sniff out a serial arsonist?

But then she remembered that wistful-yet-crazed look in Edna's eyes when she talked about burning her leaves. Kate didn't think Edna was the one setting the fires but, judging by the turnout for this meeting, there were several others around Eagle River who agreed with her, one way or another. Eagle River wasn't that big, and the rural area around it was sparsely populated. The odds seemed good to Kate that whoever was responsible wouldn't be able to stay away.

"Like a moth to a flame," she reminded herself as she made her way up the wide stone steps. "This may be our best chance to get a good look at potential suspects, at least."

And there was Bev in the front vestibule, all smiles, and Kate was suddenly glad she'd come back to town. Her comfy couch would be there tomorrow night; and besides, this could be an interesting evening. And then she laughed when she saw what Bev had in one hand.

"Popcorn? Where did you get that?"

"Down the hall by the meeting rooms." Bev helped herself to more of her snack as they made their way into the main lobby. "Kyle got a machine just last week. He said there's a bit of cash in the budget for some fun additions to the place."

Kyle Gibson was the new librarian, and his progressive ways had been a hit with most of the local residents. While many of the night's visitors were likely upset with the city's plans, most of them gave Kyle a big smile as they accepted red-and-white striped bags of fresh popcorn.

"I like this idea." Kate sampled the wares, and nodded her approval. "Adds sort of a, well, festive vibe to the evening."

Kyle leaned in. "I expect there will be plenty of drama inside that room tonight, so I thought, why not?" It was the larger of the two meeting spaces at the library, and it was already two-thirds full.

"Maybe the snacks will ratchet the outrage down a notch or two. But if this backfires, I may have quite the mess to clean up after."

"Popcorn is very popular at circuses," Bev observed. "You might be on to something there."

Kyle smirked as he added more kernels to the popper. "You're both in the country, seems like, so not voting citizens of Eagle River. What brings you out, then?"

The women exchanged a cautious glance. "We're nosy," Kate offered. Well, it was true. "But we're going to stay in the background."

"Fair enough. I'm doing the same." Kyle set three more filled bags on the kiosk, and they were quickly snatched up. He tipped his head toward the last row of chairs, just inside the door. "See you in the peanut gallery. If I'm busy stuffing my face, it might help me keep a neutral expression."

Kate understood Kyle's cautious attitude. He was a public figure in the community, for better or worse, and it wouldn't do for him to appear to take a side on such a controversial issue. She felt the same pressure, if to a lesser degree. Sharing concerns about the possibility of arson was acceptable, but this? Roberta had warned the mail carriers to stay on the fence about burning leaves, no matter how hard residents tried to entice them to jump off it one way or the other.

"Look at all these people," Bev whispered as she and Kate took their seats in the back. "Who would have thought so many folks could be so riled up about an issue like this?"

Most of the attendees were on the older side. And despite Kyle's popcorn peace offering, many of them appeared disgruntled as they chatted amongst themselves. Jaws were tight, and hand gestures were sharp.

"Edna has assembled quite the audience." Kate scanned the room for very-familiar faces, and came up empty. That was a relief. People were free to have their opinions, of course; but she was on the lookout for a potential arsonist tonight and she hoped it wasn't someone she knew well.

Edna, who paced at the front of the room, seemed to vacillate between pride over the turnout and a nervousness about how this evening might go. Promptly at seven, she clapped her hands.

"OK, everyone, let's get started." The room quickly turned quiet. "I know why you're all here. And I have to say, I'm pleased that so many residents of our little town care so much about this important issue."

This was met with a round of applause, and a few whistles.

"This is our time." Edna's brown eyes flashed with determination, and she barely bothered to consult her notes. "It's our time to stand up and speak up, honor tradition, and protect Eagle River homeowners' rights to do as they see fit with their properties."

This brought more applause, and a few residents even got to their feet. Bev sighed quietly, and Kate fought to keep her expression neutral.

Were these residents really that fired up about burning leaves, or was this meeting just an outlet for their general frustration? If this forum had been about the city raising taxes, or water quality, or a host of other issues, how many of them would have bothered to attend?

"We just need to focus on the reaction of the crowd," she reminded herself as much as Bev. "Look for someone who seems, well, overly fired up about this situation."

Bev suppressed a chuckle with a handful of popcorn.

"Sorry," Kate said, "I couldn't resist."

There was a rustle to her right, just inside the still-open door, and Kate was surprised to see a familiar face walk in. It was Alex. And even in his hoodie and pulled-low ball cap, he was still handsome.

Or maybe, she should be a little disappointed to see him here. She didn't know Alex well; at least, not as well as she might like to. But he had a sarcastic sense of humor and was very intelligent, and she wouldn't have pegged him as someone who'd get this upset over what to do with his fallen leaves.

Their eyes locked for a moment, and his lit up with something she couldn't quite name. He pivoted into the back row and started toward her, popcorn in hand.

"Hey." Alex plopped down in the chair next to Kate, and the knee of his jeans bumped hers. "What did I miss?" he whispered. "Edna's on a roll, looks like."

He rattled his popcorn bag. "Has the action started yet, or are we still watching the previews?"

"She's warming up the crowd." It now seemed likely Alex was only there as a spectator, and Kate's unease quickly passed. "I half expect a marching band to show up, or something."

"There's a fever in the air, all right."

"I guess I didn't think you'd be into something like this." Kate couldn't help but bring it up, just to gauge Alex's reaction. "I mean, I thought you had enough on your plate to not be obsessed with yard-waste disposal."

"Who says I care all that much?" He gave her an appraising stare as he munched his popcorn. "Right back at you: Why are you here? You don't even live in town anymore."

Kate gave a small shrug and looked away.

"Oh, I get it." He smirked. "Detective Duncan's on the case. You ladies are here to scan for perps, see if anyone raises any red flags. Hmm. Interesting."

Kate gave him the side eye. "Now, I wonder how you came to that conclusion. And I seem to recall your cousin's the police chief. I happened to notice, given my so-called investigative skills, that he's not here tonight. Nor are any of his officers. Are you on assignment?"

Alex only pulled his ball cap's brim lower.

"Who's running the bar?"

"I have help. Seriously, you thought I did it all alone? Besides, things don't get busy until after nine, and we'll be out of here long before then. Unless Benedict Arnold and his friends decide to stage a full-on revolt."

Alex tipped his chin toward a man in the middle of the room who was on his feet, almost shouting as he listed his grievances against the proposed burn ban. With his pot belly, patriotic tee shirt and glasses, he looked like he could be someone's grandpa. But his fire made it clear where he stood on this issue. He was angry, and he'd had enough.

"Who is that?" Kate whispered to Bev.

"Stan Winston." Bev frowned. "He was a few years ahead of me in school."

"And?" Kate was curious.

"Let's just say, I'm not surprised to see him here."

"They can't tell us what to do!" A round of applause echoed behind Stan's latest proclamation. "It's bad enough they want to raise our taxes again, and I've been trying for weeks to get someone from the city to come out and fix the storm drain along my curb."

Kate didn't know many of her fellow public employees at city hall, but there were only a handful of them. That kind of work had to be done by an outside firm, which took time as well as money.

"And this is tradition!" Stan barked. "I've been lighting my leaves for years. Do it right, and it's safe." He shook his head. "There's nothing like it. When that little flame catches, and glows, and you get that wonderful aroma. Why, I like to get my lawn chair and sit out there, just to enjoy it."

Bev elbowed Kate, and she elbowed back.

Potential suspect.

Kate glanced at Alex, and he was laser-focused on Stan. Sure, maybe the guy just enjoyed one of the rites of fall. But there was an undercurrent of anger, as well as awe, in his voice that gave Kate a bit of a chill.

One woman stood up suddenly. "What we need is a slogan! A way to get the council's attention."

"Why, Louise, that's a wonderful idea." Edna jumped in, and Kate suspected she was eager for any opportunity to regain control of the room. "Maybe we could ..."

"And I have one." Louise didn't wait for Edna to finish. "'We have the right to burn our leaves bright.'"

Bev sighed again. Alex put his head in his hands.

"Well? What does everyone think?" But Louise hurried on without bothering to get any feedback. "I'll make the signs. Anyone who wants one, I can have them done in a few days."

"I'll take two," another woman called out. "We're on a corner."

Edna studied her notes as requests for signs came from around the room.

Kate sensed that the older woman was a little eccentric, and maybe had too much time on her hands, but she was just trying to have a voice in her community. The rabble-rousers in this crowd, however, seemed intent on throwing Edna's plan, whatever it was, off the rails.

Kate spotted Kyle hiding in the far corner, his popcorn bag held up to cover most of his face. No matter how tonight's meeting ended, he was going to have to referee this debate inside the library until the council voted in a few weeks, and likely after a decision was made.

As she pondered how Kyle would manage that, she saw a younger man slip in the open door and take an empty seat at the end of the back row.

Others saw him, too. And while Louise rambled on about her signs, and someone suggested they should make tee shirts, too, a murmur of surprise echoed around the room.

The newcomer wore a faded Eagle River Wildcats sweatshirt and old jeans. His sandy hair was cropped short, and his chin and jaw were covered in day-old stubble. Nothing that made him stand out from any other guy his age in this town. But for some reason, his appearance at this meeting was drawing attention.

"Do you know him?" Kate whispered to Alex as Bev leaned in, eager for an answer.

The side of Alex's mouth twitched into a wry smile. "That's your neighbor, Brody Donegan. The one with the toasted barn and the active insurance policy."

Bev and Kate exchanged startled looks.

"Have you seen him before?" Bev murmured. "I don't know his family."

"No, I don't think I have." That was all Kate said, as she still felt a bit sheepish about how she'd been nosing around at the end of Brody's farm lane last week.

Even so, Brody's appearance at this meeting filled Kate with a measure of relief. If he were to blame for the fire on his property, surely he'd know better than to show up to something like this, even if he supported the group's agenda.

And by the way Brody slouched in his chair, and the flush that had settled in his cheeks as he tried to avoid the pointed glares sent his way, it was clear he was very uncomfortable.

So, why was he here? Kate suspected it might be the same reason why she and Bev had come into town tonight, and why Alex was next to them rather than at his bar: To try to catch an arsonist.

"I think we need to come up with a, well, maybe a platform," one man said. His measured words and calm voice made it clear he was trying to diffuse the situation, and Edna gave him a grateful nod. "You know, like how political candidates do. A list of reasons why we should be able to continue this practice in this town." He glared at Stan. "Facts, not just emotion."

"Let's do that," one woman said smoothly as she reached into her purse. "I can take notes."

Another man raised his hand. "Are there things we can point to that will build our case? Like, how many times in the past so-many years has the fire department been called out for a burning leaf pile that was out of control? I doubt there's very many. George, do you know?"

"It never happened while I was serving," an older man answered. "And that was for over fifteen years. People around here, they're smart. They know how to handle a fire."

It seemed like cooler heads were taking over the conversation, and Kate was relieved. Even Stan seemed to simmer down a bit.

"That's a good idea," he finally said. "I bet if we put our heads together, we can get that done." There was a hint of a smile, but it quickly disappeared. "I'm sure we have some fire experts here in this room that can help us with that."

Stan only looked at George, but something in his tone deepened the flush on Brody's cheeks. The younger man crossed his arms and stared at the floor, and Kate could feel the tension in his frame from several feet away. Alex apparently did, too, as he was watching Brody closely.

"George, how about you take that on?" Edna quickly delegated the task at hand. "Everyone, email him with your ideas and insight. Let's go back to this slogan."

Stan was suddenly deep in conversation with the man next to him, and they were both staring at Brody.

Edna's smile was wide, but nervous, as she nodded at Louise. "I had a slogan idea, but we don't have to use it. It was just a starting point. Yours is ... catchy. Thanks for sharing."

Brody jumped out of his chair and narrowed his eyes at the two gossiping men. "I have something to say."

"Oh, why, sure," Edna stammered as she clutched her notes close. "Do you ..."

"I'm Brody Donegan, for those of you who don't know." His hands were squeezed into fists, but he raised his chin with pride. "But I'm sure most of you know my barn caught fire not too long ago, out east of town."

He looked around the room, and stared down a few people in particular. "Everyone knows. There's no such thing as a secret in Eagle River."

"Are you sure?" An older man guffawed, but there was a hint of malice in his voice. "Anything you want to tell us?"

Kate looked over just in time to see Kyle give Alex a worried look, and Alex's barely perceptible nod in return.

Stan stood up again. "The sheriff's not here, son. If you feel the need to get something off your chest, maybe this isn't the place."

"I didn't do it!" Brody's face was red with fury. "Light my own barn on fire? Come on, man. I don't know what you think of me." Stan's sour expression said it all. "But I'm not a stupid fool. Unlike some in this town."

That did it. Four other men in the room stood up, and the insults began to fly.

Everything negative Kate had heard about Brody was brought up and flung in his face. He was lazy, didn't want to work or farm with his dad. He needed money. Didn't care about anyone but himself, or what cost ...

"I went to school with some of the guys on those crews," Brody spit out. "Right, George?" The retired firefighter nodded in agreement. "I would never, ever, put any of them, or anyone else, in any kind of danger. No matter how much money was at stake. And it's not that much."

Everyone stared at him. Brody let out a bitter laugh.

"Ooh, there's some good gossip to be had! You're all on the edge of your seats, I can tell. So I'll give it to you straight: If and when this case gets resolved, I'm due to collect a whole two grand if I'm lucky. Nowhere enough to have people thinking I'm a criminal."

Kate hadn't known exactly what to think of Brody before this, but seeing his anguish made her heart hurt. He was young, and didn't have many prospects, but she could tell he was a decent person. And not an arsonist. Not the sort of guy to light his own barn, and certainly not someone who'd turn around, less than two weeks later, and torch a farmhouse eight miles away.

"So, that's why you're here?" One man crossed his arms. "To tell all of us you're innocent?"

"I am, but that's not the reason." He squared his shoulders and glared at Stan. "I don't know who did it, but I'm damned sure going to find out. And if I had to guess, it's one of you nuts."

Brody laughed and shook his head. "All this fuss about burning some leaves! It stinks up the town and, yeah, it's a fire hazard. I say, they should have banned it a long time ago. Get a life! Can't you find something else to get riled up about?"

Stan was on the move, and the others in his row shrank back as he weaved toward the aisle. "Your dad doesn't have much sense, but I guess he got all the brains in your family."

"Funny, I've heard things about you, too." Brody took a small step back, but then decided to stand his ground. "All this talk about loving your country and our freedoms and whatever. You were quite the hellraiser back in the day. Tell us, Stan, how many times did you get arrested for criminal mischief?"

Brody looked around the room, which was hanging on his every word. "Yep, that's right. Vandalism was just the start of it, I heard."

Bev gripped Kate's arm as Stan barreled toward Brody. Alex swore under his breath, and stood up. Kyle, his face pale, put his phone to his ear and slipped out of the room.

One of the other men blocked Stan's progress up the aisle. "Hey, let's all calm down. We can't have this, not here."

"Why not?" Brody's voice rose in anger. "He accused me of arson. Which is usually a felony, by the way." He pointed at Stan. "That is, if you get caught."

Gasps went up around the room. Alex stepped in front of Brody. "That's enough. Both of you, go home."

Stan started to protest, but Alex cut him off. "You've had more than one chance to speak your mind tonight. You need to leave."

Brody backed off, but he wasn't done. "I'm going to figure out who did this," he said before he started for the door. "This isn't over."

* 12 *

After the confrontation between Brody and Stan, Edna quickly delegated a few tasks to volunteers and wrapped up the meeting.

Brody had already left by the time Kate and Bev started for their cars, and Stan's buddies had promised Alex their friend would go home and, at least for the rest of tonight, behave himself.

On their way across the parking lot, Bev gave Kate the details on Stan.

Lifelong Eagle River resident, Wildcats grad, worked on an assembly line up in Mason City as he bided his time toward retirement. Stan's dad had been a drinker, with disastrous results, Bev reported, and Stan tried to stay away from the bottle. Twice married, twice divorced; he was sometimes linked with a widow that lived outside of Prosper. Two of his three kids lived locally, but the youngest had taken off for the Twin Cities as soon as he graduated from high school.

In other words, a somewhat-typical small-town, middle-aged guy. Life hadn't always been easy, or fair; money was tight, and Stan's grip on his opinions was just as strong. But was he really angry enough to light other people's property on fire? And why?

Kate didn't know. But after what went down at that meeting, she wanted to find out.

Because despite all the debate and frustration that had been on display, no one else in the room had stood out as even a potential suspect.

But first, her furbabies deserved some of her attention. After an outside trip for Hazel, Kate picked up Charlie's favorite brush and patted her lap. Her fluffy boy hurried over to take part in their evening ritual, even though it was a bit later than usual. As Hazel listened in from Kate's reading chair, Kate gave them both the rundown on the meeting's drama.

"After Brody left, Alex marched Stan out the door like he was under arrest." The brush halted momentarily as Kate replayed the scene in her mind. "You know, he seemed to know exactly what he was doing."

His cousin, Ray Calcott, was Eagle River's police chief. But that didn't explain ...

Kate had heard Alex was from up by Austin. Who had told her that? She couldn't remember. She'd assumed he'd always been a bartender, but ...

Charlie's purr machine cut off, and then he gave her a reproachful look.

Kate shrugged and went back to Charlie's grooming. "Well, it's not that hard to step in and help, I guess. And Stan wasn't in any real trouble. At least, not legally. But he really stirred up the room. From the look on Edna's face, I think she expected things to go a bit differently tonight."

Kate had been too busy with her pets to realize the living room's heavy drapes were still open. She wasn't as nervous at night now that Hazel was there, but the emptiness of the surrounding fields and pastures could still be a little overwhelming when darkness set in. Hazel studied Kate as she went from window to window, room to room, and shut out the outside world.

"Better, huh?" Kate crouched next to Hazel and gave her a few pets. The dog wagged her tail in reply. "You really like my reading chair. I might have to get another one, just for myself. But for now, the couch is fine for me."

Kate tried to focus on the show she was streaming, but her mind kept going back to the meeting. And to Alex. She hadn't seen him much in the past few weeks. But maybe it was just as well. Because along with his good looks, Alex had an air of mystery about him.

"Catnip," she told Charlie, who'd snuggled back into her lap. "That's what he is. Catnip to this single gal who doesn't know many people around here, even though she's moved back home. She's on her own for the first time in over a decade and then, wham! Here comes Mr. Tall, Dark and Handsome. And smart."

Kate sighed. "It's probably just the allure of the unknown. Maybe he's just some sort-of-loser who runs a bar because he never found something better to do. That coolness factor? It could all be an illusion."

It wasn't just her questions about Alex that filled Kate's thoughts. She'd lived here for eighteen years before she left home. While she was relieved that no one she knew well had been in the crowd tonight, it was a little disorienting that hardly anyone even looked familiar.

Her own neighbor had slipped in the back door, and Kate had been oblivious to his identity. As for Stan ... Kate was sure she'd never seen him before in her life.

Her laptop beckoned from the coffee table, and Kate couldn't resist. Charlie moved over with a "meow" of annoyance, and Kate powered up her machine.

"If I start hanging out on the front porch all hours of the day and night, watching every vehicle that drives by and noting what time everyone is coming and going ... one of you, please, call for help."

But as she positioned her hands over the keys, Kate had to

laugh at herself. She wasn't spying on the neighbors from her porch swing, but she was about to do the high-tech equivalent. She navigated to the state's public-accessible court system and typed in Stan's name.

"Well, Benedict Arnold, let's see if Brody was telling the truth or just calling your bluff."

Stan had a handful of charges in the system, going back to when he was eighteen. Kate knew she couldn't access any juvenile records, but these incidents pointed to the possibility of others in his younger years.

The records didn't give all the details for those cases, but Kate found enough information that seemed to back up the personality and behavior she'd witnessed at the meeting. Criminal mischief and vandalism, just like Brody had said. However, those incidents had all occurred when Stan was in his late teens and twenties. Like most people, he seemed to have matured, at least a little, as he aged.

But then, she found something more recent. Charges for disorderly conduct and assault, from four years ago. The charges had been dropped, but she wasn't able to discern why. So she ran Stan through an online newspaper database, and soon came up with something of note.

The charges stemmed from an employees' strike at the factory he worked at before his current job. The mostly peaceful protest turned rowdy one night, according to an article she found, and several union members were charged in the incident.

In addition to being accused of heckling the police and the company's security guards, two of the men had allegedly punched their perceived foes. Stan's charges, as well as his co-worker's, were later dropped. Kate suspected the union's lawyers played a pivotal role in making the situation go away.

The article included another tidbit that caught Kate's eye. During the back-and-forth that night, the contents of one of the trash barrels behind the plant caught on fire. A still-smoldering cigarette was assumed to be the cause. The fire was quickly extinguished and officials kept their focus on holding back the striking employees. Of course, there'd been hundreds of angry people at the protest. What were the odds Stan was the one who'd lit the trash on fire? Not good, but Kate couldn't help but wonder.

* * *

Thursday was Kate's weekday off, and she was determined to set her musings aside. There were errands to run, including a much-needed haircut, and several outdoor chores waited at the farm if she could find the time for them that afternoon.

It was a beautiful morning, and Kate rolled the car's windows down when she reached Eagle River and welcomed in the crisp air as well as the sunshine. She hadn't traveled more than two blocks when she smelled something unmistakable. No one was behind her, so Kate quickly braked and turned into a neighborhood filled with older homes.

Three houses down, a cloud of smoke rose from a bank of leaves raked up next to the curb. At the end of the block, there was another one. She turned west, then back south, and spotted two more smoldering piles before she again met up with the blacktop on the edge of town.

It wasn't even ten o'clock in the morning. Kate assumed each leaf pile was being watched from a window or a front door. But she hadn't seen one person out on their lawn, hovering next to their burn stack, ready with a jug of water or a hooked-up hose in case things got out of control.

The city's permitted burn period had started Monday, but she was sure she hadn't noticed any fires until this morning. Maybe it was just a coincidence. Or maybe last night's meeting had spurred some in town to light their early leaf piles in a show of defiance. A reminder that, at least for this season, they would exercise their rights.

Although the residential streets were quiet, Kate had to wait to turn out onto the highway. Because along with the usual weekday-morning comings and goings, this route was favored by the farmers heading to Eagle River's co-op to unload their harvest loads.

As Kate idled there, she had to acknowledge the burning leaf piles' aromas were comforting in their own way. They held an echo of memory, of fall days at Grandma and Grandpa Duncan's farm just down the road from where Kate grew up. They'd retired and moved to Fort Dodge, and Kate still mourned the fact they weren't five minutes away anymore.

While Grandpa James, her dad and the uncles took care of the fallen leaves, Kate, Bryan and their cousins dashed around the yard, played hide and seek, and waited for Grandma Lillian's call to come inside.

With their cheeks aflame from the sudden temperature change, the kids gathered around the kitchen table. There was always ice-cold apple cider waiting for them in the kitchen, and fresh-baked pumpkin cookies with cream-cheese icing. What stood out the most to Kate now, all these years later, was the love she felt in that kitchen. Fall was always an exciting time of year for children, as Halloween was just a few weeks away. After that, it would soon be Christmas, and ...

Kate's eyes started to burn, and she coughed. With no one waiting behind her, she'd idled too long with her memories. The acrid smoke from the yard on her right had gained strength, kicked up by a wind that, as it did so often on these October days, couldn't decide exactly which way it wanted to go. With another cough and a sigh, she powered up the windows and turned toward Prosper.

* * *

Getting an appointment with Stella Adair hadn't been as difficult as scoring chair time with Kate's favorite stylist at her

Chicago salon, but there had still been a bit of a wait. All Kate needed was a trim; it was the perfect way to see if Stella lived up to her glowing reputation.

Stella had been the top assistant stylist at the only true beauty shop in Swanton, and Emmett and Patricia Beck had been savvy enough to lure her away when they relocated their own business from Swanton to their hometown of Prosper.

The Becks promised Stella the freedom to set her own hours, as well as first rights to purchase the business when Emmett was ready to hang up his shears. And since his close-cropped locks had gone gray several years ago, that time wasn't that far off.

Emmett's new shop was in an old building on Main Street, and Kate was pleased to see the historic, hexagon-tile floor was still intact. Even better, the gleam of the chrome chairs was matched by the sparkle of the porcelain sinks. The setup reminded Kate of how Austin had transformed an empty Eagle River storefront into The Daily Grind, and she was as happy to support another locally owned business as she was to give her strands a fresh start.

Stella manned the station closest to the window, and Emmett reigned over the other. There was just one on-deck spot near Stella, an overstuffed chair whose side table offered a vase of fresh flowers and a selection of fashion magazines.

Down the way, Emmett offered three faded waiting-room chairs and nothing else. It suited his customers just fine, since they usually came early and liked to hang around after. He was an experienced snipper, but they were just as interested in the conversation.

And the guys were certainly riled up today. Stella and Kate barely had a chance to exchange greetings and get settled before the debate across the room kicked into high gear. Word had spread fast about the showdown at last night's pro-burn meeting, and the opinions flew as fast as Kate's split ends hit the floor.

"They've been at it all morning." Stella raised an eyebrow at Kate in the mirror. "It's been a madhouse in here since that first fire, but between the one last week and that meeting last night? We've moved on from expressing shock to sharing conspiracy theories."

With her black-framed glasses and sleek blond hair, Stella had a cosmopolitan vibe that wasn't common in such a small town. Kate liked her immediately. "Well, this must be quite a change from your last salon."

Stella laughed. "That's for sure. But we don't have fights about who stole someone's favorite hair dryer, or tears when a fresh manicure gets chipped on the cash register's keys. I find it refreshing, actually. You always know where you stand with these guys."

Kate was tempted to mention she'd been at the meeting, but worried the men would bombard her with questions because it seemed none of them had attended. After all, Roberta continued to warn the carriers not to contribute to the gossip mill.

So she just took a deep breath and relaxed into the chair as Stella snipped away. If this went well, and Kate had high hopes it would, maybe she'd come back in a few weeks and have Stella freshen up the color.

"We know there must be a pattern to all this," one guy said as he lifted his coffee cup. Emmet always had a pot percolating on a side table. "I wouldn't just assume the properties' owners acted alone."

Emmett paused with his electric razor in one hand. The man in the chair didn't mind, as he was as embroiled in this conversation as everyone else. "As far as I know," Emmett said, "they don't know each other. You think they were in on it together, somehow?"

"Not exactly," the first guy said. "Everyone's going on and on about insurance money, which I get. But I can't see either Brody or the Snyders having the gall to go out there with a can of gas and light their own stuff on fire. I'm talking about, what if someone's doing it for them?"

The youngest man chuckled. "You mean, like a gun for hire?"

"But this would be a firestarter for hire," the guy in the chair said. Then he shook his head. "Man, I don't know about that, seems kind of far-fetched to me."

Stella widened her eyes at Kate, but kept her shears moving.

The oldest man in the on-deck circle had been mostly silent so far. Kate thought he looked familiar; he might have been a friend of Grandpa Wayne's. "Now, wait a minute. I remember hearing about something like that one time. Maybe it's not such a crazy idea after all."

That brought the debate to a halt. Kate knew harvest was Auggie's favorite time of year, but decided he'd move heaven and earth to be at the barber shop right now. There was a story about to be told, and it was sure to be a juicy one.

He was retired now, but this man and his family had farmed north of Prosper for several decades. A former neighbor had collected antiques, including old farm implements and advertising signs, and networked online to sell his wares. Prospective buyers came out to his farm to look the goods over, and he'd never had a problem. But the two young guys who showed up one afternoon gave the seller a bad vibe.

"They seemed really shifty, that's what he told me later." Everyone in the room, including Stella and Kate, was hanging on his every word.

"They wanted this one old tractor seat, it was a collectible, and they wanted to pay cash. But as they all chatted out there in the yard, those two seemed to be sizing up everything they could set their sights on."

The neighbor had put up a large metal shed, mostly for his cows but also to shelter his antique wares, because the old wooden barn was beyond repair. The youngsters seemed overly interested in this situation, although it was very common. The seller couldn't figure out why they kept asking him about the barn. Until one of the visitors made him an astounding offer.

"So the one kid says, 'sounds like you wouldn't be too heartbroken if the barn came down, it would save you a lot of work.' And he wasn't talking about an act of God; lightning, tornado, you know what I mean. He meant a fire. And not an accidental one."

Wouldn't it be convenient if the barn burned down one night? the young men suggested. It was in bad shape; once a blaze got going, it would be a goner. Light it the right way, and no one would be the wiser. Besides, it's just an old barn. No reason the fire marshal, or the insurance company, would invest too much time and energy in the situation. They might be able to arrange something ... for a cut of the payout, of course.

Gasps went up around the barber shop.

"They came right out and said that?"

"That takes some real nerve."

"What did your neighbor do?" Emmett wanted to know. "Did he call the sheriff?"

"Well, first off, he told them he'd decided to keep that tractor seat for himself," the older man reported. "Then he told those punks to get off his land, and never come back. Quite honestly, he was too spooked to call the authorities. Those two dropped their nice-guy act quick when he sent them packing."

The neighbor sat up late for several nights, a coffee cup in one hand and a hunting rifle in the other, worried the pair would come back and try to steal some of his stuff, or worse. They didn't.

But he'd learned a hard lesson about trusting people he met online.

Here was an angle Kate hadn't considered. But then, there was always someone looking for a quick and easy payday. Even so, volunteering to commit arson wasn't a simple matter. The strike would have to be carefully planned and executed. There were logistics to consider, and the secrecy ...

"Karen told me you were in Chicago for a decade," Stella said as she shaped up Kate's ends. "Must have been a big change to come back. Ever get bored?"

Kate had to smile at that. "Not yet. The pace is slower here, sure, but there's always something going on."

"Especially lately." Stella frowned. "I guess it's true that evil is everywhere." Then she squared her shoulders. "Well, there's not much we can do about that right now. So, how much do you want off the front layers?"

* 13 *

Distracted by this chilling new theory, Kate forgot a few things at the Swanton superstore. Thank goodness Eagle River's pharmacy, which also carried groceries and household products, would have a few options in stock.

But Hazel and Charlie had been left alone together for a few hours already, and Kate decided a check-in at home was required before she finished her shopping.

There were no howls and barks beyond the kitchen door when she came into the back porch. Her "hello" went unanswered as well.

Fearing the worst, Kate hurried through the kitchen and into the living room.

Hazel was stationed at the front window, where she kept watch over a trio of squirrels gathering fallen bounty from the walnut trees on the lawn. Charlie dozed on his stuffed-bed throne by the fireplace. Both of her furbabies barely gave Kate a glance when she came into the room.

"Well, I'm glad to see the two of you aren't duking it out." They were eager to accept her pets, at least, before they returned to their afternoon plans. "I have to head back into town, but I'll be home long before chore time."

Hazel's brown eyes lit up and she wagged her tail. "Chore time" was code for "run around the yard, sniff stuff, and see what the other kitties are up to." It had quickly become one of Hazel's favorite activities.

"Yes, we'll have some fun then," Kate promised as she offered another scratch behind the ears.

Scout wanted some attention as well before Kate got back in the car. When Maggie and Jerry couldn't resist joining in, Kate was happy to spend several more minutes sitting on the back steps. She was glad to see the other two cats becoming more confident in her presence, and this was an opportunity too good to pass up.

The day was getting away from Kate. But before she reached the stoplight, she turned off on a side street and headed toward the river.

"Maybe this isn't a good idea." She gripped the steering wheel tight and shook her head. "But I need to talk this through with someone. I mean, arson for hire? Here in Hartland county? And Bev won't be home until this evening."

Kate took another right, and Paul's Place came into view. In the bright sunlight, the single-story, cinderblock building really showed its age. There was only one truck in the parking lot this early in the afternoon, and Kate hoped it was the one she wanted.

The bar didn't open until three. Alex was probably busy, but maybe they could chat while he got ready. At this point, she'd offer to wipe down tables and stock the napkin dispensers if it gave her a few minutes to discuss what she'd heard this morning. And process what happened at last night's meeting.

"I could still leave," she bargained with herself as she cut the engine. "I have plenty of other things to do this afternoon."

She was still in her run-around uniform of a fleece pullover and old jeans. Which was just as well. She wasn't here to impress anyone, and would feel like a fool if she had been. Then why was she so nervous?

Someone walked past the bar's only front window, and Kate knew it was too late to ditch this impromptu errand. Alex missed nothing, and he'd already spotted her car.

"I won't stay long," she muttered as she approached the entrance. "Just a few minutes."

The door flew open. "Hey." Alex wore his usual, jeans and snug tee shirt. His brown hair was a little disheveled, but he looked just fine to Kate. Given his frazzled appearance and curt greeting, she wondered again if this was a good idea. He was busy, she shouldn't have dropped in like this.

"Nice apron," she blurted out. The faded cotton one tied over and around his trim torso was splattered with the washed-out remains of too-many stains.

"Nice haircut."

Kate blinked. Stella had only taken off an inch. This guy *really* noticed everything. But then, that's why Kate was here.

And while she'd obviously interrupted Alex's pre-opening routine, he didn't seem surprised to find her on his bar's doorstep. Maybe he'd been expecting her, somehow.

Or maybe he just had an excellent poker face. Kate suspected the latter.

He jerked his chin inward, and she followed. "Sorry to drop in like this, but after last night ..."

Alex went behind the bar and pulled two bottles out of the glass-door refrigerator on the back wall. "This good?"

He held up the brews, but didn't wait for her response before he popped the tops and set them on the edge of the counter. Before Kate could say anything, he gestured for her to take one corner stool, then came around to command the other.

Alex hadn't said much yet, nor had she. But here they were, beers in hand. Kate hadn't known how this would go, and she was pleasantly surprised at how comfortable she felt. At ease, like she was hanging with an old friend rather than butting in on an almost-stranger's workday.

Alex took a swig of his beer, then gave her a big smile. "Let me guess, Detective Duncan. You're wanting to debrief regarding last night's incident."

"Yeah. It was interesting, for sure. I don't think the monthly book club or the knitting circle meetings cause that kind of commotion at the library."

"No kidding. I'm glad I was able to stop by and help out. We figured things might get a little ... heated."

The situation was serious, but the puns were too easy to resist. They had a laugh over that one before Kate decided to press for details. In a roundabout way, of course. "I'd ask who 'we' refers to, but I think I have a pretty good idea."

Alex nodded. "The presence of an in-uniform law enforcement officer might have been a bit much. There were security concerns, but no one wanted to create more drama than was necessary."

Interesting. Before Kate could try to find out if those concerns were general, or perhaps focused on certain individuals in the crowd, Alex quickly changed the subject. "Hey, are you hungry?"

"Maybe a little. Lunch was a few hours ago. But you don't need to make a fuss."

"Be right back."

Whatever Alex knew, Kate decided as she waited at the counter, he wasn't likely to give up that information. And she could understand why. If the sheriff and the fire marshal had their eye on a certain someone, or more than one person, they couldn't jeopardize the case by letting word get out. Even so, Alex was a shrewd judge of character; he might offer some personal opinions that could shed light on the situation.

Alex returned five minutes later with a plate stacked with small slices of three kinds of cheese, and quartered hamburger buns that had spent a brief stint in a toaster oven.

"You didn't need to go to all that trouble." Kate was taken aback. "And I know you have to get ready to open."

"Come on, it's not a charcuterie board. And look around. We always clean up well before we close. I'm not that busy." He stacked some bread and cheese, and motioned for Kate to do the same. "Besides, who else am I going to chew this situation over with? My patrons aren't exactly known for their discretion."

"In that case, I'm honored to help out." Kate took a bite. The simple snack really hit the spot. But then, the company might have had something to do with it. "So, what's your take on Brody Donegan? And I found out something interesting about Stan Winston last night. But you go first."

Alex was pretty certain Brody didn't light his barn on fire. "He's a little lazy, that doesn't seem quite his style. It takes guts to roll up on a building like that, douse it with gasoline and torch it." He chewed for a second, then corrected himself. "No. It's a cowardly act, when you get right down to it. And selfish. Fighting a fire takes money and man hours, not to mention that someone could be injured, or worse. Someone in your community, someone you know."

Kate nodded. "Makes me wonder, then, if it's not a local. I mean, would it be easier to justify such behavior to yourself if no one you knew would be affected?"

"That's possible. Either way, I just don't believe it's Brody. If he needed money, I think he'd swipe it from his parents somehow. Or wheedle them into giving it to him outright, or bum it off a friend."

Kate shared what she'd discovered about Stan. When she finished, Alex set his bottle on the bar and gave this news some serious consideration. "That is really interesting. Good work!"

"Thanks." She shrugged. "But it may not mean anything."

"That's true. It can be dangerous to jump to conclusions."

Kate quickly realized that while Alex had praised her efforts, he hadn't seemed truly surprised by what she'd found. Of course, he had access to the internet like everyone else.

And given his connection to Eagle River's police chief, way more access than that. Once again, Kate wondered what Alex knew.

"Stan's behavior last night was troubling, to say the least," he said. "There he was, shouting and waving his arms like a madman, like he's at a rally or something. We were in a *library*. Talking about *yard waste*."

"That was bad enough." Kate shook her head. "But when he accused Brody of burning his own barn, right in front of everyone? I couldn't believe it."

When it seemed Alex wasn't going to say more on that subject, Kate took a deep breath and moved on to her second item on the agenda.

"I got more than a haircut when I was in Prosper this morning." She found herself whispering, even though they were alone. "I heard something really troubling. The worst part? I think the source is pretty reliable."

Alex's eyebrows shot up as Kate told him the retired farmer's story.

"That guy never told the sheriff," she hurried on as Alex took it all in. "And I don't know who else he confided in. It might not mean anything, but please don't spread it around, OK? It was pretty clear those creeps didn't like being told no."

"I won't say anything." But Alex now looked as worried as Kate felt. "I haven't heard anything like that and, as you can guess, a lot of gossip flows through this bar. But I believe it, one hundred percent."

"I guess that was a few years ago," Kate said, as much to comfort herself as anything else. "Whoever they were, they may not be around here anymore, anyway."

"I'm glad you told me, though. Sometimes those things are hard to keep to yourself."

And Kate did feel better. "But, here's the thing: Should I call the sheriff and tell him what I heard? What if it's important? The night of Brody's fire, I ran into Deputy Collins near the scene. He specifically asked that I let them know if I came across anything. Even if it didn't seem like an obvious clue."

Alex considered this for a moment. "You want to stay out of it, but you never want to feel that you somehow aided and abetted a criminal, or more than one, by keeping silent."

"Yes."

"And they like silence. Criminals, I mean. They like it when people look the other way." Before Kate could press him about his apparent knowledge of this subject, he offered a solution.

"How about this? I'll pass it on." He shrugged. "All I have to do is say I overheard it at the bar." Then he laughed. "Well, it's the truth."

"It is, isn't it? I guess I'm glad I stopped by." And Kate meant it. In more ways than one.

"Me, too." He was staring at her again, with that intense look that thrilled her down to her toes. "How are things at your new place? It must be hard, being alone out there at night, after all those years in the city. And then, with all this going on ..."

"Yeah. I've been scared at times, I'll admit it."

"Nothing to be ashamed of," he said gently. "Most people would feel the same, in your shoes. I have people coming in here who've lived in the country all their lives. Tough guys, hunters, not the type to be spooked by their own shadows. But even they are on edge, especially after what happened Friday night."

"Well, I do have a new security assistant." Kate smiled. "I'm up to five now, including three sassy barn kitties and a house cat who's more concerned with how good his coat looks than protecting his owner."

She told Alex about Hazel, and he nodded his approval. "Sounds like a perfect match, for both of you. What sort of commands does she know?"

"Well, I think she knows several. But she doesn't always feel like following through on requests; that was the problem. It's going well, though. I'm glad I decided to adopt her."

"So you have some backup. I'm glad." He reached for his phone. "I'm a night owl, as you might guess. If I'm not here, I'm usually awake into the wee hours. I'll text you my number. If something doesn't feel right out there, but you're not sure you need to call it in, just reach out."

"Oh, hey, you don't have to ..."

"No, it's fine." He nudged the plate closer to Kate, and indicated she should take the last bites of cheese and bread.

"If you get really spooked by something, don't hesitate to use it."

"OK," Kate promised. "And thanks."

Alex was smart and charming, and very handsome, but she'd never expected him to be this ... caring? Although she could look after herself, this offer of support was as welcome as it was unexpected.

As she was mulling all this over, Alex's phone chimed. "Helen" flashed on the screen, and his eyes lit up just as bright when he saw the name.

"Hey, how's it going?" He gave Kate a smile, but it was one she couldn't really read. "Good, good. I'm in the middle of something, can I call you back in a few minutes? Thanks."

"I should go." Kate was already reaching for her purse. Alex was an interesting guy, but she didn't know him well enough to start making assumptions about him. "Thanks for the beer and the snacks. And the advice."

"Anytime." He got up from his stool, too. There was work to be done. "Hopefully things get resolved soon, and everyone can settle down."

Just before she left, Kate thought of something. "Do you like pears?"

Alex gave her a quizzical look. "Uh, I guess I do." Then he laughed. "What's this all about?"

"I have a little orchard, out at my place. Just pear and apple trees, a few of each, but I can't keep up with the baking and canning."

Maybe Alex was seeing someone, maybe he wasn't. But Kate wanted to repay him for his kindness, at least. "I'll bring some by, if you like."

"Sure. They're too good for the bar. I'll keep them for myself."

Kate laughed. "Unless you're looking to elevate things around here." The bar only served burgers, fries and coleslaw. The in-the-shell peanuts were always free. "Get some cured meats from the locker in Swanton, throw in some sliced apples and pears with that cheese, and you're well on your way to a charcuterie board."

"I don't know if you're enough of a regular here to give me pointers about my menu," Alex said wryly as he walked her to the door. "Maybe you should come by more often."

"Maybe I should." Between the chance to share her concerns, the just-right snacks and the interesting company, Kate already felt much better. This was one time when forgetting to buy a bottle of shampoo and a box of baking soda had actually improved her day. "And thanks again."

* * *

Kate heard rain drumming on her farmhouse's roof sometime in the middle of the night. She woke to find heavy skies and a blanket of fog over the half-harvested fields. As she and Hazel trudged across the brown yard to feed the outdoor cats, Kate wished for more than the hood of her chore coat to cover her ears.

"Guess I need to get out the stocking caps," she told Hazel, who had inspected the softest spots in the gravel driveway, as well as several puddles, as they made their way to the machine shed. "Would you wear little doggie boots if I could find you some?"

The Three Mouseketeers had wisely decided to wait for their breakfast inside the machine shed. The gravel-flecked mud that covered Hazel's paws and lower legs drew a look of disdain from Maggie as Kate and the dog came in the "non-cat" door.

"I know, she's messy." The cats quickly turned their attention to the warmed-over chicken gravy and extra kibble, but Kate stayed focused on how to get Hazel "work-ready" in as little time as possible.

While Hazel and Charlie's interactions had warmed a degree or two, Kate wasn't quite ready to let her new dog have the run of the house and yard all day. So with Roberta's good-natured blessing, Hazel was about to embark on yet-another shift as Kate's ride-along assistant.

"I'm going to have to find extra old towels to clean you up before we leave for work. Good thing there's all those worn-out blankets in Bertha's trunk. The back seat will have to be covered today."

Kate always carried a wide selection of gear in her postal vehicle, and was as ready as she could be for just about everything, weather-related or otherwise, that might come her way on a rural route. Last week, she'd added extra cold-weather gear to the stash and, with a sigh of resignation, tucked a snow shovel in the trunk as well. It was a little early. But she always wanted to be prepared.

As they headed back to the house, Kate pondered the other challenge of having Hazel with her for the day. Jared was off, so Kate had his southern loop. That included the nine-stop walk through Mapleville, a tiny, unincorporated village a few miles outside Eagle River. Would Hazel be patient and calm enough to wait in Bertha's back seat while Kate hiked the short "in-town" route? It was certainly chilly enough for the dog to safely remain in the car, but still.

Of course, Kate could take Hazel along on her on-foot rounds, but that might be a recipe for disaster. Hazel's interest in commands seemed to come and go when it suited her, and there would be plenty of distractions, both in the trees and on the ground. Kate imagined being dragged around Mapleville by a mud-splattered and excited dog, trying to keep a tight grip on her mail bag while Hazel made overly friendly introductions to every person, dog and squirrel along the way.

What about the co-op? The office at the Mapleville outpost, which was the only business in town, was barely bigger than a postage stamp. Its proprietor was a longtime friend of the local mail carriers, and Kate wondered if Gerard would welcome Hazel's company for twenty minutes or so. Of course, it was still harvest time, and his little shop would be loud and crazy.

"We'll have to figure that one out as we go," she told Hazel when they got inside the back porch. "Just like everything else these days, right? Now, hold still! You can't go inside until I wipe your feet. Charlie won't approve of you running around like this."

Haze's arrival at the post office was met with warm smiles and ear scratches, and she offered several of her trademark butt wiggles in exchange for all the attention. The mood in the back room was as mellow as the hushed landscape outside, where there was no breeze to push the fog away.

Roberta admonished her rural carriers to be extra careful, although the forecast called for visibility to improve by midday. "It's just common sense, but I need to remind you, anyway."

"It's in the handbook, right?" Aaron asked with a smirk.

Their boss was smart and caring, but her disdain for some of the federal rules and regulations was well known among the team. And they admired her for it. Well, except for Jack, on occasion.

"Yep." Roberta smiled. "Every once in a while, they get it right." That brought groans and laughter from the group.

"But seriously, folks, safety does come first around here. Slow down; this isn't a race. Fog reduces our visibility out in the country. That applies both to people seeing us, and our ability to see who else is out there."

"Or *what* else," Marge broke in. "It's not just the other vehicles, and the school buses, and the combines and such. Yesterday afternoon, I came over the crest of a hill and had to hit the brakes. Turns out, some cows had been crafty enough to get their pasture fence down. Eleven of them were already out on the road when I came along."

"Exactly eleven?" Jack was impressed. "You must have taken a quick head count, then."

Marge rolled her eyes. "They had me surrounded. There was plenty of opportunity to evaluate the situation. I had to honk several times before I could ease through the roadblock."

Kate's parcel haul that day was surprisingly light. Which was good, because Hazel liked to sprawl out on Bertha's back seat when she could.

"With everyone in the fields, no one has a lot of time to be shopping online," Bev observed as she sorted the day's boxes on one of the metal-topped counters. "Of course, if you get stuck in a long queue at the co-op, your phone can become your worst enemy."

"Guilty as charged." Roberta held up a hand. "That happened to me, two days ago. But I'm happy to say my Christmas shopping is already half done."

As Kate started sorting mail for her route, she leaned in closer to Bev. "Did you ask Clyde about ... you know? What did he say?"

Bev had been shocked by what Kate had heard in Prosper, and promised to ask her husband if he recalled that incident or anything similar.

"He said it didn't ring a bell," Bev whispered to Kate over a stack of packages. "And he can't imagine he'd forget something like that. But he's going to keep his ears open."

Then she chuckled. "Well, one good thing has come from all of this. He's been determined to clean some old machinery and stuff out of the barn, and thought maybe one of those online marketplaces was the way to go. But he's now realized that may not be the safest way to downsize. I think I've convinced him to add his things to a consignment sale at the auction barn, instead."

With her mail car loaded down, her thermos filled with coffee and Hazel's bathroom break out of the way, Kate was ready to hit the road. Slowly.

Fog hadn't been much of a hindrance in Chicago, and Kate had forgotten how thick it could be out on the country roads. Even though she drove this route at least once a week, and had become familiar with its landmark houses and bends in the gravel, the thick haze made too many of the intersections look the same.

Despite the chill, Kate rolled her window down at most of the rural crossroads to listen for the sound of an approaching vehicle rather than rely on her limited vision.

But true to the forecast, the sun began to peek through the blanket of fog within the hour. The view out Bertha's windshield slowly improved and expanded, and Kate turned up the radio as she and Hazel rolled through the countryside. It wasn't long, though, before her phone trilled from the side pocket of her purse. Hazel barked an announcement.

"Yep, I hear it. Let me pull over, first. Too bad I can't train you to answer it for me. But then, it doesn't ring that often when I'm on a route."

Despite the lighter skies, Kate's mood dimmed a little. Was something wrong? What if it was one of her parents calling? She breathed easier when she saw it was only Roberta. "Hey."

"How far out are you?" Her boss sounded a little winded.

Kate's brow furrowed with concern. "About four miles

from town. I think I'll have an early lunch today. Or better yet, I'll push on with some more stops until I come in. What's going on?"

"I'm glad you're not swamped. I'm going to need you to pick up part of Jack's afternoon deliveries."

"Is he sick? He seemed OK this morning."

"Well, no, but he's beside himself, for sure." Roberta took a deep breath before she continued.

"He found something, not ten minutes ago. Oh, I can't believe this is happening!"

Hazel shoved her head over the back of the front seat, and Kate absentmindedly scratched the dog's ears. "Found what?" Her pulse started to race. "What's going on?"

"There's another one. Another fire." Roberta's voice wavered with fear. "Or at least, someone tried to start one last night. An old, abandoned house, just like the last time. Up along Flood Creek, not far from the railroad junction. Do you know where that is?"

Kate did. The waterway northeast of Eagle River had once shared its name with an early settlement along its banks. A general store and church had sat on opposite sides of the road until, one night about a hundred years ago, the creek lived up to its reputation and took out the tumbledown shell of the former mercantile. The church was spared, and its small congregation somehow managed to hold on.

The place was in the middle of nowhere, and hadn't appeared on any maps other than those in local residents' minds for decades. But as she sat there on the side of the road, Hazel whimpering as she sensed Kate's concern, Kate knew the spot must hold some sort of meaning for the arsonist. But what?

"Do you need me to come in now? I can if you want."

"Well, you might as well drop what you have." Roberta's voice steadied somewhat. "Jack refuses to leave the scene until a deputy can get out there, he said it's so ..."

Roberta faded out for a second, and then Kate heard her talking to someone else.

"I have to go," she told Kate. "I guess the sheriff's on the landline."

"Who will take the rest of Jack's route?" Kate tried to steady her own nerves by focusing on the details. "Maybe Marge?"

"Perfect. Can you call her for me? Thanks a million."

"It's never a dull moment," Kate told Hazel as she checked her mirrors. Just as she'd suspected, they were alone on this stretch of gravel. "Too bad you flunked out of doggie training. I'm starting to think the sheriff might need your assistance."

* 14 *

Kate's mind buzzed with questions as she continued her route, absentmindedly opening mailboxes and leaving parcels on front porches.

What exactly had Jack found? Why was he so sure it was an arson attempt? And how was the situation just now coming to light?

Even though the Flood Creek house was in a remote location, massive flames would be visible from a long distance away. With so many farmers still in the fields, at all hours of the day and night, surely someone would have seen something and called the authorities. It just didn't add up.

Kate didn't have an emergency scanner to keep tabs on every regional incident. But Auggie did.

And she was certain that, even if no one else had thought to call her and share news of another fire, he wouldn't have missed his chance.

At least the question about how to make today's stops in Mapleville was resolved. Kate decided to drive from house to house, just as she did in the rural areas, to speed up the process and keep Hazel in the car.

As they turned off the highway and headed for the first mailbox, the dog took in the change in scenery with a few yips of curiosity.

"A new town, huh? It's even smaller than Prosper. Way smaller. Sorry we can't go exploring. Maybe I can give you a tour some other day."

At the Mapleville co-op, the line of farmers waiting to cross the scales stretched out to the highway. With only one way in, and one way out, Kate decided the fastest delivery option was to park Bertha on the shoulder of the road, leave Hazel in the car, and hike the mail and packages to the office.

Gerard looked up in surprise when she came in the door. "Kate! Where did you find a parking spot?"

"I didn't. I'm out on the road." For a moment, Kate considered dropping a crumb of fire-related gossip with the letters and package. Between Gerard and the farmers filling every aisle of his tiny shop, someone surely would have a tidbit of news from Flood Creek.

Or maybe not. Maybe it wasn't common knowledge yet. And what if the sheriff had told Roberta and Jack to keep this quiet?

"Wow, it's really busy here today," was all she said, then took a cookie snack pack from the small rack by the register. Gerard liked it when the carriers made a purchase, and his bathroom was the only public one for miles. "What's new?"

Gerard sighed, and Kate's ears perked up. "That rain last night brought everything to a halt." He rubbed the gray stubble on his chin as he shook his head.

"We don't need any more delays. And as you can see, everyone decided it was a good time to bring in another load while the fields dry out."

This observation wasn't what Kate had hoped for, but it reinforced her assumptions about Sheriff Preston's position on the Flood Creek incident. Gerard knew nothing.

"Isn't that farm life?" She gestured for him to keep the change. "When we want the rain, we don't get it. And when we don't need it, it shows up."

Gerard's laughter followed Kate as she hurried out of the

shop. She was eager to wrap up her own route, as part of Jack's now awaited her that afternoon. And the sooner she made it back to the post office, the sooner she'd know what had happened.

But when Kate ushered Hazel through the post office's back door a few hours later, she found the opposite of what she expected. It was calm and quiet, and Kate's portion of Jack's afternoon deliveries was neatly stacked on the end of one of the metal counters.

Roberta looked up with a wry grin when Hazel and Kate popped into the lobby, which was otherwise empty.

"Hey, Hazel! It's my newest recruit. Are you staying out of trouble?"

"I need to eat, then we need to get back on the road." Kate took a deep breath. "But I have to know: What is going on?"

Roberta glanced out the plate-glass windows and searched up and down the sidewalk before answering. So it *was* a secret, at least for now.

"Here's the deal. They're trying to keep it off the radar for as long as they can. There's enough panic as it is. But, oh, this is unnerving, to say the least."

Kate was right; no fire had been reported the night before. But Jack's keen eyes and habit of sticking his nose where it didn't belong had served the community well that morning.

It was the deep, fresh tracks in the gravel lane that gave it away, Roberta said, as there was no reason for anyone to turn their tires up that drive. The rundown farmhouse had been vacant for years, just like the last one, and easy access to the surrounding fields was available through a handful of gates along the road.

With no mailbox to service, Jack never paid the place much mind. But for some reason he couldn't explain, he felt the need to slow down as he approached it this morning. Then he caught sight of the fresh ruts in the now-muddy lane, and couldn't resist.

"He shouldn't have gone up there." Roberta rolled her eyes. "That would have been the right time to pull over and call it in. But you know Jack."

Other than the tire tracks, which stopped just short of the house, nothing seemed out of the ordinary at first. The tumbledown house was forlorn and empty, its limestone foundation visible through a tangle of weeds that had already gone to seed for the season. The rest of the structure was just what one would expect: sloped walls, busted-out windows, rot and decay.

But Jack felt something wasn't right, and he got out of the truck. The sagging steps and porch were nearly separated from the house, and the downstairs floor had long ago fallen into the cellar. There was no safe way inside, but he decided to walk around the house before he left.

And on the northwest corner, he found what he was looking for: a black, angry streak that snaked across the rotten clapboards and inched toward the second story. The side of the house was charred and, even though the blaze had been snuffed out hours ago, Jack caught the faint smell of smoke and something chemical he couldn't name.

"Whatever it was, he said it made the hair on the back of his neck stand on end." Roberta's face was grim. And tired. Kate realized she couldn't remember the last time her boss looked rested and content.

"He glanced around, felt certain he was being watched, but didn't see anyone. Other than an owl staring him down from a dead tree not ten feet away."

"They hunt in the mornings, sometimes," Kate said to soothe herself as much as Roberta. "With that rain last night, and the fog ... even an owl would have had a tough time finding enough snacks in that kind of weather."

Jack's untrained gaze couldn't tell him if the fire had been doused by nature or an arsonist with cold feet. But he was spooked enough to end his investigation. He hurried back to his truck, locked the doors, and called the sheriff.

"It took me forever to get him to go home," Roberta said. "First, he wanted to be there when the deputy showed up, which makes sense. And then, he had to come back here to drop his case. The landowners know, of course; and the sheriff has folks up at the scene, they have it secured. But I guess he sent them in an unmarked vehicle."

"Smart move," Kate said. "Word will get out fast enough." A car had just pulled up in front of the post office, and a man was about to enter the lobby. "Well, here comes our next customer. It'll be interesting to see if he's heard about this."

"If he has, he's sure to blab it." Roberta gave a wry smile, then suddenly turned stern. "I have my poker face on, I won't give away a thing."

Kate turned to guide Hazel toward the back room, but something about the man made her pause. He carried a laptop bag over his arm, as well as an air of importance that was rarely witnessed in a town like Eagle River.

She couldn't quite place him. But then he came through the door, and ...

Well, that was fast, she thought. *Mayor Benson certainly can't complain about you dragging your feet.*

"Gage Werner, state fire marshal's office." He extended his hand to Roberta. When the postmaster shook it, Kate could swear Roberta stood up just a little straighter. "You know why I'm here."

Caught off guard, Roberta merely blinked.

"We certainly do." Kate stepped in. "How can we help?"

"Yes, marshal." Roberta was back at the helm in a second. "What can we do for you today? I'm sure the sheriff has debriefed you on this morning's ... incident. Or, I mean, last night's."

"We'll determine a timeline as soon as we can. Hopefully, that'll help us narrow the investigation, at least a little. I'm here to talk to Jack O'Brien. Is he around?"

"He went home, about an hour ago." Roberta was now more at ease. "I finally got him out of here, he's pretty wound up. But then, I'd be, too, if I came across what he did this morning."

"That's just what it is going to take to put an end to this ... ongoing situation." Gage looked to Kate, then back at Roberta. "People sharing whatever they come across, no matter how small it might seem. What Jack found this morning is significant, to say the least. He's a credit to his community."

"He certainly is." Roberta was proud. Even so, she had a word of caution for the marshal. "But he's also stubborn and full of himself, most of the time. Please don't let on to him that he's saved the day, or we'll never hear the end of it."

Gage chuckled. "Got it." He turned his attention toward Hazel, who gave a bark of greeting and that trademark butt wriggle that always melted hearts. The marshal seemed amused, but a little taken aback.

"Is this your dog?" he asked Kate. "I'm guessing it must be. But I've learned the hard way not to assume anything."

"Oh, she is." It was Kate's turn to nearly burst with pride. "This is Hazel. I've only had her a few days, and I'm not ready to let her have the run of the farm yet when I'm not home."

"She rides along with you?" He frowned. "Interesting. I didn't think public employees were allowed to bring their pets to work. I mean, unless ..."

"Hazel's a service dog," Kate blurted out. "Well, a service dog in training."

She gave Roberta a knowing look.

"Yes, absolutely." Roberta nodded emphatically. "There's a facility on the other side of the county, Hazel's from there." Well, that was actually true.

"Part of their training, as you can imagine, is getting acclimated to a regular home life. After all, once they graduate, they'll be someone's constant companion."

"That's wonderful that you help out with such a program." Gage gave Kate a genuine smile. "What a great cause! She's certainly a fine dog."

Then he laughed and looked at Hazel. "I bet you're very smart. You know all kinds of cool tricks, right?"

Hazel answered with a happy whimper, and Kate knew it was time to go. Her dog was loveable and smart, but following prompts wasn't her thing. Given the story Kate and Roberta had just concocted for the marshal, it was best he never found that out.

"Well, time to get back to work," Kate trilled as she reached for Hazel's collar. Simply telling Hazel to "come along" would only net Kate a blank stare. "I'm picking up part of Jack's route, and people will be looking for their mail."

The marshal offered a quick wave, then turned back to Roberta. "Since Jack's already left, I'll just give him a call. What's his number?"

Kate hustled Hazel into the back room and sighed with relief.

"That was close," she whispered to the dog. "There are all sorts of rules and regulations around here, and I think you're violating at least a few of them."

Then she smiled. "But Roberta doesn't care, and the marshal doesn't have to know. Besides, we're a federal shop, and he's only a state employee."

It had been a jam-packed day, but it wasn't over yet. Kate loaded the rest of Jack's deliveries into Bertha's front seat, settled her gear and Hazel, and headed north up Main Street.

But suddenly, she was so tired. The adrenaline of the morning had drained away, leaving her with miles of gravel to travel and dozens of deliveries to make before she and Hazel could head for home.

Roberta had promised overtime pay, of course, but Kate's mood dimmed as Eagle River faded in Bertha's rearview mirror.

The fire marshal seemed capable enough, from what everyone said, and his arrival in Eagle River gave Kate a measure of comfort. Even so, she glanced at the dashboard clock and calculated the hours since Jack's discovery.

Marshal Werner had to be incredibly busy, especially with a coverage area that spanned a large swath of the state. Of course, this fire was discovered on a weekday, during regular business hours, but Kate was still impressed by how swiftly the marshal must have dropped whatever else he was working on to drive down from Mason City.

On one hand, she was glad he was so invested in what was happening here. On the other, it made her wonder what he suspected about who was doing this, and why.

Three fires so far.

Four, if the cattle-shed blaze made the cut.

So far. Kate gripped the steering wheel tight and took the next gravel road to the east. If she went north at the first crossroads, she could pick up where Marge left off.

And something else bothered Kate, now that she thought of it.

Why had the marshal come to the post office? Jack had obviously given a detailed account of his findings to the sheriff's department, and they would have his phone number on file. The state investigator could have simply asked county officials for Jack's contact information, and saved himself a stop.

"Maybe he just wanted to talk with Jack face-to-face," Kate told Hazel, who'd curled up on the back seat. "But again, one of the deputies had already taken his statement. What good would that do?"

And then, Kate remembered Mayor Benson's comments about how difficult it could be for various levels of government to work together.

What if the marshal didn't have a good rapport with Sheriff Preston? Was there tension, even dissention, among the ranks? Was it possible that, for whatever reason, the marshal didn't quite trust what the local folks were telling him?

"I'm tired." Kate shook her head and reached for her coffee thermos. "My imagination is getting the better of me."

Then she sighed. "I just wish there was something I could do to help. Any little thing." Another glance at the dashboard clock told her it would be dark again in less than six hours. "Something more productive than sitting on the sidelines, wondering what might happen tonight. Or tomorrow."

* 15 *

When was the last time Kate had been out and about long after midnight? Probably years ago, and in Chicago, and celebrating someone's birthday or enjoying another kind of revelry. A situation very different from tonight's errand.

But here she was, navigating her personal vehicle through the pitch-black darkness, clad in layers of warm clothes and wearing her heavy chore boots. She slowed at the next crossroads, hesitated for a second, then turned left.

"This must be it." Hazel perked up in the passenger's seat, as if she sensed Kate's unease and excitement. "I don't know if I've ever come this way on a route, there's no one living on this mile. And it's so dark out here!"

When the alarm on Kate's phone dinged half an hour ago, Hazel had been quick to hop down from the foot of the bed and watch Kate get dressed. Charlie had graciously accepted Hazel's recent change in sleeping habits, but his reaction to this disturbance had been one of annoyance. Who turns on the bedroom light in the middle of the night? And why would Kate leave the house at such a crazy hour?

Hazel had been eager to follow when Kate gestured to the stairs, and waited patiently in the kitchen while Kate retrieved the walking harness and leash. It was as if Hazel sensed they were on a mission. On assignment.

And they were, Kate decided as they crept down the gravel, her eyes straining to see as far down the road as possible. Her headlights had already reflected the glowing eyes of a few wild critters, and the last thing she wanted to do was to hit a raccoon or opossum who was on its nocturnal rounds. Deer tended not to roam as much in the middle of the night, but that was always a possibility, too.

"I can't believe I used to drive in the dark like this all the time, and thought nothing of it," she told Hazel as they crept through the next mile. "I grew up on a farm, for goodness' sake. That's what you do when you live in the country."

The car's beams lit up a mailbox just ahead, and Kate studied the metal nameplate on its top.

"This is the place." She let out a deep sigh of relief. "Civilization. We made it this far, at least."

Even at this hour, a few lights glowed inside the comfortable-looking farmhouse up the lane, and there was a cluster of vehicles along the driveway.

Corey's truck was right there, under the yard light, and spotting her cousin's vehicle made Kate feel a little better. Besides, this had been her idea. She'd wanted to help out, do something useful. When she'd called Corey, Kate had expected an invitation to drop off baked goods for the first responders, or something of that sort.

Not asked to join a stakeout at a crime scene. If she really wanted to make a difference, Corey had said, this was the best way to do it.

"Bring Hazel the Wonder Dog with you," he'd pleaded. "She might be able to help us." And Kate hadn't been able to say no.

Local emergency leaders and law enforcement officials shared residents' concerns about the recent string of mysterious fires, but they also saw an opportunity too important to pass up. Pyromaniacs were notorious for returning to the scenes of their crimes to watch the flames and bask in the chaos they had caused. An ignition that had somehow been snuffed out before it turned into an inferno? That was an itch they'd want to scratch. So this was the third night volunteers had spent at the Flood Creek site, watching and waiting to see if the arsonist might come back to finish the job.

Two-hour shifts were about all anyone could stand, between the October chill in the overnight air and trying to stay alert, and no one was allowed to keep watch alone. But everyone had day jobs, and harvest was still happening.

With resources stretched so thin, Corey insisted Kate wouldn't be the only "civilian" taking part. She was surprised by that at first, but Corey said the sheriff and the local fire chiefs would take all the volunteers they could get to keep surveillance going.

They hoped to catch the arsonist, of course, but that wasn't their only concern.

The old house wasn't worth anything, but the reckless behavior of the arsonist had the farmer who owned the land up in arms. Literally. He'd told Sheriff Preston that he and his grown sons were prepared to keep watch themselves, hunting rifles in hand, and vigilante justice was the last thing any of the emergency officials wanted.

Hazel barked when she spotted Corey and a woman on the front porch, and Kate soothed her with her right hand. "It's OK! My, aren't you on alert tonight. But I guess that's why Corey asked for you to come with us."

Hazel gave a happy whimper. "Oh, yes, he did! Let's go see if we can catch a bad guy."

Although Kate really hoped that wouldn't happen on her watch. She already felt she was in over her head.

"I'm Cindy Talbot." The woman offered Kate a friendly handshake before she leaned over to greet Hazel.

"Look at you! Such a pretty girl. Thank you for coming tonight to help us."

Cindy looked back up at Kate and, even in the faint glow from the porch light, Kate could see the appreciation in the older woman's eyes. "Both of you." She dipped her head to include Corey. "All of you. I can barely sleep, worrying."

"We'll keep at this until ... well, something happens," Corey promised Cindy. "In a perfect world, we'd catch this creep in the act."

Cindy would give Corey, Kate and Hazel a ride to the drop-off point, which was beyond the back pasture's gate and halfway through the cornfield. It wouldn't be wise to have any vehicles or general commotion near the abandoned farmhouse, which meant the volunteers had to hike to the lookout post. The first night shift always toted a battery-powered lantern and camp chairs to the site, as well as an initial stash of bottled water and snacks. Kate had brought a coffee thermos and some cookies, as well as a water bowl and treats for Hazel.

While the goal was for the volunteers to be as comfortable as possible, the lantern was only for emergencies. As Kate pondered two hours in total darkness out in a field, she wondered if she was up to the challenge.

"We've only had a few ladies helping out," Cindy broke into Kate's thoughts. Then she smiled. "Maybe you'd like to come inside, use the bathroom before we take off? The men have it easy, as they always do."

Kate had to laugh. "You know, I was wondering about that." She handed Hazel's leash to Corey. "I'll gladly take you up on that offer."

Corey sat in the bed of the truck so Kate and Hazel could squeeze into the cab, and he offered to hop out to open and close gates as they went along.

"I wish this was all over," Cindy said as they bumped and thumped through the pasture. "Not just to bring closure to the community, but Wade? He's beside himself. Angry, frustrated, the whole nine yards. So are the boys. I keep telling them, give it time. Let the sheriff and the fire marshal do their jobs."

"I get it." Kate gripped the edge of the worn cushion as she braced for another dip in the field drive. "It's not just an old, abandoned house. Your sense of security has been violated. That first burn, the old barn? It's just down the road from my place."

She told Cindy about how she and Hazel walked their yard's perimeter every night before sundown. "I'm scared, too. Who's doing this, and why?"

"Hopefully we'll get some answers soon." Cindy downshifted as the two dark shapes along the fence line morphed into men. "Here they are. Cold, tired, I can't imagine. But the coffee's on in the kitchen. I'll make sure they're fueled up before they head home."

The previous shift consisted of one of Eagle River's volunteer firefighters and his brother. There had been no activity at the burn site, they reported, but they'd spotted headlights down along the road about an hour ago. The vehicle had gone on by, didn't seem to slow down at all, but you never know ...

"That is why we're here," Corey told Kate as they gathered their gear and left the headlights of Cindy's truck behind. "The minute we take our foot off the gas, something could happen."

In the gloom, Kate could barely make out the dense windbreak that surrounded the old farmhouse.

No lights, Corey had said, and she understood why.

In this thick blackness, any little glow would be visible from some distance away. The sky was clear, but the moon was only a sliver of light high above the fields.

They began to slog through the tall, dead grass on the edge of the pasture and, as Kate's eyes adjusted to the dark, she kept them focused on Corey's back and her hand tight on Hazel's lead.

"Good girl," she whispered. "You're being so brave, and quiet. Almost there."

A sagging fence crossed their path, but the Talbots had snapped the rusty wires from the closest post Friday afternoon. The trio passed through the makeshift gate, hiked for a few more minutes, and soon found the house's windbreak looming ahead of them.

Trudging across the open field had made Kate feel nervous and exposed, and she'd hoped that unease would fade when they at last approached the shelter of the trees. But her anxiety ratcheted higher as they took their final steps through the edge of the pasture.

Still cloaked in its veil of overgrown vegetation, the house had yet to reveal itself. She'd never been here before, she was sure of it. So why was there something so familiar, and so ominous, about this place?

And then, she knew. A story song she'd learned long ago, in elementary school. Something about a "dark, dark wood." And a house inside that wood. There had been something, or someone, inside the house ...

Corey might remember. But Kate was too scared to ask if he knew how the story ended.

He paused at the edge of the woods, and searched through the gloom for the faint break in the vegetation that marked the path to the lookout site.

"It's creepy, right?" He was whispering now, and a shiver ran down Kate's spine. "Last night, I have to say, I was so freaked out that I wished I hadn't volunteered. But once we settle in, it won't be so bad. And we have Hazel to protect us."

"She flunked out of the doggie academy, remember?" Kate reached down and gave Hazel a pet. "But I'm so glad you're here."

Even with most of the trees now bare-limbed to the dark and the cold, the windbreak was so thick that hardly any moonlight came through its canopy. Every step brought a *crunch* from the blanket of dead leaves smothering the ground. It occurred to Kate that the sound of their boots would alert anyone who might be hiding among these trees.

No one is out here but us, she told herself. But then: *At least, not yet.*

Corey finally motioned that they were where they were supposed to be. It took a moment for Kate to make out the two camp chairs in a trampled-down patch of dead, unruly grass, and the plastic tote that held their provisions.

"The house is just ahead," he whispered as they took their seats and Hazel stretched out at their feet. "This last stand of trees gives us some cover." Corey pulled out his phone and shielded its screen with his other hand as he checked the time. "Do you want to do shifts, or both stay awake for now?"

They were on duty until four, when the night's final volunteers would arrive to keep watch until sunrise. Kate couldn't imagine being lulled to sleep given the immense silence that pressed in around them. And the thought of Corey dozing off was more than she could bear.

"Stay awake together. Absolutely."

"Good, I was thinking the same."

A twig snapped somewhere in the underbrush. Kate sensed a spread of wings gliding over them somewhere above. They were far from alone out here. Kate just hoped they were the only humans wandering about on this night.

She could barely make out the hulking shape of the abandoned house just ahead of them. This farmstead sat on a small ridge, and their position offered a sight line to the left that encompassed the lane as well as part of the front pasture and the gravel road beyond. Or, it would have in daylight. Of course, someone could come up behind them, and ...

Kate turned quickly in her chair. There was no one there. At least, no one she could see.

Hazel was down in the leaves, her head on her paws, and Kate tried to take that as a sign that danger wasn't near.

Maybe ten minutes had passed, although Kate couldn't be sure, and her eyes had adjusted better to the dark. This place was forlorn and foreboding, but Kate's curiosity was getting the better of her.

"Can I ... could we go look at the house?" The inspector had concluded his investigation Friday evening, and the site had been turned back over to the Talbots. Any evidence deemed important had already been collected. "Is that allowed?"

Corey let out a low chuckle. "Sure. I didn't want to push it, wasn't sure you'd be comfortable."

Kate slid back in her chair. "Is it that bad?"

"Well, it's ... unnerving, let's call it that." He picked up the unlit lantern, just in case, and Hazel jumped to her feet. "Come on."

A few paces through the tree line, and the old house suddenly loomed over them in the dark. The broken-out windows were like watchful eyes, and Kate sensed that she, Corey and Hazel were being studied as they carefully inched their way forward.

A gust of wind rustled through the tall, dead grass. *What was that?* It was almost like a whisper, but Kate couldn't make out the words.

Corey turned toward the closest corner of the house. "This way. Watch your step."

Kate found the courage to follow. Hazel put her nose to the ground as they zigzagged through the brush in the dark. One second, she pulled on the lead, eager to forge ahead. The next, the line went slack as she studied something at her feet. What was it? Had she found something? But before Kate could try to check, Hazel moved on.

"Here." Corey stopped so suddenly that Kate nearly ran into him. He pulled out his phone, tapped the screen and then, with his free hand cupped over the top of the phone, aimed its weak light at the rotten clapboards long enough for

Kate to get a glimpse of the damage. "I've never seen anything like it."

Burnt-black slashes snaked up and away on the rotten clapboards. Smaller veins ran down from them like angry tears. Kate's fingers tingled as she imagined someone splashing gasoline on the side of the house before reaching for a lighter and setting everything aflame.

How many seconds or minutes had it taken for the incinerated pattern to appear on the side of the house? And more importantly, how and why was the fire extinguished?

Corey tucked his phone away, and they were again left in the dark. Kate was relieved, and not just because the light could have drawn attention to their presence. What she'd already seen was terrifying enough.

"Last night, when my buddy and I were out here, we started talking about this house," Corey said in a low voice. "Who lived here, long ago? Why did they leave?"

"Probably the same sad story, like for so many of these old farmhouses."

Kate leaned over to rub Hazel's ears. The dog had moved into a "sit," but her focus was fully on the structure before them. "Too much upkeep, the children didn't want to farm, so everyone moved on. Literally and figuratively."

Corey's friend had grown up not far from this place, and he'd heard things over the years. Oh, you never knew if those stories were true.

But something about a rich farmer who'd built this fancy house for his status-seeking wife. He thought Flood Creek was going to be the next big thing, that the railroad would put his little kingdom on the map and keep it there. Then bad crops doomed his dreams. Anger, madness, heartache; it was as if this place was cursed.

He drank himself to death, everyone was sure of that. And some swore his spirit was still here, unable to let go, unable to leave.

Corey's voice dropped to a whisper. "It gets to you, doesn't it? The silence. The dark. That feeling that you're being watched."

"Yes." So she wasn't the only one who'd sensed that. She wasn't sure if her cousin's confession made her feel better or worse. "You couldn't pay me to be out here alone. And not just because there's an arsonist on the loose. I've seen enough, let's go back."

Kate had never been so happy to see a camp chair in her life. She welcomed the distraction of getting a drink for Hazel and some coffee for herself. When Corey twisted open a bottle of soda, he tried to smother its telltale *hiss* with his hand.

Talking would help them both stay awake, but it would likely distract them from the rustle of any potential approach. Kate recalled Grandpa Wayne's stories about mountain lions roaming the area, and decided silence was probably the safer way to go.

More time passed. All of them began to relax a bit as their hair-raising trek to the house faded into the background. The damp and cold took over, and Kate was glad she'd brought a blanket for herself as well as a smaller throw for Hazel.

Corey shifted in his chair, then sighed. "Fun times, huh?"

"The best," Kate whispered back. She was cold, worried, and still more than a little scared. But this was a bit of a thrill, too. And she was contributing, in some small way, rather than curled up in bed at home, staring at the wall and wondering what might happen next. "I mean, I couldn't find this kind of excitement in Chicago."

Corey snickered. "Yeah, no kidding. It's good to have you back, by the way. We should all get together more often. You know, all the cousins. In the daylight, doing something normal."

"Or if it's at night, we should at least be at a bar." Kate thought of Alex and wondered where he was, what he was up to. Paul's Place would be closed by now. Then she pushed that thought away. It was none of her business. "I wasn't sure if I should sign up for this, but I'm glad I did."

A twig snapped somewhere to their right, where the edge of the tree line met the pasture, and they both jumped in their chairs. Hazel quickly raised her head off her paws, but soon settled down. Kate and Corey took it as a sign they could do the same.

"We need all the help we can get," Corey said once the possible threat was discarded. "These fires have stretched everyone to the breaking point."

"I know, that's why I took you up on your offer. All of you have day jobs, people are in the fields. This couldn't have come at a worse time. There just aren't enough hands to go around. And one way or another, this has to stop."

It wasn't just the strain on local emergency resources, the long hours and fatigue and stress. This person wasn't just torching old buildings; they were threatening the sense of safety that small-town folks often took for granted.

Domestic terrorism, Auggie had called it. Kate could see how that argument was starting to hold water.

"I know I told you not to tell anyone what you were doing tonight," Corey said slowly, "what we have going on up here on this ridge."

"Only Charlie knows I'm not home." She rubbed Hazel's ears. "I mean, that *we're* not home."

"Good. We're hoping the arsonist doesn't get wind of what we're doing, of course, but it's not just that."

"What's going on? Can you tell me?"

"Well, we can't ask all of the crew members to help out." He paused, as if measuring his words carefully. "Because not all of the Eagle River and Prosper departments know what we're up to."

It was the middle of the night, and dark and cold, but Kate picked up on the hesitation in her cousin's voice. And maybe, there was a bit of fear, too.

"There's a list," Corey said quickly. "I'm not on it, so I'm allowed to be here. The chiefs and the fire marshal drew it up. I haven't seen it. They're the only three who know what's on it. I mean, *who's* on it."

Kate's chest squeezed with dread. "They think it's a firefighter."

"It's possible. Anything is possible, at this point. And so, here we are."

Corey didn't seem eager to say more. Kate let it drop. But as they sat there in silence, she tried to recall as many faces as she could. Who was on the Eagle River fire department these days? What about Prosper's crew?

How difficult it must have been for the local chiefs to sit down with the fire marshal, run through their rosters, and flag their own volunteers as potential suspects. Of course, there was the Swanton fire department to consider as well. And the crew in Charles City, and others around the region ... and the fact the arsonist may not be a firefighter at all.

Kate thought of Stan Winston, and the behavior he'd exhibited at the library meeting. She wondered if the marshal had any potential suspects yet, or if he was as in the dark as, well, Kate was right now. But all she could do was hunker down, pull her fleece blanket closer around her shoulders, and keep watch.

And then, it occurred to her that Corey hadn't mentioned Sheriff Preston. Had the sheriff even been involved in this review of the firefighters? Was there a possibility the list reached beyond the local emergency departments to those in law enforcement as well? Had Corey told her everything he knew, or just ...

Corey yawned, and Kate couldn't help but do the same. She picked up the faint sound Hazel made as she yawned, too. That broke the tension, just a little.

"How much longer?" Kate turned in Corey's direction. "Dare I ask?"

He checked his phone. "Fifty minutes, maybe." Then he chuckled softly. "You know, you're getting the hang of this stakeout thing. Like I said, our staffing options are limited. Care to sign up for another shift? Because I'm afraid we might be at this for a while."

"Let me check my schedule," she said wryly. "But I might be a one-and-done."

An owl hooted from a nearby tree. Kate thought of the one Jack saw Friday morning, and wondered what that majestic creature had witnessed the night of the fire. Another owl answered from its perch closer to the front pasture, and Kate entertained herself by imagining what they must be thinking: These silly people, with their chairs and totes, and grumbles about the cold and damp! They should try sitting up in a tree all night, in all kinds of weather, hunting a mouse or gopher for supper. And that lazy dog! It had its own blanket and was nearly asleep.

Really, Kate decided, this wasn't so bad. For years, she'd walked mail routes in Chicago no matter the weather, with just brief breaks in the truck to warm her toes and fingers. Two hours up on this ridge? It could be worse.

Like Corey said, they needed help. Maybe she could do this again. Not two nights in a row, but …

Something far out in the darkness caught her attention. It came so quickly, and disappeared just as fast, that she couldn't say for sure if she saw something, heard something, or both.

Hazel jumped to her feet. Kate snagged the leash just before the dog let out a low growl. And this time, Kate knew she *saw* something: a flash of light. Two, in fact.

Corey was already out of his chair. "Headlights," he whispered. "I thought that's what it was! Then they disappeared into that little dip in the road."

They stood in a huddle, Kate's feet braced in the dead grass and both hands in a tight grip on Hazel's lead, and waited. The beams remained visible this time, as the vehicle inched down a long grade just west of the abandoned farmstead.

Who would be out at this hour? Some of the farmers were taking shifts around the clock. It could be one of them heading out to, or on the way home from, their fields. It was now after three; all the region's bars would have closed an hour ago. Drunk people tended to drive too fast, or too slow ...

The lights disappeared again, another dip. Once the vehicle chugged up the next grade and crested the hill, it wouldn't be long before it rolled past the end of the lane.

They waited again. But this time, nothing.

Kate blinked, several times, willed her eyes to peer farther in the dark, strained to see down toward the road. There were a few trees between them and the gravel, but the rest was only overgrown pasture. It was a better sight line than the one they had of the house.

"Did we miss it?" she whispered to Corey. "Where did they go?"

Maybe there was a field entrance not far from the end of the drive. But if the vehicle had turned off the road, shouldn't its headlights or taillights be visible?

"I don't know." Corey sounded worried. "Something's not right."

Hazel bounced from one front paw to the other, like a boxer eager to enter the ring. Then she let out a high-pitched whimper that Kate had never heard her make.

"They didn't go on past," Corey said through gritted teeth. "I'm sure of it." Then he swore. "That means they ..."

Hazel growled and bolted into the darkness. Kate had no choice but to run after the dog, as the woven leash was wrapped around her hand. "Corey!"

"Right behind you! Does she see something?"

"I don't know." Kate's heart thumped in her chest and her body surged with adrenaline. "Hazel, what is it?"

The dog plowed on through the dead grass and weeds, which were nearly as tall as she was, then nimbly stepped over a half-buried tree limb that almost took Kate down. Seconds later, Hazel tacked slightly to the right and increased her speed.

Suddenly, Kate knew her dog wasn't running blindly into the darkness. She'd smelled or heard something, if she hadn't yet seen it, and was taking Kate right to it.

If not something, then someone.

Kate was scared, but she held on. She wouldn't let go of Hazel's lead, and she couldn't see a thing. Her breath came in gasps, and she tried to fill her lungs on the next inhale. All those daily runs came to her aid now, even though it felt like Hazel was about to rip her right arm out of its socket.

Corey, who was still behind them, was now on his phone. "Yeah, someone's out here! Hazel's trying to track them. No. I don't know. She just …"

They had to be halfway through the front pasture by now, Kate guessed. Heading at this new angle, they would eventually meet up with the lane. Her mind tried to run ahead, picture this place in the daylight, but it was no use. No deliveries were made here; hadn't been for decades.

Was there a waterway in this pasture? A fence that marked the field's boundary with the lane? The dead grass was so tall, she couldn't see her feet. And she couldn't see what was ahead of her, and that could be dangerous for all of them.

"Hazel!" she gasped. "Stop! Wait!"

The only answer was another bark, louder and stronger than before. Then two more.

Something reached up from below and grabbed Kate's left ankle. Before she could think, could take another breath, she hit the ground and started to slide. Rough weeds and orphan twigs clawed at her face, and she closed her eyes. Her foot was on fire, her arm was sore, but she held on.

No matter what happened, she couldn't let go of Hazel's lead. There was danger out here, somewhere ahead of them in the dark, and Kate wouldn't let her dog face it alone.

She heard Corey behind her, shouting her name, then Hazel barked again. Another hard jerk on the leash, and it scraped Kate's palm raw as it disappeared into the dark.

"No!" she screamed. "Corey, help her!"

More barking up ahead, a *whoosh* in the grass as Corey flew past. Kate tried to get up, but couldn't get on her feet. Instead, she laid there on the damp ground, panting with exertion and fear.

The arsonist had come back, just as everyone had hoped he would. He'd cut the lights when he got close to the lane, turned off his vehicle, and had been creeping toward the house on foot when Hazel sensed his presence.

Hazel continued to bark as she and Corey rushed on toward the road. Kate managed to raise up on her elbows, but she couldn't see anything in the darkness. And then, just east of the lane, she heard the howl of an engine.

Tires spun and gravel rattled, and a vehicle roared away into the night. Its headlights were still off, and Kate was suddenly filled with rage instead of fear. "They could hit someone!" she gasped. This person apparently cared as little about loss of life as they cared about loss of property. Kate prayed no one was coming down this road at this hour, and tried to steady her breathing.

A few minutes later, a rustling sound came toward her. "Hey, where are you?"

"Over here. It's my ankle."

The too-bright beam of a flashlight dazzled Kate's eyes. Hazel whimpered when she spotted Kate down in the grass. "I'm OK," Kate told her. "Good job! You found the bad guy."

"I just called the rest of it in." Corey was still breathing hard. "One of the deputies is headed this way, but without a vehicle description ..."

"It's too dark." Kate slid her left leg out and managed to sit up. Hazel was still at her side, in the grass, and wasn't about to budge. "I couldn't see a thing. You?"

"Nope. A truck, I'd say, based on the sound of the engine. That's all I got. They'll pop their lights back on once they think they're far enough down the road. Turn out on the highway, and away they go."

Sometimes, it was handy to have a cousin who was a first responder. Especially if you were down in a damp field in the middle of the night with a bum ankle.

"It's only sprained, nothing's broken." But Corey groaned as he held his lit phone up to Kate's face. "Man, something scratched you pretty good! A twig, maybe. You have blood running down your face."

Kate gently touched the spot, and it stung. Great.

"You don't need an ambulance, at least, just a sag wagon." Corey scrolled through his contacts. "Hey, Cindy. We've had a little excitement up here. No, it's OK. But after you drop Ken and Trent at the fence, we'll need you to come back around and up the lane."

16

Kate leaned back against Bertha's headrest and closed her eyes. "Well, we made it out to the car. But the day is just getting started."

Hazel made a noise of sympathy from the back.

"Or is it that the day's more than a quarter over?" Kate rubbed the side of her face, but then stopped. Her scrapes were still tender. "I mean, we start all over at midnight."

Efforts to catch the arsonist would also need a fresh approach after Hazel's antics last night. But, as Corey had told Kate while they waited for Cindy to arrive, that was a good thing.

The perpetrator now knew the Flood Creek site was being guarded, so it was highly unlikely they would return. The Talbots shouldn't have to worry about their property going forward and, with resources stretched so thin, it would be a relief for many to justify giving up those overnight watches at the old house.

Kate was certainly one of them. She and Hazel didn't get home until four-thirty, and then Kate spent half an hour picking burrs and weed seeds out of her dog's thick coat. Hazel had been surprisingly calm during the procedure, and Kate had been grateful for that. Charlie's furry face had registered only confusion and disapproval when he'd ambled down to the kitchen and found his housemates looking so bedraggled.

And Charlie was just the first of many who'd seek an explanation today for Kate's appearance. Ice, antibiotic ointment and makeup might help, but they weren't going to give Kate the coverage she needed. Although her mind was clouded on so few hours of sleep, a plausible story needed to be drafted.

"I'll think of one on the way to town," she told Hazel as Bertha's engine roared to life. "I'm just glad Roberta said I could bring you along again today."

Last night's events were so strange and scary and unusual, Kate could almost wonder if she'd imagined that terrifying dash through the pasture. Her scars and bruises were a tangible reminder it had really happened, but it was Hazel's reaction that kept Kate on edge this morning.

The dog sometimes followed Kate around the house, but otherwise was content to observe her still-new surroundings from Kate's reading chair or one of her plush pet beds. But ever since they left the Talbots' farm, Hazel hadn't left Kate's side. Even when Kate had carefully hauled her aching self into the shower, the dog remained stationed on the other side of the vinyl curtain.

That told Kate everything she needed to know: Someone had definitely been out in that field. Someone dangerous.

Today wasn't the right time to give Hazel her first unsupervised stint at home. It seemed likely she and Charlie could now peacefully share the house, but being separated from Kate might be too stressful for Hazel given the protective behavior she'd exhibited since last night.

Kate tried to clear her mind and come up with a game plan as she and Hazel started for town. Her ankle was feeling better, thank goodness. Kate considered herself blessed that she'd twisted the left one, not the right, as she was still able to drive. It was another stroke of luck that her day's assignment was Jack's rural route. Other than a few to-the-porch package deliveries, she wouldn't have to get out of the car.

But first, she had to appear at the post office without drawing too much attention to her appearance. Easier said than done.

"What happened to you?" Bev gasped with sympathy when Kate and Hazel ambled through the back door. Randy shook his head, then let out a hoot.

"So, who's the guy you got in a tussle over?" he asked good-naturedly as Bev rolled her eyes. "I wouldn't peg you as someone who hangs out in bars, getting in cat fights over some dude. Just goes to show, you never know about people."

Kate laughed. Or at least, she tried to. It set the scratches on her cheek aflame. "Randy, you have the feline part right, at least." She took a deep breath and tried for a serious expression.

"I tripped over a cat."

It was ridiculous, but it was the best story Kate could concoct in just a few minutes and on so little sleep.

Her tall tale began with her usual trip to the machine shed last night to feed the Three Mouseketeers. Scout was right under her feet like always, demanding his supper. Trying not to topple over Scout, she'd made a misstep and toed one chore boot on a crack in the uneven concrete floor.

Down she went, and landed on her left ankle. In her frantic flailing to grasp anything that might keep her upright, she'd scratched her own face.

The performance must have passed muster, as everyone seemed to buy it. Anecdotes began to circulate about the perils of country life, and Randy had just launched into an account of one uncle's unfortunate run-in with a pitchfork when Roberta came in the door.

Hazel hurried over and gave her usual greeting, and Kate had to shake her head. Her dog hadn't made the cut at obedience school, but she certainly knew how to work a room.

"There's my girl." Roberta rubbed Hazel's ears. Then she looked at Kate. "My goodness!"

Kate told the story again. Really, it wasn't that bad. Some humor, a crazy animal, the sort of mishap her listeners might fall into themselves.

All this practice was a good thing, she decided, as customers who were at home today when she dropped a package were likely to ask the same questions. Scout would be notorious around several supper tables tonight, but Kate decided her big barn cat couldn't care less about his soon-to-be-tarnished reputation.

And if it saved Kate from having to admit she'd been roaming around with her cousin in the middle of the night, trying to catch an arsonist, it was all worth it.

Talk around the tables soon turned to Eagle River's Friday-night football chances (pretty good), if the city council would ban leaf burning (likely) and the town's upcoming Halloween celebration (now just over two weeks away). Randy offered to give up his stool to Kate, and she settled in with a grateful "thanks" and began to sort her route's deliveries.

But it wasn't just her injuries that weighed on Kate this morning. There had to be some connection between the fire sites, but she couldn't figure it out. Simply being a vacant structure down a gravel road didn't seem to be enough of anything to elicit this sort of violent response in someone. Besides, there were too many similar locations around Hartland County. Why target these three?

As the other carriers packed their cases and headed out into the cool fall morning, the post office went from bustling to quiet. Kate yawned, then yawned again. She was moving slowly today; thank goodness her load was rather light.

She glanced over at Hazel, who was nearly asleep in what had apparently become her favorite corner of the back room. They'd both had a long night; maybe she should have left

Hazel at home. The dog's reticence to leave Kate's side had tipped the scales in this direction, but now, Kate noticed a change in Hazel's behavior. Once they'd arrived at the post office, Hazel had seemed less concerned about Kate's welfare.

Maybe she was just eager to soak up all that attention. But then Kate had another, disquieting thought: Was Hazel's watchfulness at the farm prompted by something other than residual worry from last night's stakeout? Did she think there was a potential threat at home?

The truck had fled the scene, but now Kate wondered if the driver could have doubled back to do some investigating of their own.

Hazel's keen senses had alerted Kate and Corey to this person's presence. The problem was, that discovery went both ways. If the arsonist had indeed been behind the wheel of that truck, they might attempt to uncover exactly who was guarding the Flood Creek site.

While the Talbots had taken several precautions, the merry-go-round of late-night visitors to their farm couldn't be concealed. And Kate remembered what Corey said about the list.

License-plate registration information wasn't easy for most people to get their hands on, but any first responder could access those details within minutes. Especially if they didn't care to play by the rules.

Kate tried to comfort herself with the fact she hadn't met any other vehicles on her farm's gravel road during the wee hours. Even so, she recalled a few sets of headlights behind her on the state highway, and then the blacktop, as she'd made her way back from the Talbots' farm. Kate hadn't sensed any danger when she and Hazel arrived home. But given her exhaustion and bumps and bruises, she wasn't as observant as she could have been.

As she recounted her parcels for the day, Kate took a deep breath and tried to steady her nerves.

No one followed me home, she told herself, then tried her best to believe it.

I'm exhausted, my ankle's swollen, my face feels like it's about to peel off. I'm turning into one of those crazy people in a Hitchcock movie, paranoid and jumping to conclusions.

Roberta was at her desk, frowning at her computer screen. "All this paperwork." She sighed. "And we still have to finalize plans for the Halloween open house. Do I really have to wear a costume?"

Kate snorted. Now, this was one question she could answer.

"You run this shop, so I suppose you could abstain. But Austin is really counting on you to be in the Halloween spirit. Just dress as a witch; get a wig, wear all black, easy-peasy."

"Have you been talking to my kids? Apparently, that's what I am these days." Then Roberta laughed. "I know! I'll dress up as, oh, what's her name? The girl from that horror novel, the one that starts fires with her mind."

Kate stared at her boss. "Have you *lost* your mind?"

"Well, it's timely. Would give everyone something to talk about." Roberta's phone buzzed. "Oh, hello. Yeah, I sure can."

As Roberta moved toward the back door, Kate started to pack her mail case. But maybe that wasn't a good idea.

It was always so heavy. She should take everything out of it, load the empty case into the car, then ferry the items in a few trips. That meant more walking, but maybe she needed to stretch things out, just a bit. Once she was in the car, she might be sedentary for several miles at a time.

Roberta was back, with a familiar face in tow. Even so, Kate was surprised.

"Marshal Werner." She blinked and tried for a smile. "What brings you in?"

It was a dumb thing to say. Why else would a state investigator drive all the way down from Mason City? She really needed more coffee.

Gage simply nodded in greeting and studied Kate's scratched face. For one terrible second, she wondered if he was there to talk to her. But Corey said everything was on the down-low; the fire marshal would know better than to ...

And then Gage smiled. It wasn't much of one, but there was a hint of humor in it. While he'd obviously been debriefed on last night's drama, he wasn't about to discuss it now.

"I'm in need of a quiet place to work in this town, and Postmaster Schupp has graciously offered one end of your break room table." His grin widened when Hazel sauntered his way for some attention.

"Who's a good girl?" Kate heard him whisper to the dog. "Way to go!"

A quick glance showed Roberta beaming with aunt-like pride after Hazel went into a "sit" and then offered one paw for a shake. Kate nearly burst out laughing. Little did her boss know why Marshal Werner was showering Hazel with praise this morning.

While the investigator fussed over Hazel, Roberta explained to Kate why she'd offered him professional sanctuary.

"There's too much commotion down at city hall. Beyond the usual activity, Ward says so many people are stopping by to complain about the proposed burn ban, one way or another." She tipped her head toward the marshal. "And he's been in town enough times that people are starting to recognize him, they want to badger him about the cases. He can't get a moment's peace, I guess."

"Makes sense. That would rule out the library and the coffee shop, too."

City hall was certainly cramped, but Kate suspected there was another reason the marshal didn't want to hang out there. The theory that a firefighter could be behind the arson incidents had likely ruffled some municipal feathers. Kate had lived in Eagle River for more of her life than not, and knew local leaders would rather entertain the notion that a random outsider, or at least someone who wasn't a servant of this community, was behind these fires.

"I'm glad you offered him a spot. Unfortunately, I think his work in our town is far from done."

"I wish it was over." Roberta shook her head. "But until it is, well, I figured all the public employees need to look out for each other." Then she laughed and raised her voice, just a bit. "It's the federal government's responsibility to give the state folks a hand from time to time, when they need it."

"I heard that!" But Gage was laughing, too. Then he gestured at the to-go cup he'd set on the counter. "I can't work there, but I did stop at The Daily Grind when I got to town."

"Is our in-house coffee really that bad?" Roberta was giving him a hard time.

"You know it is," Kate broke in. "Strong and bitter. But it's hot. It's the fuel that keeps this shop running."

By the time she had the case in Bertha's front seat and the bundles of mail and packages transferred as well, Kate felt like she'd already logged in a full day. All she needed to do was collect Hazel, and it would be time to hit the road.

She peeked into the break room, and saw a sight that warmed her heart: Gage was at one end of the table, papers spread around his laptop, wearing a look of worried concentration. Hazel was at his feet, sprawled out on the linoleum with her head resting on her paws.

He had to be under an enormous amount of pressure to solve these cases, with very few leads to follow. As far as Kate knew, authorities had no possible suspects, no reports of a specific vehicle, nothing yet that could lead them to anyone. Tensions ran high in the community, and property owners were anxious. To make things worse, the specter of Halloween, with its traditions of tricks as well as treats, loomed on the horizon. It would be hard to believe the arsonist was finished, especially with such a holiday only days away.

Kate was exhausted and weary, but maybe someone else needed Hazel's companionship today more than she did.

"Aren't they a cute pair?" Roberta asked when Kate popped into the lobby. "As soon as he put his laptop on the table, it was like Hazel knew he was going to stay for a while."

"I can't disturb them." Kate rubbed her eyes, then winced when her hand caught the rough edge of her biggest scratch. "I think we can justify it by saying part of Hazel's alleged training is becoming comfortable around the hustle and bustle of a business, as well as interacting with strangers."

"Very good." Roberta nodded her approval. "I was thinking of something along the same lines. But I don't think he'll question it; he has more important things to worry about this morning."

She reached for the dust cloth kept behind the counter, but turned back to Kate before she set to work.

"You know, he seems very smart and perceptive, and I still hold out hope he'll get to the bottom of all this. But I was really surprised he didn't say anything about your face. No offense, but it's hard to miss."

Kate only shrugged. She knew why, of course, but wasn't about to share that with her boss. "He has a lot on his mind, I guess."

* 17 *

Living in a smaller community certainly had its perks. Kate had never expected to find a contractor who did double-duty as a dog sitter, but that's just what she had in Richard Everton.

"I'll keep an eye on her," Richard promised as he made some notes on a pad of paper. "Hazel and I are good friends, aren't we?"

Hazel answered with a happy whimper, then looked up at Kate. "It's OK," she told the dog. "Richard will be here off and on for a few days. You can come and go as you please. But he'll be watching to make sure you stay close to the house."

With her hopes for a second bathroom on hold, Kate had decided she'd better replace the ancient toilet in the only one she had. Some vinyl planks would replace the burgundy carpet, and that was it. Surely she could find some neutral bath mats and towels that would tone down that pinkish tile.

"Hazel's such a good girl." Richard showed his revised estimate to Kate, and she nodded with relief. Now this, she could afford. "I don't think we're going to have any problems."

It was a frosty morning, and Kate needed to gather up her warm layers and get to the post office. Friday was Aaron's regular day off, and she'd be walking his town route. Thank goodness her ankle had healed up enough over the weekend to make such a trek possible.

She spun around to find Charlie perched on the closest edge of the kitchen counter, watching Richard with an evaluating stare.

"This will keep you entertained. You can supervise." Charlie responded to her pets with a loud purr. Kate leaned in and whispered, "I put Big Mousie and Mr. Birdy in your safe room upstairs. Hazel won't be able to get at them there."

While Hazel and Charlie had slowly warmed to each other, the dog wasn't content to play with only her own toys. Two of Charlie's favorites had been deemed especially interesting, and Hazel liked to snatch them up and hide them around the house.

The duo got along best when the dog respected the cat's boundaries and routines, and Kate was determined to do whatever was needed to foster harmony in her home.

"The dog and cat treats are in that top cabinet, there on the end," she told Richard. "One or both may ask you to take pity on them, and they can be very persistent. But what one gets, the other has to have, or things get rough around here. Your best bet may be to not give them any, at all. They have plenty of food."

"Good to know." Richard looked out the nearest kitchen window, to where a faint etching of frost outlined the blades of browned grass and marked the edges of the sidewalk. "It's chilly out there. And it's supposed to kick up a big wind by tonight. Makes me glad to be in here, doing this. Outside jobs are only great when the weather's nice."

He whistled as Kate stuffed two extra sweatshirts into a canvas tote. She had a town route today, and one of the mail trucks, but she'd spend most of her shift on foot. "I don't know how you all do it, walking all day when winter arrives."

"We're a tough bunch, I guess." Kate thought of the day-in, day-out hikes she'd made in Chicago, and was glad to be back in Eagle River. Most of this post office's routes were rural, which brought their own challenges in less-than-pleasant-weather. But Bertha's heater would make her work so much easier when the next season arrived.

"I'll be back around four-thirty," Kate promised. "Good thing Scout and the gang can't see you from the front porch's windows, or you'd have even more supervisors than you do now."

"I'm used to it." Richard laughed. "Have a good day. And watch out for that sneaky Scout on your way to the garage. You don't need to take another tumble!"

✳ ✳ ✳

Cold air blew in with Kate when she opened the back door of the post office. A scattering of dead leaves hitchhiked along, and they weren't the first to make it inside the vestibule that morning.

"George needs to stay up on his raking," Jack grumbled. "Those leaves are everywhere."

"That's the truth," Bev said. "They *are* everywhere; because they're everyone's leaves. How are you so sure these came from George Tindall's backyard? Seems like we have our own two maples out in the parking lot."

Jack frowned. "We're on public property, but who has time to do yard work? Can't the city send someone over to gather them up? I mean, they mow our lawn."

Roberta set a stack of boxes on the counter. "They will, but they'll wait until all the leaves are down. And we aren't there yet."

"Ward has enough on his plate," Allison reminded Jack. "Let it go. I don't think this is the best time to be running over to city hall and asking for favors."

Mae came out of the break room, her travel cup full and her coffee thermos fully stocked. "I don't know about anyone else, but I can't wait until the council meets at the end of the month. I'm sure they'll ban leaf-burning, but some folks in town are going to raise the roof when they do. I say, let's get this over with."

Jack gave a wry grin. "Maybe they can get out their broomsticks and pitchforks and dance around the flames on Halloween. One last gasp before the leaves are done for the year, and the practice is outlawed for good."

"Well, I'm proud to set my leaves out in those collection bags." Marge raised her chin. "I won't put a sign in my yard, but I think I'm still making a statement." When the pro-burn people mounted their campaign to fight the proposal, a handful of residents on the other side of the fence created their own banners. "It's just as easy, and far safer, than burning them up. Besides, after you're done with a fire, you still have to dispose of what's left."

"What about mulching them into the lawn?" Kate asked. "That seems to be the easiest of all. I'm doing it with most of mine, and my parents always have, too. In Chicago, it's considered acceptable, socially as well as environmentally."

Bev laughed. "Clyde and I do the same when we can, but folks hate change. It's hard enough to get some people to stop dumping them in a pile and lighting them on fire."

"What you mean," Jack insisted, "is that people hate change *most* of the time, unless they can clearly see how they'll benefit from it. Mulching leaves is an idea that hasn't taken root here yet, for most people."

Allison squared a stack of letters and began to sort her next pile. "Tradition is hard to break, especially in a town this small. Sometimes, that's a good thing. Take us, for instance; if everything, and everyone, went one hundred-percent electronic, we'd be in trouble."

"Except for parcel delivery." Jared had two boxes stacked in his arms, and he seemed to struggle under their weight. He dropped them next to Kate with a grin of relief. "It's keeping us in business."

"Well, I'd better get the truck loaded." Kate took another swig of her coffee and picked up only one of the boxes. She'd be smart to not wear herself out at this early hour, and her arm was still a bit tender from when she took that tumble in the pasture during the stakeout.

"No Hazel today?" Jack asked hopefully. Then he looked around. "No marshal, either, I guess."

"We've made it a week without a fire." Allison pointed at Jack. "Don't jinx it."

"Hazel is settling in now, so I'll be leaving her at home. Most days," Kate added after she saw the disappointed faces of her coworkers. Roberta gave Kate a secretive smile that indicated Hazel's stint at the Eagle River post office hadn't ended for good.

* * *

Just as Marge had said, Kate noticed several homes on her town route had yard-waste bags on the curb. It was pickup day, after all, but the sheer number of sacks seemed to indicate how most of Eagle River's residents felt about this issue.

The filled bags were lined up in neat rows, sometimes two or three deep. They reminded Kate of soldiers on duty, silent but stalwart, a show of force against the yards around them marked by pro-burn signs and the ash heaps from last night's fires.

The other sights along her route, however, certainly brightened Kate's day. Seasonal decorations were everywhere, from the subtle autumn colors of potted mums and stacked pumpkins to the flashing lights and spooky sounds that marked the commercialized Halloween displays.

Goblins peeked out from beyond the trunks of trees, and a few of the undead popped out of their caskets as Kate passed by. One yard on Ash Street sported an eight-foot-tall, one-dimensional plywood spooky house. It was painted a shiny, weatherproof black and featured cut-out windows and doors. Cheesecloth cobwebs were draped over its angles, and a host of lopsided headstones were clustered in front.

Several residents had taken the merry-not-scary route, with inflatables of cute ghosts, grinning jack-o-lanterns and depictions of popular animated characters celebrating the upcoming holiday.

Most farm yards were like Kate's, decorated in natural themes rather than the abundance of celebratory spirit that was on display in town. And while she enjoyed those understated acknowledgements of the season, all of these impressive efforts really had her in a festive mood by the time the afternoon rolled around.

How would she celebrate Halloween this year? She'd promised to help out at the post office's open house during the town celebration, but hadn't made any plans beyond that. Kate didn't expect to find many trick-or-treaters at her farmhouse's door. Growing up, she and Bryan had made the rounds in town, but only dropped in on their closest rural neighbors on that special night.

Gwen's boys were probably a little old for trick-or-treating. But what about the rest of her rural neighborhood? Some of the residents were older, with adult children, which made Kate wonder if there might be any grandkids wanting to canvas nearby farms for candy. Who had young kids within a few miles of Kate's place? She wasn't sure, and it made her a little sad that she didn't know.

At least, Kate decided, she no longer had cause to be afraid of any of her neighbors. At this point, Brody's only role in his barn's fire seemed to be that of an innocent victim. She didn't know everyone as well as she'd like, but there was no indication anyone living close to her farm was up to no good.

Now, this group up the block, however ...

It was only a cluster of teenage boys, huddled on the front porch of one of the once-grand homes that had long ago been partitioned into apartments, but Kate's nervous system went on high alert. The teens lounged in the weathered porch swing and against the railing, and Kate wondered if either was sturdy enough to hold anyone's weight for very long.

The boys were smoking, a bad habit that probably marked their biggest attempt at after-school rebellion. As far as Kate could tell, and smell, only cigarettes were being passed around on that porch.

But the boys' pulled-up hoodies and stony glares told her she was being evaluated. And discussed.

Kate pulled her mail bag closer and raised her chin. No, she wasn't going to be scared. Not today. Not after what happened in Chicago, what she went through earlier in the year.

But that was just the problem, Kate decided as she made her way down the block, unwilling to slow her stride or show any other sign of hesitation. Any one of these boys could leap from his perch at any moment, rush down the rotten porch steps, and pull a gun from the waistband of his jeans.

Kate took a deep breath and looked away, just for a second. She couldn't control what these teens might, or might not, do, but she could keep her emotions in check.

They're just some bored kids, she told herself. *There's no reason to be afraid.*

Her mail bag suddenly seemed twice as heavy, but she couldn't turn back. There were two bundles of letters to drop in the lobby of this building. Kate had them in order to save time, like always, but she still had to cross that porch and go inside. And after her drop, she'd have to face those stares all over again.

Kate decided that since she had to go up those steps, she might as well put this opportunity to good use. The latest gossip had the Flood Creek fire pegged as a copycat case, a stupid prank pulled by some bored kids looking for a thrill and a little notoriety among their peers.

How many of the teens on this porch looked capable of such a thing? More than one, she decided.

"Hey, lady," one of them called out, then took a quick drag on his cigarette for dramatic effect. "You got mail?"

It was a dumb joke, but his buddies laughed anyway.

"I sure do." Her voice came out louder than she intended. "And the postal service is a great career, you know."

Where had that come from? But she was here, she might as well try to spread the word. "Good pay and benefits. Steady work. But you need to graduate first, then meet their standards to be considered."

This unexpected speech quieted the crowd, maybe even gave the boys something to ponder as she marched through their group and pushed open the front door.

She hated to play into stereotypes, really she did, but Kate wondered what these kids would do with their lives if they didn't get it together before senior year came and went. Factory jobs? Maybe work as hired hands for one of the corporate farms?

Not everyone needed to land a white-collar position. But Kate couldn't help but think about Brody, of the already-defeated resignation she'd sensed in him at the pro-burn meeting.

He was very young to be so cynical about life, but many opportunities seemed to have already passed him by. Some farming with his dad, a little auto-body work, never enough money for what he wanted or needed. No wonder a few beers at Paul's Place were likely the highlight of his week.

And then, all the pointed stares, the whispers about his barn. It wasn't fair, but if Brody worked at the bank, or was a teacher at one of the local schools ... Kate wondered if people would have been so quick to judge him guilty of a crime that, as far as she could now tell, he hadn't committed.

So, what about those boys out on the porch? If any of them had been involved in the Flood Creek fire, they surely thought it was all some kind of joke. It was just an old house in the middle of nowhere, of no value. What's the harm in a little fun? They likely didn't care about the fear sweeping through their community. And the sleepless nights, the hours put in by local firefighters and law enforcement.

But these kids weren't going to listen to a lecture, especially from her. Kate shook her head as she deposited the mail into the boxes. Those were life lessons they'd have to learn on their own.

The rusting hinges on the old front door alerted the boys to her return. Only a few of them even looked at her, this time around, and no one said a word. Whether they were still processing her speech, or just thought she was a weirdo that wasn't worth further consideration, she didn't know.

As Kate continued her route, however, she decided the assumption that the Flood Creek fire was a prank didn't hold up. The idea that some kids did it for a thrill, then got scared when they saw how fast the flames consumed the rotten clapboards and rushed to snuff them out, could make sense. But Kate possessed information that few others had, and she couldn't imagine some spooked teens would have felt compelled to come back three nights later to finish what they'd started.

Because at that age, the thrill was the thing. Thumbing your nose at authority, sneaking out of your parents' house. That first night, bored kids would have accomplished what they set out to do. They got a shot of adrenaline, had a good story to whisper to their friends in study hall or at football practice. And they didn't get caught. Their work was done.

Kate felt fairly confident about her assessment of who didn't set the fire at Flood Creek, although she still had no idea who did. As she stepped around stacks of porch pumpkins and pulled her cap lower against the rising wind, Kate instead pondered why that old house hadn't gone up in flames.

Of course, it had rained sometime later that night. The insistent drumming on her farmhouse's roof woke her up in the wee hours, but all she knew was the skies were still dry when she'd gone to bed. Could the rain have put out the blaze if it hadn't yet taken a good hold?

With harvest in full swing, there was always the possibility the arsonist spotted a combine or truck in a nearby field, lost their nerve, and doused the flames themselves.

Kate didn't know much about arsonists, but it stood to reason that the smart ones would have some source of water with them in case things got way out of control, or they were in danger of being discovered. Because while they wanted to burn something to the ground, they also wanted to walk away unscathed.

It didn't seem likely, however, that the arsonist had been disrupted by another person. Because while the thick stand of trees behind the old house partially obscured it from the field, the flames still would have been visible for some distance. If anyone had come down the road at the right time, they certainly would have spotted the fire.

But no one had called it in, and there was no proof anyone knew about the fire until Jack's discovery the following morning.

There was another option, as far-fetched as it might be, that gave Kate a chill.

What if something else had spooked the arsonist, caused them to abort their mission and run for the safety of their vehicle? Kate hadn't been able to shake off the strange presence she'd sensed Sunday night up on that ridge. It had felt like the house was watching them; there wasn't any other way for her to explain it.

As Kate greeted the manufactured ghosts that hovered over the yards on her route, she decided anything was possible. Especially this time of the year.

* 18 *

Sunday was a golden day: cobalt-blue skies, warm sunshine, miles of amber-hued fields in every direction. It was a little chilly to roll down the window; but otherwise, the weather couldn't be better for this late in October.

"I can't wait for you to meet Hobo," she told Hazel, who tracked everything they passed from her perch in the back seat. The dog had surprised Kate by allowing a rust-shaded calico bandana to be tied over her collar, which gave her a festive air for today's party.

Well, "party" might be too strong of a word. This was going to be a rather low-key event, according to Melinda, but it was one Kate didn't want to miss. The Schermann family had owned Melinda's acreage for over a century before she moved there, and she'd since grown close to its current members. That included Horace, the elderly bachelor farmer who was taking a now-rare trip to his lifelong home this afternoon. He was in his mid-nineties, Melinda said, and his advanced age made it increasingly difficult to come down from Elm Springs, even though the nursing home was only twenty minutes away.

The family used to hold a reunion every October and, while the number of attendees and level of revelry had both diminished in recent decades, Melinda had graciously kept the tradition going. And began to invite a few of her friends and family members as well.

There would be a buffet of chili, side dishes and desserts, lots of visiting, and that was about it. But Kate had been looking forward to this for weeks. A securely packed pear-apple tart was nestled in the passenger seat, and her camp chair and a fleece blanket were in the trunk.

"Well, this must be the corner." Kate turned south off the blacktop. "She said it's two miles, over a creek bridge, and then the first place on the right."

Kate soon saw a white farmhouse winking at her through the sparse-leafed trees in its windbreak. Steep gables anchored the house's second floor, and an enclosed porch jutted from the front. The dark-green steel roof was new, along with a fresh coat of exterior paint. Several sheep dotted the front pasture, but it was the critter stationed at the fence corner closest to the lane that made Hazel bark and Kate laugh.

"That must be Pepper!" The speckled donkey had apparently nominated himself as the gathering's official greeter. When Kate turned up the drive, he opened his jaws wide and let out a boisterous "hee-haw!"

Hazel was excited about this curious creature. "Easy, girl. Pepper loves Hobo, I guess, but I don't know what he thinks of other dogs."

Several vehicles were parked in the farm yard, and Kate added her car to the row. Karen was already here, and her Collie, Pumpkin, sat calmly at her side as Karen talked to a few other visitors by the back porch's entrance.

A brown dog with white feet soon barreled around the corner of the machine shed, barking all the way. "That's him," Kate told Hazel. "Let's get out and say hello, huh? But I'd better go first."

"Hobo!" Melinda jogged across the yard, waving her arms. "Stop that! It's fine!" She shook her head at Kate. "He has no manners, whatsoever. Not like Pumpkin and Hazel." Melinda waved at Kate's dog, who was still in the front seat of the car. "I love her bandanna. And she's so regal!"

Kate snorted. "Well, maybe. 'Obedience' is a word that apparently means different things to her, at different times."

She longed to tell everyone about the night Hazel chased away an intruder at Flood Creek, but she couldn't. Kate's face had healed considerably over the past week, thank goodness, so makeup now easily covered the scratches. And her ankle was back to normal, too. It seemed like the days of Scout having to play the villain were over.

Pumpkin ran over to join the fun, and the three dogs were soon sniffing the lawn for whatever scents they could find. Hazel had spent yesterday at home with only her sensor-activated doggie door to control her activities and, as far as Kate knew, there hadn't been any trouble. So she took a deep breath and unhooked Hazel, and the trio of pups wandered off across the yard.

Two well-fed barn cats sunned themselves on the edge of the sidewalk between the house and the garage. The orange tabby was Sunny, and the gray tabby was his assumed brother, Stormy. Both grudgingly accepted one pet from Melinda, but Kate's overtures of friendship were mostly ignored.

"They're just mad because I made them get off the picnic table," Melinda explained. "That's their favorite spot. But we have company, and lots of it, so they'll have to suffer, I guess." She grinned. "Are you ready to meet Horace?"

The ladies went in through an enclosed back porch, one very similar to Kate's as well as just about every farmhouse around. But when they stepped into the kitchen, Kate had to laugh.

"Oh, my! Yours is as outdated as mine. I'd say more so. But it's vintage enough to be retro-cool, while mine is just kitschy."

"I painted the walls and the cabinets, and left everything else." Melinda shrugged. "The linoleum will last forever, I think. I figured, why not go with the flow?"

The kitchen was filled with the aromas of spicy chili, pumpkin and apples, and fresh-baked bread. Kate couldn't wait to dive in and enjoy all of it. She added her tart to the spread of desserts on one side of the kitchen counter, and the ladies continued their tour.

While the farmhouse's kitchen was practical and rather drab, the dining room's wallpaper certainly made a design statement. "Well, there they are." Kate looked around with wide eyes. "The bluebirds you told me about."

In a quick burst of decorating she'd later regretted, Horace's mother had long ago applied a garish wallpaper to the space. The life-size birds swooped through a tangle of vines and leaves, a dramatic pattern that Melinda had tried to mute by painting the adjacent living room a soft, light blue. But both the dining room and living room held oak built-ins and trim similar to those in Kate's house, and the hardwood floors still gleamed.

"When I get all my wallpaper down, this is what I want," Kate declared. "Simple, peaceful. Keep the focus on the architectural details."

She spotted a thin man with a shock of white hair in the next room. He looked so at home, resting in the overstuffed chair by the fireplace, that Kate knew it had to be Horace.

A man about Melinda's age with glasses jumped up from the sofa and shook Kate's hand. "It's so nice to meet you. I'm Kevin Arndt, Horace's nephew. Uncle Horace," he called over his shoulder. "Kate's here."

A pair of blue eyes turned in her direction, and Kate was glad to see intelligence and curiosity in Horace's gaze. Wilbur, who was just two years older than his brother, had suffered from dementia for some time now. But Horace seemed as spry as someone who was a decade younger.

Well, maybe not quite. He made a small effort to get out of his seat, but quickly settled back into it. Kate hurried over to sit on the footstool by his chair, and Horace's grateful smile said it all.

"So, you bought a little farm too, huh?" He was pleased. "I know your grandpa Wayne."

"Everyone does, I think. Seems like you grew up here; how does it feel to be back?"

Horace didn't answer right away. Kate knew he'd heard her, and that he was as full of opinions as ever. But there was a little shyness there, as well; a reticence to share his true feelings with a stranger. Kate understood.

"It's such a beautiful day." She quickly moved on so Horace wouldn't feel awkward. "Have you been outside yet?"

Horace was waiting until after lunch to make the trip. While most of his relatives and Melinda's friends would eat outside, at the picnic table or in their camp chairs, he and his immediate family would enjoy their meal at the dining-room table.

It wasn't original to the house, he said, but Melinda had found this one at the consignment shop just outside Eagle River. Wasn't it nice?

"It's beautiful," Kate told Horace. "I have all these rooms to fill at my new place, too. But I can't decide if I should get the wallpaper, paint and carpet taken care of first, or just find the extra furniture I need now."

Horace barely nodded, so Kate went on. "I'd like to put a half bath on the first floor, since there isn't one. But everything is so expensive! And then, I have so much to do outside, before winter. I don't know how I'll get it all done in time. My family farms and they're still in the fields. I'm helping out when I can, but maybe after that ..."

"Slow down, I'd say." Horace's voice was gentle. "Time flies fast enough as it is. Things will work out, one way or another."

Gasps of admiration went up around the living room as a long-haired calico sashayed down the stairwell.

"Well, if it isn't Princess Grace," Kevin announced with a deferential dip of his chin.

Kate admired Grace, but only from a distance. She apparently had a regal temperament to match her looks. "Where's her sister? Hazel, right? That's my dog's name, too."

"And a fine one it is," Horace said. "She's in the den." He gestured through a half-open door into the back room. "She made the rounds just before you came, then went in there to curl up on her round bed. It's her favorite spot."

Ada Arndt, her cheeks still flushed from the autumn breeze, patted her short white hair into place before she settled next to her son on the sofa. "We didn't expect the girls to be too social today, with so many strangers coming and going."

Grace claimed Ada's lap, and the older woman smiled at Kate. "My husband and I farmed just a few miles from your parents for many years."

"Really? I wonder if we've met before. Small world, huh?"

"It's possible. Isn't that fun to think about?" But then, Ada sighed. "I know the Snyder family, too, the ones who own the first house that burned." She shook her head. "Not much left but a pile of rubble. What a terrible mess for them to clean up."

"This whole thing is just unbelievable." Kevin held out one hand, and Grace allowed him to scratch her chin. "It's been, what, ten days since the fire up at Flood Creek? There's always hope, I guess, that this is all over. But this community deserves closure. Who's responsible? And it must be one person. I can't imagine there's multiple people around here crazy enough to do something like that."

Horace made a noise that landed somewhere between a laugh and a snort, and Kate thought of all the people he must have known in his ninety-plus years.

"You can never tell about people," he finally said. "Sometimes the offbeat ones aren't that crazy, and it's the quiet ones you have to watch out for."

Kevin leaned toward his uncle. "Speaking of suspicious fires, what happened over in Hawk Hollow all those years ago?"

Hawk Hollow was just a few miles south and west of Melinda's place. Or at least, it used to be. It was never more than a creamery, school, general store and post office, and those buildings had disappeared decades ago.

"Oh, now, let's see." Horace settled back in his chair, ready for a trip down memory lane. "There was just that one farm, across the road from the store. Big house, fancy, especially for way back when." He nodded with approval. "Old Mr. Peabody really outdid himself when he built it."

Peabody? Kate was all ears. The surname was unique enough. In an area this rural, that long-ago resident was likely an ancestor of the family that operated the Eagle River restaurant.

"The house was in bad shape by the time the sixties came along," Horace said. "Then one night, there was a fire. It was too far gone by the time crews came all the way out from town." He paused for a bit of dramatic effect. "They never did figure out exactly what happened. The Peabodys' shirttail relations owned the place by then, and they were quick to bulldoze what was left."

"I remember that." Ada shook her head. "It was quite the mess."

Kate thought of Marshal Werner. "Maybe they didn't want people asking too many questions. Was anyone living there when the fire happened?"

Horace shook his head. "Nope. They'd moved out the year before, it seems like, went to a nursing home." He gave a rueful laugh. "It happens to the best of us, sooner or later."

"And it was such a big house, and in such terrible shape,

that no one wanted to fix it up." Kevin gave Kate a pointed look. "So it just sat there, neglected and empty. Does that sound familiar?"

"It sure does."

"Hold on, now." Horace put up a hand. "You've been watching too many of those true-crime shows. The Peabody house went up in smoke sixty years ago."

Then he chuckled. "Goodness, if someone lit it back then, they'd have to be way up in age these days. Doubt they could even lug a gas can around, much less carry out a plan like that."

"You're right," Kevin admitted.

"Of course, I am. These situations can't be related, too many years have gone by."

Ada turned to Kate. "Henry and Eloise still have their restaurant, right? Goodness, they have great food. Haven't been there in years."

Kate nodded. "Their breakfasts are legendary, and the broasted chicken and steak specials bring people in from miles around, especially on the weekends."

She couldn't imagine those Peabodys being mixed up in anything sinister. But their family had lived in this area for generations. Just like hers, and the Schermanns as well. And you never knew who might be hiding in the branches of your family tree.

* * *

Melinda soon announced it was time to eat, and Kate joined Karen in the queue of friends and Schermann family members waiting to make their way through the potluck line.

Karen elbowed Kate when another truck turned up the lane. "There's Josh. I hoped he could get away long enough to eat lunch, at least." Josh Vogel and Melinda had been dating for nine months now, and his Swanton veterinary practice had a partnership with the Prosper clinic.

"The elusive boyfriend." Kate smiled. "I've heard so much about him, but have yet to meet him."

"He needs to take on a partner, I think. His practice is going gangbusters. It's a good thing Melinda is really independent and can entertain herself."

In addition to his work, Josh had a young son who lived about two hours away. Melinda had found a way to have someone in her life, yet was happy being on her own at the same time. It was a balancing act Kate found rather appealing these days.

She and Ben had been together since college, and he'd been at her side for over a decade before their marriage fell apart. She was lonely sometimes, but Kate had learned over the past several months that there were certain benefits to having a little emotional, as well as physical, space in her life. She could now make big decisions, like coming home to Eagle River, buying a house, and adopting a dog, without having to consult anyone else.

Melinda hurried down the back porch steps and edged her way through her guests, her face alight with joy. Josh stepped down from his truck, and Kate was impressed. He certainly was handsome, with dark brown hair and brown eyes.

Josh was as happy to see Melinda as she was to see him, and they embraced in the driveway and shared a quick kiss before, hand in hand, they started for the house.

Kate felt a tug at her heartstrings. There, right in front of her, was what she missed the most. Someone who lit up when you walked into the room. That person you could tell everything to, any hour of the day or night, and know they had your back.

Despite her evolving emotions, or maybe because of them, Kate was starving. Four varieties of chili waited on the kitchen counter, and she picked one and vowed to return and try at least one more. Along with the expected cornbread, veggies and dip, and cheese-and-cracker tray, there was one slow cooker filled with scalloped potatoes and another loaded to the brim with macaroni and cheese.

Kate was proud to see her pear-apple tart next to the other fall treats, which featured pumpkin and chocolate as well as more fruit. But there was one offering that stood out among the rest.

"Is that your coconut cake in there?" Kate asked Mabel Bauer as she took a seat on the lawn next to Melinda's neighbor. "I'll have to try it."

Mabel nodded and beamed. "Can't have a neighborhood party without it, I guess." She took Ed's plate so he could focus on settling in his chair. "Melinda specifically requested I make one for today. How are your pumpkins holding up?"

"They're as nice as when I brought them home. Thanks for sharing with me. I hope to keep them out there until Thanksgiving, if I can."

Karen shook her head. "That's barely a month away. Where does the time go?"

"And it goes faster as you get older," Ed promised. "I can't even think about the holidays yet. We have one big thing to check off our list before then."

The Bauers had purchased a tumbledown acreage southwest of Melinda's place a few months ago with plans to turn it into a wildlife refuge. Another neighbor's relative, who worked in conservation out of state, helped them draft ideas before the project was handed off to Hartland County's staff.

No one else wanted the property, so the Bauers got it cheap. But it was still a lot of work to remove all the buildings, so they'd decided early on to let the local fire departments burn the house for a training exercise.

The recent arson cases had some people questioning if the controlled burn should be delayed, Ed told Kate, but early November was still a good time to get the house leveled before winter.

Harvest would wrap up soon, so the surrounding fields would be empty in time.

"We decided, we might as well let the fire crews get in their training," Ed said with a sigh. "Who knows how long they might have this threat hanging over their heads?"

Kate leaned over the arm of her camp chair. "Are you nervous, even a little?" she asked Mabel. "I mean, unless things get resolved ..."

"We'll take each day as it comes." Mabel paused long enough to return a neighbor's wave of greeting. "There have been some sleepless nights lately, for sure."

The controlled burn had always been expected to draw a crowd. The Bauers still hoped the occasion would motivate others to support local first responders, as well as the need for natural habitat, but the intentional blaze had now taken on greater significance.

"We've been talking to the sheriff," Mabel told Kate in a low voice. "He's prepared. So's the fire marshal."

Kate understood. Law enforcement officials would be watching closely to see if anyone's reaction to the controlled burn made them stand out as a potential suspect.

One of Kate's had apparently been busy in the past week. Stan had authored an inflammatory opinion piece in support of in-town burning that had appeared in Thursday's Swanton newspaper. Several other residents had added their names to the bottom of the letter, including Edna.

"Anyway, I'd like you to come." Mabel patted Kate's arm. "I think your grandpa and grandma might be there, Harvey invited them."

Then she laughed. "I can't promise a chili feed, but it's bound to be an interesting time, one way or another."

"If I can get off work, I'll be there. Oh, and there's something else I wanted to ask you about. Melinda says you have an excellent recipe for canning pears, and I don't want to let the rest of mine go to waste."

Mabel shared her time-tested process while Kate scribbled notes on the back of a receipt from the depths of her purse. Then it was time for another round of chili, followed by dessert. Mabel's cake lived up to its glowing reputation but, after Kate followed it with a small slice of pumpkin pie, she was about to doze off in the gentle warmth of the autumn afternoon.

"I have to pace myself, or I'll be in trouble," she told Karen and Ed. Mabel was in the kitchen, helping Melinda and Ada sort the leftovers, as there would be endless snacking until the gathering wound down in a few hours. "I think this would be a good time to take a walk around the farm."

"Go ahead." Karen yawned. "I'm staying right here in this chair."

The dogs were now milling around the picnic table, gathering pets and praise. It made Kate happy to see Hazel so comfortable with Pumpkin and Hobo. Several playdates should be in Hazel's future, she decided.

Kate's first stop was the pasture fence just west of the barn. Pepper had long ago decided all his visitors had arrived, so he'd moved from the front pasture to a spot where he could keep an eye on the celebration.

After he'd been acknowledged, Kate turned her attention to the handful of sheep who'd ambled over to the fence to see what was what.

"Look at all of you." She rubbed the black forehead of the closest ewe. "A donkey, sheep, chickens; it's never dull around here, huh?"

Another sheep let out a demanding "baaa" and stomped one front hoof.

"You must be Annie." Kate laughed as she moved down the fence. "Don't worry, I won't pass by without saying hello."

As Kate continued her walk, she tried to imagine her own little farm populated with more animals. Sheep? Goats? Chickens? A donkey was probably out of the question. But winter would soon be on its way, and Kate decided to use the coming months to consider what she wanted her place to be like by summer.

The cold, snowy weather would be the perfect excuse to start peeling off all that wallpaper, and do some painting, too. Richard and his sons could remove and replace carpet. Could they refinish the floors instead, if they were in salvageable shape? Probably; she'd have to ask.

As Kate rounded Melinda's machine shed and headed north, her sneakers rustled through the fallen leaves that spilled out of the windbreak. The summer had been so full of upheaval and activity that she'd barely had time to think. Beyond the updates at her little farm, what else in her life did she want to change?

A "meow" rose from somewhere to her left, and an orange-tabby blur rushed out from behind the trunk of a nearby maple tree.

"Well, Mr. Sunny!" Kate had barely offered her greeting before the kitty was at her feet, rubbing his cheek against one leg of her jeans. "Are you coming with me on my walk?"

His loud answer made it clear he intended to do just that. On impulse, Kate reached down and picked him up, and was thanked with a loud purr.

"Look how friendly you are, even with strangers." Kate entered the stand of trees. "Scout's friends need to take a page from your playbook. But it takes time, I know; we'll get there."

She paused where the back of the windbreak met the cornfield. Combines crossed the yellowed field in orderly rows as they brought in the harvest. The Duncans expected to have their work completed this next week and, while Kate would be glad to have a little more free time again, the end of the growing season was always a little bittersweet.

Or at least, it had been during her growing-up years. Through college and then her time in Chicago, late fall had been marked only by the evolving weather. But now, being home again, Kate sensed the change in the air.

It was time to let go of her expectations, and let things be as they were. Horace had suggested the same. And, ninety-some years in, he knew exactly what he was talking about.

For his part, Sunny just wanted more attention. When Melinda first rented this little farm, both cats had wanted nothing to do with her outside of breakfast and supper. And look at them now! Time, patience, and a lot of love could work miracles, it seemed.

"Aren't you the love bug?" Kate cuddled Sunny close, then started back toward the house. "Let's go find Hazel and see how her afternoon is going."

✳ 19 ✳

Kate reached for two more apples, dropped them into the basket perched on the ladder's shelf, then checked behind her before she began her descent.

The way was clear, as all three of the cats were occupied with other pursuits.

Jerry was stretched out on the blanket of leaves on the ground, his orange belly turned toward what little warmth was offered by the late-afternoon sun. Maggie's approach caused him to bolt upright and give his cat sister a sniff.

"I'm glad you could join us," Kate told Maggie as she added the last of the apples to the large metal bucket at her feet. "It's too nice of an afternoon to spend lounging in the shed when you could be out here, helping me gather the last of the fruit."

Maggie wasn't interested in chores, however. She sashayed over to Hazel, who watched the cat's approach with keen eyes but a relaxed stance. Kate seemed to be the only one holding her breath, but she let out a sigh of relief when Maggie touched her little nose to Hazel's snout and the dog only blinked in return.

"Good girl," she told Hazel. "You too, Maggie. I'm glad you are starting to get acquainted. We might just be one big happy family yet. Where's Scout?"

Kate looked around and among her fruit trees, which were so few in number that she could hardly call it an orchard. Two with pears, three with apples; more than enough for what Kate needed or could even begin to give away.

The rustle of fallen leaves in the adjacent windbreak caught her attention, and then she spotted the big tuxedo cat dashing in her direction.

"There you are! Where have you ..."

The mouse in Scout's jaws was clearly dead, but Kate cringed just the same. "Now I know what you've been up to."

With a gleam of triumph in his eyes, Scout dropped his trophy in front of Kate's work boots.

"Way to go! I don't think there's been any cats around here for some time. Those rodents better watch out, huh? Mr. Scout is on the lookout."

There was just one pear tree left to check, and Kate felt a mix of satisfaction and melancholy as she moved her ladder. The trees were nearly dormant at this time of year, with only a few edible fruits remaining on their branches.

The rest were too small to amount to anything. They would eventually drop to the ground, where the wild critters that roamed her little acreage would find some passable snacks for the coming cold weather.

"The good ones are for us," she told Hazel, who'd come over to inspect the metal bucket of fruit. "I have more than enough for some pies, and there's that cookie recipe I want to try. Maybe I can take them to the post office. I'm sure they'll disappear fast if ... Hazel, what are you doing?"

The dog had her snout down in the galvanized bucket. Before Kate could even believe what she was seeing, Hazel snapped up one of the pears and took off across the yard.

"Hazel!" Kate hurried after the dog. Or at least, she tried. Her old work boots were stiff with dirt and mud, and their heavy soles were nowhere near as nimble as Hazel's paws.

"You don't need to eat that pear. Drop it!"

Hazel pretended not to hear, but she did stop long enough to give Kate an amused look before trotting off toward the now-barren garden.

"Leave it!" Kate tried again when she caught up with the dog, who only made a happy whimper around her prize and wagged her tail.

"Flattery won't work with me." Kate's firm tone was lost on Hazel, who dropped the pear in the dirt and, before Kate could snatch it up, took a bite out of its side. "No, don't do that!" As soon as Kate lunged toward the pear, Hazel picked it up again and ran for the far corner of the garden with Maggie at her heels. By the time Kate caught up to them, the dog had already pawed a hole in the cold dirt.

"You're going to save it for later?" Kate rolled her eyes. "Yeah, I can just imagine you'll want to come out here when there's a foot of snow on the ground and dig up a rotten pear and have it for dessert." She snatched up the fruit and put it, dirt and all, in her sweatshirt pocket. "I think you've been spending too much time watching the squirrels gather their nuts. You don't need that thing."

Kate expected a round of whimpers accompanied by a sad-eyed look meant to induce maximum amounts of guilt, but Hazel instead found something of interest to sniff under the now-barren bridal-wreath bushes.

"I guess that's one less pear I have to do something with." Kate started back to the orchard to retrieve the last of the season's bounty. "And I better get started on clearing out those flowerbeds."

With the last of the apples and pears safe inside the house, Kate rummaged around in the garage for a hoe and hedge clippers. The wind was picking up, and she raised the hood of her sweatshirt and tied its strings under her chin.

She'd been outside most of the day, walking a town route, but all that movement had kept her warm. But here, crouched on the north side of her home's foundation, her hands threatened to turn stiff with cold inside their chore gloves. Kate pulled and pruned as fast as she could, and the dried stalks soon began to pile up in the wheelbarrow.

Hazel was still running around the yard, and Maggie and Jerry had disappeared with no notice the way barn cats often did. Scout, however, lived up to his name. He stayed just ahead of Kate's progress, gave everything a good sniff before it was added to the wheelbarrow. When he decided their haul was big enough, he jumped up and settled in for a ride.

"Who's the king of the world? Or at least, this farm yard?" Kate laughed. "I have a feeling you've done this sort of thing before."

Scout only stayed on his perch for a few feet before he decided to abandon ship. But he ran on ahead, turning back several times to be sure Kate was still following him to the brush pile behind the chicken house. As Kate righted the wheelbarrow, and waited to see if Scout wanted a lift back to the house, her phone began to ring.

"It's Gwen!" Kate was pleased, but a little surprised. Although the ladies had exchanged numbers, they hadn't had a chance to chat. "I wonder what the deal is."

"Hey, are you at home?" Kate's neighbor sounded winded.

"Yeah, sure." Kate crossed her arms against the chill, as well as the unease she heard in Gwen's voice. "Scout's helping me clear out the flowerbeds around the house. Is everything OK?"

"I don't know, I just ..."

Gwen's next words cut out in a blast of wind, and then she was back. "I'm down here at the bridge with Maisie. We went for our walk and, oh, Kate! I'm really scared!"

"What happened?" The wheelbarrow was forgotten as Kate ran for the house.

"I found something in the ditch. I mean, Maisie found it." Gwen's voice rose in pitch. "I already called the sheriff, someone's coming over. But I'm supposed to wait right here until they do, and the boys are at practice."

Hazel had already started in Kate's direction with a wary look in her brown eyes, and Kate motioned her toward the back steps.

"I'm on my way," Kate promised Gwen as she hustled Hazel inside and grabbed her purse. Before she left, she locked all the doors. "I'll be there in a few minutes."

✳ ✳ ✳

Gwen sat on the bridge's metal railing, with Maisie settled at her side.

"Thank you so much for coming." Gwen raised her voice over the driving wind. The soybean field on the west side of the road had yet to be harvested, and the stalks swayed and roiled as if moved by an unseen hand. "Deputy Collins should be here soon, but I just couldn't ..."

"Don't worry about it." Kate raised her sweatshirt's hood and wished she'd reached for a heavier coat before she dashed out the door. "You shouldn't have to wait alone. What happened?"

Gwen and Maisie had passed over the bridge, which wasn't much more than a culvert with railings, as they made their way south for Maisie's afternoon walk. A pheasant had startled out of the bean field not long after they turned back toward home, and Maisie bolted after the bird.

While Gwen had Maisie on a leash, she hadn't had a firm enough grip on the lead to keep the dog at her side. Maisie never gave her any trouble, and little side trips into the ditches weren't a problem since it was rare to meet a vehicle on this road.

Gwen had waited on the gravel's shoulder as Maisie tunneled through the ditch's brown grass, ducked around the edge of the fence where it met the waterway, and tracked the pheasant along the creek. As expected, Maisie quickly lost interest and, after only one call of encouragement, started back along the waterway.

"But then, she stopped right there." Gwen pointed a little way up the creek. "I didn't know what she'd seen or smelled. No matter how I yelled to her to 'leave it,' she wouldn't. I worried she had some poor rabbit cornered, or something. So I went down there after her."

It wasn't an animal that Maisie had found along the creek's edge, hidden in the layers of decaying vegetation. It was a gasoline can. Red metal, with a bit of rust on its visible side. Gwen didn't know about the other; she was too terrified to touch the container.

"It's been there a while, I think." Gwen clasped her hands and gazed north toward the county blacktop, as if willing the deputy to hurry. "It doesn't look new, but I don't think it's been there for decades, either, if you know what I mean."

"It would be rusted through if it had been." Kate searched for an explanation other than the one already lodged in her mind. "Maybe some farmer tossed it. We need to keep these waterways clean, but that happens."

"It's too small." Gwen's certainty made Kate's stomach clench. "I know what you mean, but this isn't that kind. It doesn't hold much." She blinked away tears. "But it would certainly be enough to douse the side of a barn and set it on fire."

Maisie whimpered and Gwen reached down to give her dog a comforting pet. "You're a good girl, despite what I said earlier. We're supposed to leave the birds alone, remember? Especially that kind. But you were smart to point out what you found."

A cruiser came over the rise in the road, and Gwen sighed with relief. "There he is. Thank goodness."

Kate returned Deputy Collins' wave as he parked on the shoulder of the road. "I'm glad he got here as fast as he did." Trash along a creek wasn't normally even worth a call to the authorities, but the speed with which Steve arrived spoke to the fact the arson cases were a top priority.

"Good afternoon." Steve didn't bother with his hat when he got out of his cruiser. The wind on this wide-open road was strong enough to blow it away.

"Gwen, I'm glad you called this in. Let me get some gear, and we'll go see what's what."

Steve opened the trunk of his car and pulled out a plastic bag and gloves. Kate held Maisie's leash while Gwen guided the deputy down into the ditch and over to the creek. As they trudged off through the dead grass and weeds, Maisie whimpered and strained against her lead.

"I know, I know, you want to be right in the middle of everything." Kate soothed the dog with her free hand, then tightened her grip on Maisie's leash and stepped back into the weeds. "Someone's coming, let's stay out of the way."

An older-model sedan, likely a shade of burgundy under its layers of gravel dust, slowed and then came to a stop behind the cruiser. With a brief wave and a nod, a man with close-cropped gray hair got out of the car and started toward Kate and Maisie.

"Chester Donegan." He held out one calloused hand, and Kate shifted Maisie's leash to return the greeting. "You must be Kate."

"I am." Kate was a bit surprised, but then remembered no one had moved into this rural neighborhood in years. Process of elimination, along with a little gossip, made her a good guess. "Nice to meet you. I'm sorry I haven't made it around to everyone yet."

"No worries." Chester shrugged. "Everyone's busy." He was already focused on the sight of Steve and Gwen trudging through the tall grass. "I was on the blacktop, on the way home, when I saw the deputy's car up ahead. I went on after he turned south, but then I had to double back and see what was going on."

His blue eyes, so like his son's, turned back to Kate. They were full of questions.

"Maisie found something." Kate didn't know how much to say. "We're not sure yet if it's ... well, if it's important."

Chester said nothing, just looked at the dust-covered toes of his work boots. But his curiosity was palpable, and Kate wondered if he was only concerned about what had been found, or if he was also worried about who might have left it in that field.

Brody didn't do it, she reminded herself. *I can't believe he's behind all this.*

"I'm sorry things have been so difficult lately." Her words tumbled out in a rush. "This must be very hard for you. For your family."

"My son's been dragged through the mud." The lines on Chester's forehead deepened. "Maybe we could have raised him better, but we did the best we could. He's not a crazy fool, and he's not a criminal."

Kate didn't know what to say, so she simply nodded in understanding. Steve and Gwen were on their way back through the ditch, and his sack was no longer empty.

"Well, here they come now," Kate said lamely, desperate to fill the awkward silence. "Let's see what's going on."

Kate sensed Chester was eager for a better look at what was inside Steve's evidence bag, but the deputy barely broke his stride long enough for a nod of greeting before he went straight to his cruiser.

Gwen told Chester about the gas can, but cautioned it apparently held more questions than answers. "He doesn't know if it's of value, or not."

"It's unusual to find one of those these days," Deputy Collins said when he rejoined the group. "But not unheard of. Most people don't dump stuff like this, not anymore. I can remember when every farmer, my grandpa included, had a trash pile under a tree out in their field."

"That's why I was so shocked when Maisie found it." Gwen was more relaxed now that the errand was completed. "Why not just recycle it? Unless, of course, you didn't want anyone to find it."

Chester crossed his arms in a defensive gesture.

"I didn't mean ..." Gwen's voice trailed off as she shook her head sadly at her neighbor.

"Can you get fingerprints off it?" Kate asked Deputy Collins.

"I doubt it. It's pretty beaten up. Sun, rain, wind, wild animals; fingerprints are more fragile than most people realize. Even after a few days, out here?" He gestured at the empty fields around them. "We'll give it a go, of course, but that would be like winning the lottery."

The gas can was noticeably smaller than most, Steve reported, but there were no markings on it anywhere. Nothing that could help authorities trace where it had been purchased.

"Well, this just makes me mad." Gwen sighed with frustration. "And here I was hoping it would be some kind of lead." She gave Deputy Collins a level stare. "Do you have any at this point?"

Steve shook his head in defeat. "I wish we did, that we had something solid to go on. I'm sorry."

Chester's wind-whipped cheeks went from ruddy to an angry red. "So, let me get this straight. This guy, whoever he is, just rolls up on some old barn in the dark, dumps fuel on it, lights it and drives off?"

Steve didn't answer. There wasn't much he could say.

"And then," Chester continued, "he gets a wild hair, or whatever, and so-many nights later, he goes out and does it again? And again?" He threw his arms up in defeat. "When does this stop? What's it going to take?"

Kate understood Chester's frustration. She tried to focus on work, and the to-do list that would get her little farm ready for the coming winter. But sometimes, she'd wake in the wee hours and stare at her phone, there on the nightstand, and wonder if it was going to ring.

"It's been two weeks tonight since the fire at Flood Creek," Gwen reminded Chester. "Maybe we're lucky, and it's over."

"I'd like to think so." Chester's words were clipped and angry. "But even if there isn't another fire, what about those of us who've been affected? Where's the justice? This person needs to pay for what they've done!"

"I know this is difficult." Deputy Collins then paused for a moment, as if choosing his words carefully. "We appreciate any tips the public can give us, but we need to do this the right way."

There was no doubt his message was aimed at Chester. "People need to let us handle things. It won't help any of us if we end up with more trouble around here."

Chester looked down at the gravel, and Kate wondered what had been happening behind the scenes. Given the way Brody had shown up at the library meeting, angry and willing to confront Stan in front of dozens of other residents, she suspected both the father and the son had been conducting their own surveillance on the side.

"I want you to know that we're working this thing, everyone who's available, all hours of the day and night." Steve glanced at Kate, just for a second, but Gwen and Chester didn't seem to notice.

"But the truth is, arson cases are very difficult to prove. The vast majority are never solved. We can test samples from the site, confirm that an accelerant was used. But unless we can prove a certain person was at the scene when the fire occurred ..."

Steve put a hand on the arm of Chester's chore coat. The older man didn't shrug it off, and Kate thought she saw tears in his eyes.

"You may not be interested in this," the deputy said gently, "but there's support available for people who've been victimized by crime. There doesn't have to be bodily harm to do damage, if you know what I mean."

Chester only nodded. Given what little Kate knew about her neighbor, she suspected he and his son weren't likely to take advantage of such an offer. Keep a stiff upper lip, be a tough guy, don't talk about your feelings. She wondered how either of them would find a way to move on from this ordeal.

With a quick nod and a mumbled "see you around," Chester got in his car and drove away. Steve soon left, too. Once the ladies and Maisie were alone, Gwen looked at Kate and shook her head.

"I can't take much more of this. I know, my house is occupied, we shouldn't be a target. But I can't help it." She glanced toward the west, where the sun was dropping into a blanket of low clouds. "When it gets dark, my nerves amp up. The boys are usually with me, but they're so young; I try not to show how I'm feeling, how scared I get sometimes. How are you managing it, being alone?"

"I don't know," Kate said simply, then told Gwen about her nightly perimeter walks with Hazel. "We get inside before the sun goes down, and we stay there." She gave Maisie another pet. "Except for potty breaks, of course."

"We shouldn't have to live with this fear. But the deputy's right. I don't know what else they can do, at this point."

Kate thought of Alex's offer. Some nights, it was the one thing that kept her calm. She didn't intend to take him up on it, knew it wasn't likely to come to that, anyway. But it was a lifeline of sorts, the comfort that someone had her back, just in case. A lifeline she could extend to someone else who needed one.

"Tell you what." Kate smiled at Gwen. "We ladies need to stick together. You get too scared, really scared, you call me, OK?"

"Thanks." Gwen nodded. "You do the same."

"I will," Kate promised.

"I can't thank you enough for coming down." Gwen looked at Maisie, who was growing restless. "We should get home, there are chores to do." Then she gave Kate an unexpected hug. "We're having a few friends and their kids over on Halloween. If you aren't busy, try to join us."

"I'd like that." Kate waved as she started for her car. Suddenly, the wind out on this gravel road wasn't so cold. "When I'm done at the post office's open house, I'll stop by."

✳ 20 ✳

Kate's dad rolled the machine shed's door closed, and the rumble of its wheels on the metal track pierced the chilly air.

"Well, that's the end of it." Curtis looked up toward the building's peak and nodded with a mix of satisfaction and resignation. It was Sunday evening, and the harvest was over. "And just in time. Looks like rain is on the way."

"We always finish 'just in time,'" Kate said. "One way or another."

She had to smile at the "we." This was the first time in over a decade she'd been home for all of harvest season, and the hours clocked driving meals out to the fields and waiting in the drop-off line at the co-op had been worth it. She glanced around the farm yard, at the now-resting fields that surrounded it, and felt a sense of peace. And, maybe, a little loss.

Halloween was just three days away. Then Thanksgiving, Christmas ... where had the year gone? This time last year, her life had been very different.

Like night and day, she thought as the sun's last rays peeked out from behind the gathering clouds. Kate tried not to think about Ben too much; and her emotional pain had eased. But when she was in a reflective mood, the feelings all came rushing back. The good, as well as the bad.

Waylon nosed her jeans for a pet, and she knelt down to rub his ears. She glanced up to see her dad watching her closely, and brushed at her eyes before she stood. Was he getting misty-eyed, too?

Apparently, yes. But for a different reason.

"It means so much to have you back," he said as they started for the house, Waylon in the lead. The last of the fallen leaves skittered before them in the gathering breeze, and crunched under the soles of their work boots.

"To have both our children here, for harvest and everything else, well … Honey, I know the last year has been hard for you, several times over. Your mom and I, we just want you to be happy. That's all we've ever wanted. But if you can be happy here, well, that makes *us* really happy."

The ham-and-potato soup simmering in a slow cooker and the cinnamon rolls still in the oven made Kate's mouth water. Her cheeks were aflame thanks to the quick switch from cold wind to warm kitchen, but she didn't care. Right now, there was nowhere else she'd rather be.

The rest of Kate's immediate family had already gathered around the dining-room table, and a card game was in progress. "We're in here!" Anna called out to Kate and Curtis. "Is everyone tucked in for the night?"

Curtis took his usual chair. "Yep. The combines and the cows, both."

"And Waylon has his supper, and so do the cats." Kate found her seat at the table. It was the one she'd occupied for years, growing up, and it was always waiting for her. "Deal me in." She smiled at her mom. "It smells amazing out there. When do we eat?"

* * *

Kate was tempted to attend Monday night's council meeting, but decided she was too tired, and too stressed, to listen to any more arguing and yelling about burning leaves.

Besides, it had become clear in the past few weeks which way the council wanted to go.

While the pro-burn residents were numerous and vocal, they were clearly in the minority. Most residents favored scrapping one of Eagle River's long-standing traditions to gain increased safety and improved air quality, so Kate wasn't surprised to get a text just after eight relaying the council had just voted 4-1 to snuff out residential burning in their community.

Who the message was from, however, was a pleasant surprise.

I thought you might be here, Alex's text said. *I was sure you'd attend to see the circus, if nothing else. There isn't any popcorn, but Stan put on quite the show during the comments before the vote.*

Detective Duncan needed a night off, she replied.

Kate hadn't had time to take those apples and pears to the bar, and offered to do so the following afternoon. But Alex said he planned to come by the post office during the Halloween open house, so she could save herself a trip.

"He's an odd one," she told Hazel, who thumped her tail in response. "A little old to be out trick-or-treating. Well, I guess that's one less thing on my to-do list for the rest of the week."

A velvety brown paw batted the brush that lay idle in Kate's lap, and she laughed. "Yes, King Charles, we were in the middle of something, weren't we? I promise, no more disruptions until we're done."

* * *

Kate was snapped out of a deep sleep by the chime of her phone. Charlie startled on the side of her pillow, his guttural "meow" a clear indicator he didn't appreciate this intrusion, either. Hazel remained at the foot of the bed, but watched Kate with cautious eyes as she fumbled to pick up the call.

"Kate!" Auggie shouted. "My God, I can't believe this is happening!"

She knew there was another fire. Had to be. The only question was: where?

"Is it the co-op?" she blurted out, still half-asleep.

A loud gasp was the only answer at first. "Oh, no, thank goodness." Angry silence. "They'd better not get any ideas. We're shut down in the wee hours, of course, but I have cameras up everywhere. It's another old house this time, just west of Mapleville."

Kate dropped back on her pillow and closed her eyes. Maybe it was the late hour, or the weeks of worry and cumulative exhaustion, but the usual wave of fear and dread, mixed with anticipation to hear the details, had yet to arrive.

Numb. That was the best way to describe how she felt. Maybe it was good not to overreact, as this situation was out of her control. At the same time, Kate realized this was exactly the reaction the arsonist hoped to elicit from the community as the number of cases continued to grow.

If people resigned themselves to the violence and upheaval, let down their collective guard, the arsonist truly had the upper hand. Who knew how long this might go on? Whoever it was, they certainly hadn't been deterred by the failed burn up at the Flood Creek site.

"What happened this time?" She sighed. "I can't believe I'm saying this, but is there anything new? Did they spray-paint graffiti on the house before they lit it, or something like that?"

"Nope. Same pattern of behavior as before."

Empty old house set back from the road. Overgrown vegetation that made it harder to get the pumper trucks close to the structure. Multiple fires set inside.

"I've got half a mind to head up to the old home place and take my hunting rifle with me. This guy had better not get it into his head to pay the Benniger homestead a visit."

Kate blinked. She hadn't thought about that. That house had been empty for years. And it was at the end of a long lane, over a quarter-mile from the road. If someone was looking to make a statement by setting places on fire, Auggie's ancestral farm would be hard to ignore.

"Do not go up there! Are you listening to me? Don't do it." She was out of bed now, and padded to the window to stare out into the night.

There were no answers outside, just the moon and the bare-limbed trees of her windbreak shivering in the wind. "You're crazy, Auggie, but you're not stupid."

He guffawed at first, then turned petulant. "You sound like Jane."

"Jane's a smart woman," Kate countered. "And she puts up with you, so she's a saint. Besides, this guy has a pattern. He only hits one place a night."

It had been over two weeks since the last fire, but the arsonist apparently wasn't done. Halloween was only two days away; actually, since it was already past midnight, the holiday was tomorrow. Kate wondered if this nightmare was building toward some sort of grand finale, like a fireworks show.

But she tried to focus on the practical side of things to ease her rising fears and hopefully keep Auggie from doing something foolish. "Wait a second; that house is brick. And the roof is, what, tile? It wouldn't burn the way the others have. And I think this guy wants a big show. He wants a structure to collapse like a house of cards."

"You're right." Auggie was relieved, but he hated to admit it. "The home place must be off the list, then. Good thinking, and for the middle of the night. Are you sure you're not a detective or something?"

Kate had to smile in the dark. "I'm a mail carrier, so you're close. Which means I have a long day ahead of me tomorrow. So do you, I'm sure. We're done harvesting, but I bet you have some customers still in the fields. Go back to sleep. Let the authorities handle this."

"OK, fine. At least, for a few hours. And I bet you'll have an interesting day, what with your top-secret visitor showing up at the post office again. Might as well give him Roberta's desk. See ya."

And with that, Auggie hung up.

Kate crossed back to the bed and stroked Hazel's coat. "It's OK, let's go back to sleep. And he's right, I'm sure the marshal will be there in the morning."

Then she looked at Charlie. "Wait. How does he know about that? No one's supposed to ..."

Auggie always said he knew everything that went on in Hartland County. She shouldn't be surprised. So, who spilled the beans? Kate decided if she had to place a bet, she'd put her money on Jack.

* * *

The mood around the back-room tables at the Eagle River post office was clearly subdued the next morning. Even Randy's outlook was dim. "Makes you wonder if people will even turn out for our little festival tomorrow night. I'm certainly not in a celebratory mood."

Jack nodded. "It's bad enough for us adults, but what about the kids? You know even the little ones have overheard something, by now. Are they going to be too afraid to go trick-or-treating, even if their parents are with them?"

"That would be a real shame." Bev frowned as she prepared her packages for delivery. "The fires themselves are destructive enough. But people were getting their hopes up that this was over. And here we are, dealing with this again."

Mae pulled a sheet of foil off the large pan she'd set on the end of one counter, revealing a tray of caramel-covered apples rolled in chopped nuts and miniature chocolate chips.

"I couldn't resist, even with how things are going around

here." She thought for a moment. "Or maybe, I was determined to make them despite what's going on."

"I'm so glad you went to all that trouble." Bev gave Mae a warm smile. "They look delicious."

Kate yawned. "These are just what we needed! It's going to be a long day. Auggie called me with the scoop, first thing. After that kind of wake-up call, it's nearly impossible to get back to sleep."

"Same here." Randy rubbed his chin. "Once you're awake, at that hour, all the thoughts start to circle around, don't they? The worries creep in, then the doubts. And before you know it, an hour's gone by. Or two."

Always practical, Mae had also brought a box of zip-top bags for the carriers to take their treats on the road. Allison took an apple off the tray with a nod of thanks to Marge. "Who needs ghosts and goblins when there's an arsonist lurking about?"

"Empty houses only," Aaron reminded everyone. "Ours are all occupied, of course. So, I'd say we're safe."

Mae raised an eyebrow. "Well, I don't know. Last night's fire could indicate a change in pattern."

Kate doubted that, but Mae raised an interesting idea. While the most-recent house was unoccupied and its lawn overgrown with weeds, it had only been vacant for a month or so. The property's owner, a man in his seventies, had recently moved to New Hampton to live with one of his daughters. A widower, he'd been at the farm for several years with a girlfriend until his adult children convinced him the property was too rundown to be habitable much longer, especially with winter coming.

While it had been difficult enough for the man's family to convince him to leave, word was it was even harder to get his girlfriend to vacate the property. It took threats of having the sheriff serve her with eviction papers before the woman could be convinced to pack her bags.

"I know where you're going with that," Randy told Mae. "But I don't think Geneva's capable of such nonsense."

"Well, she's hurt, and angry," Jack put in. "Her boyfriend dumped her. She had to get an apartment here in town. Even so, I don't think that's enough motivation to set the place on fire."

Allison glared at Jack, and Kate wondered if their disagreement about Brody still simmered, several weeks later. "And even if she did it; what about the others? She'd have no reason to burn the rest."

Roberta soon came in the back door, her cheeks aflame from the cold wind. "Barney is on his way in." She didn't have to say more, as everyone knew Jared was out due to last night's fire. "But I don't think this should wait, the rest of you have to get on the road. We need to chat for a moment."

"What did I do now?" Jack asked around a mouthful of caramel apple.

"Nothing, but the day is young." Roberta unloaded her coat and purse, then motioned for the carriers to gather around one of the tables. "I know things have been tough around here lately. And I'm afraid it might get worse before it gets better. Sheriff Preston called this morning."

Kate's sluggish mind snapped to attention. What now?

"He wanted me to remind all of you to be on guard until this is resolved, one way or another," Roberta said. "Someone is behind all this, but the authorities don't yet know who."

"Or at least, they won't say," Randy added.

"I asked about that, specifically, and was told they have no suspects as of this morning." Roberta threw up her hands. "Take that as you will. Last night was number four! But this person is, as you all may have guessed, becoming bolder by the day."

She seemed to choose her next words carefully. "We need to be vigilant, as always. But whatever happens, do not engage in conversation or speculation about what is going on." Roberta looked around the table. "We are not to put ourselves in harm's way. He specifically told me to share that with all of you."

On one hand, Kate thought, that was obvious advice. Safety always came first. But in all her years with the post office, she'd never been given a warning quite like this one.

Roberta rubbed the side of her face. "And then, just as I was about to leave home, I got a call from the shift leader at the regional parcel delivery warehouse. Sounds like everyone's been put on alert."

It wasn't just the mail carriers and package crews, Roberta said. Milk-tank drivers, propane-delivery services, everyone with routes in the rural areas of the county had received the same ominous message.

"So, drop your packages with a smile, as always. But do your best to skirt these conversations. And if you feel uneasy about someone, or sense any sort of threat or suspicious behavior, retreat to your vehicle immediately. Once you are down the road, pull over and call me, right away. I'll handle it from there."

"Did somebody confront someone?" Jack wanted an answer.

"What did they ..." Aaron started to say.

"I don't know." Roberta cut them both off with a wave of one hand. "Honestly, I don't. All I know is, we're all supposed to be very careful."

"You know, old Mac Feldman carried a gun, sometimes," Randy mentioned casually. "I mean, not on the days when Shep was with him. Just his hunting rifle. Kept it under the seat, I guess."

Kate wished she'd met Mac. What a character! Grandpa Wayne surely had stories to share. But Roberta just put her hands over her face and shook her head.

"What's the matter, boss?" Jack elbowed her in an attempt to restore Roberta's usual good humor. "Would that be against federal regulations? I don't recall you caring too much about the handbook."

Roberta rolled her eyes, but then she smiled. Just a bit. "Must I say it more plainly?" She set her sights on Randy this time. "Don't do anything stupid."

"Are you going to be OK out there?" Bev whispered to Kate as they went back to sorting their stacks. "I've never given much thought to the fact that we work alone, but we do."

"I'll manage." Kate was grateful to have such a supportive friend. "Do you want to text each other, say, every hour or so, just to share our locations?"

"I'd like that. The buddy system is a good one."

The caramel apples continued to disappear from the tray. Just before the last of the carriers headed out, Mae went into the break room and came back with a plastic food container.

"For the marshal," she told Kate as she boxed up the last two apples. "He's part of the team these days, and somehow I think he's going to need a treat or two once he gets in. I'll leave them in the fridge and put a note on the door."

* 21 *

"It's the night for ghosts and goblins to be lurking about." Kate pulled on her black sweatshirt and adjusted her matching leggings. "Hazel, I hope you understand why you can't have free rein tonight. We'll do a potty break before I go, then I want you locked inside until my return."

She glanced at the kitchen clock, and exhaled. "Which will be many hours before the stroke of midnight, thank goodness."

Despite the talk around town about the last victim's lady friend, Kate continued to lean on her hunch the arsonist was a man. And just like the secretive creatures that folklore claimed roamed about on All Hallows Eve, he might be out tonight, as well.

Even so, Kate was determined not to let her fears ruin the fun. This was supposed to be a night of calculated frights, lots of treats, and a little seasonal spirit thrown in for good measure. Eagle River's Halloween celebration ran from six until eight and, once the post office was tidied up and ready for tomorrow, she wanted to stop at Gwen's for at least a few minutes.

Social invitations, other than those extended by her family, had been nearly nonexistent since Kate returned home that spring. The carriers were a tight-knit bunch but they rarely gathered outside of work, and attending Melinda's fall celebration had reminded Kate how much she enjoyed being out and about and meeting new people.

Supper at her farm had been early tonight, as Kate had to be back at the post office at five-thirty. The quick holiday meal had been boring at best, consisting of frozen pizza for Kate and the usual kibble for all her pets, but there'd been a bit of warmed-up chicken gravy added to the barn cats' snacks for a Halloween treat. Charlie had been rewarded with a generous helping of his favorite organic catnip, and the new pumpkin-shaped stuffie seemed to be a hit with Hazel.

"Sorry, I need that." Kate reached for the end of the fake black tail Charlie batted about on the kitchen's linoleum floor. "It goes with my headband's ears. I hope you don't mind that I'm channeling Scout tonight, instead of you. I don't have a white patch on the front of my sweatshirt, but I do have white shoes and socks. Your brown-and-tan fluff is too hard to replicate."

Charlie just stared at her, lost in a catnip-induced haze, and only managed one flip of his tail in response.

Kate checked her tote bags for the umpteenth time. Had she forgotten anything? Along with bags of candy and some decorative items for the lobby, she'd packed a dozen of the last of the pears and apples for Alex.

As Kate started for the garage, she noticed that the wind was rising and a chill was in the air. She glanced toward the machine shed, and saw the dark silhouette of a feline in the closest window, surrounded by the glow of the lone light left on inside. It was one of her barn kitties, keeping watch in the night. And rather than being a frightening sight, it warmed Kate's heart.

Gwen's home was lit up, too. Kate spied several cars in the yard as she rolled past, and spotted a handful of costumed kids running around on the lawn with Maisie.

More merriment was on display in Eagle River. Several of

Main Street's storefronts glowed from within. Strings of orange and purple lights outlined some of the windows, and the festive vibe made Kate tap the steering wheel along to the tunes on the radio. By the time she came in the back door of the post office, she was certainly in a celebratory mood.

"Well, hello, Pooh Bear!" she called to Bev, who had wedged herself into Roberta's office chair despite her rotund costume. "When will your transformation be complete?"

"The very last second before the kids show up." Bev gestured to Pooh's head, which waited on the closest counter. "That thing is hot, even with those vents on the side."

"It looks a little morbid. Like someone beheaded the poor guy. He's still grinning, though." Kate gestured at her black sweats. "I have to commend you for getting, so, well, into the spirit of things. This was all I could come up with. I'll have to 'meow' a lot to make it seem more real."

"One of my teacher friends recommended Pooh. She's rented this getup several times for literacy programs in her classroom. 'It's comfortable,' she said." Bev waved a hand in front of her face, fanning herself. "I'm not sure I agree."

The carriers each carved a pumpkin yesterday afternoon, and their creations were now aglow along the front counter. Lit only by battery-operated candles, of course. To boost the spirit of competition, Roberta had promised a Peabody's gift card to the carrier who won the public vote.

The plan to offer apple-bobbing for the kids had ebbed away due to questions about food safety and sanitation, along with the possibility of having to mop water off the lobby's floor. Instead, Roberta had settled on Pin the Tail on the Donkey. All in all, it would be an old-fashioned Halloween at the Eagle River post office.

"Who goes there?" Roberta cackled as she came in from the parking lot, then made a dramatic sweep with her red-lined witch's cape. "Well, my pretties, I see you're all ready for tonight's festivities!"

"I like your warts," Kate said. "Is that hat going to stay on, though?"

"It had better." Roberta tipped her head and its pointy topper this way and that, testing her efforts. "Haven't had this many bobby pins on my scalp since the last time I used those scratchy rollers to curl my hair. Which has been decades, I'd say."

Kate reached for one of the oversized plastic bowls that waited on the counter, and ripped open a pouch of individually wrapped chocolate bars. "I'm not going to be able to resist these. I think I can take a few in the form of a tip. After all, I found them on sale over in Swanton."

"I'm going to add some to my growing stash," Bev said. "I mean, if we have leftovers."

Many residents had left treats in their mailboxes that day. At a few farms on Kate's rural route, some of the little ones had even offered greeting cards.

"Be sure you fill out that reimbursement form," Roberta reminded Kate. "You're too young for this; but, Bev, I'm sure you remember when Halloween treats had more variety."

"They sure did. One of our neighbors made the best snickerdoodle cookies." Then Bev's smile faded. "Of course, times have changed. Now, everything has to come shrink-wrapped from a factory. You can't trust people nowadays, not like we did back then."

The post office's jubilant mood vanished, just like that.

"So, what do we think is going to happen tonight?" Kate brought up the ghost in the room. "My neighbor invited me to stop by her party on my way home. I'd like to go, there's no reason not to. But, I don't know."

Roberta and Bev exchanged a worried look.

"I'm wondering that, myself." Roberta shook her head. "Tonight's the night for mayhem, and not all of that is the good-natured kind."

"Will the arsonist strike?" Bev wondered. "Or will he pass

up that opportunity, knowing everyone expects him to do something? After all, this is supposed to be the scariest night of the year."

"That's just it." Roberta squared her witch's hat. "He's got us in a tizzy, every one of us. Night after night, watching and waiting. I don't know if I'm more scared at this point, or just angry." She sighed. "And poor Marshal Werner. He's becoming quite a regular around here. As nice as he is, I keep hoping we'll never see him again."

She glanced at the clock. "I'm going to try to forget all this nonsense, at least for a few hours. We're about to have a couple hundred little ghosts and goblins come through here, and I don't want any of them to sense that something might be wrong."

The ladies hurried to wrap up the last decorating details. Or, at least, Kate rushed around the post office. Roberta's cape kept threatening to get caught in the swinging door into the lobby, while Bev tried her best to toddle back and forth. "I'm getting into character, I guess," she told Kate. "Pooh doesn't exactly sprint around, does he?"

Lengths of ragged black cheesecloth were draped in the corners of the lobby windows to resemble spooky spider webs, and an oversized arachnid was added to one side to bring the theme home. The already-hung leaf garlands, as well as the carved pumpkins on the counter, added to the festive vibe. An additional coffeemaker Bev brought from home was set up on a side table to offer warm cider to their guests.

With the candy bowls in place, Roberta brought out what she expected would be the real treat of the night for the adults.

"The holiday stamps have arrived!" She set the stack on one end of the counter. "We have some of the fall special-edition sheets left, too. But these will get everyone looking ahead to the next season."

Bev waddled over to give the Christmas-themed designs a look. "Oh, those are cute. I really like the reindeer one. You know, some years, the post office goes with more of a serious, religious theme. But I think I like these whimsical ones the best."

Roberta had already made a sign for the holiday stamps, which she taped to the front of the counter.

"A few of our serious collectors were asking about these weeks ago, already. I suspect some of them will swing by tonight."

The post office was bright and festive, and the warm cider filled the air with a comforting, spicy scent. Although a cloud of uncertainty loomed over Eagle River on this frightful night, Kate couldn't help but clap her hands with glee. "Well, it's showtime! Here come our first little visitors now."

"Pooh, you'd better go find your head." Roberta tried another sweep of her cape as she went to unlock the front door. "Maybe I'll get the hang of this thing yet."

The next two hours were filled with fun and laughter. Kate was surprised at how many of the little ghosts and goblins had never played such an old-fashioned game. It was a world away from the screen-based activities they were accustomed to, and they found it fun to put on their blindfolds and, with the assistance of Pooh Bear and their parents, try to hit their target.

Kate kept the candy bowls full and handed out cups of cider, while Roberta presided over the counter and helped out with whatever was needed.

The holiday stamps were a hit, just as Roberta had predicted, and several customers even asked about shipping deadlines for Christmas deliveries.

How time flies, Kate thought as she peered out the plate-glass windows long enough to enjoy the sight of all the trick-or-treaters parading up and down Main Street. *It won't be long before this year is over, and another one begins.*

And then, she spotted a sort-of-familiar truck pulling up in front of the post office. Her heartbeat sped up, just a little; but this time, it wasn't from fear or worry.

Alex came in the door and gave her a big grin. "Nice costume." He chuckled. "Does the infamous Scout know you're channeling him tonight? Are you going around tripping people to keep in character?"

Kate frowned. "How did ..."

"Oh, I hear all kinds of things." But as he stepped closer, he lowered his voice. "Way to go, Detective Duncan," he said sincerely. "And I think Hazel deserves an award for her bravery that night. Too bad she can't get the recognition she deserves."

Between running a bar and being the police chief's cousin, it was no wonder Alex had the scoop. Roberta was possibly listening in, so Kate only smiled. "And where is your costume?" she asked.

He looked down at his faded Wildcats sweatshirt and shrugged. "Grumpy bartender doesn't count? We'll be busy tonight. I gotta be able to stay on my toes."

Kate handed out cider to a young princess and a little ninja, then tipped her head toward the back room. "I have your apples and pears; I'll bring them up."

When she returned to the lobby, Alex was at the counter, chatting with Roberta.

"You got here just in time," Roberta said. "It's a good thing I have more of these holiday stamps on order, we're just about out."

"Helen would never forgive me if I didn't pick these up for her." Alex then turned to Kate. "My aunt is quite the collector."

"Your aunt?" Kate was caught off guard. Ray Calcott had been Eagle's River's police chief for several years now, but he wasn't a local. Other than the fact that Alex was his cousin, Kate didn't know anything about Ray's family. Until now.

"Helen's usually one of the first in line when there's a new edition," Roberta explained to Kate as she swiped Alex's credit card. "How's her knee doing?"

"Much better, thanks. But she didn't want to mess with the crowds tonight. Besides, I'm taking some groceries over there tomorrow. I told her I'd bring these along. Working on her stamp books helps pass the time these days."

"Well, I'm sure she appreciates you stopping in. And Ray, too. I know the sheriff and the marshal are leading the investigations, but our town's resources have been stretched thin."

"They sure have." Alex tucked the package of stamps carefully under his arm and reached for Kate's sack of apples and pears. "Thanks again. I'll get this tote back to you soon."

"Sure, no rush." She returned his grin. "Happy Halloween!"

As Kate went back to her duties, a big smile remained on her face. Of course, there could be more than one Helen in Alex's life. It could all be some sort of Halloween-night joke. A trick of the mind, a distraction that might send Kate down a dead end of getting any sort of hopes up about Alex. And where, if she decided she wanted him to, that he might fit into her life.

Just as likely, however, was that this was an unexpected treat. The name was rather old-fashioned, not common for women from Kate's generation. Kate decided she'd had enough doubt and fear lately to last for some time. Maybe she needed to look on the bright side again, if only on this special night, and give things a chance.

* 22 *

Kate was glad she took the time to stop at Gwen's party. She met a few other neighbors, and her costume sparked more good-natured laughter about Scout. But despite her high spirits, there had been a bit of trepidation when she turned up her own lane just before ten. Would anything happen that night? If so, where?

But nothing did.

November rolled in with a day of dark clouds and howling winds; but by Friday afternoon, the weather settled into a pattern of calm, clear skies. There had been talk about having to delay the Bauers' controlled burn, but the sudden switch to near-perfect conditions made many in the community, including the elderly couple, breathe a sigh of relief.

"I'm glad you suggested we ride together," Kate told Melinda as Lizzie, Horace's old farm truck, bumped down the gravel on Saturday morning. "I'm not sure how many people will be there that I know. It's too bad Karen had to work today, or she could have joined us."

"They're expecting quite the crowd." Melinda gripped the leather-clad steering wheel tight as she started to turn west toward the Wildwood farm. Lizzie grunted in protest, then finally complied. "It's going to be like riding a roller coaster, or watching a scary movie. You'll get the rush of adrenaline, but know you're safe, at the same time. People won't pass up the chance to gawk at something like this."

Dozens of vehicles were already parked in makeshift rows in the mowed-down front pasture. Melinda pointed out how the unruly grass and weeds around the house had also been cleared away just days ago to provide a generous safety zone for the fire crews and the spectators.

Kate had never seen the old Wildwood place, yet her sinking heart recognized its forlorn appearance. An old barn leaned so far to the east, it looked as if the next strong wind would cause its collapse. A few sheds, their red paint nearly worn away, dotted the yard. Only one had an intact roof.

Melinda said the house was one of the oldest in the township, built not long after the Civil War. Its second story wasn't much more than a steep-pitched roof with a narrow window at each end. The front porch listed at an odd angle, like a broken arm, and the stoop's floorboards looked as if they wouldn't support more weight than that of the squirrels and raccoons that now called this desolate place home.

"I can see why Ed and Mabel thought it would make a good wildlife refuge." Kate leaned forward to get a better look through Lizzie's dust-covered windshield. "Look at all those old trees. And nature has pretty much taken over here already."

"Bart and Marge couldn't keep up with all the work as they got older." Melinda turned down the newest row of vehicles and eased a chugging Lizzie into line. "She has dementia, and his health's not good. They had a farm sale this summer, but the house was too far gone for anyone to want to fix it up."

Dozens of firefighters milled around an impressive array of pumper trucks east of the driveway. Corey and Jared were somewhere in that crew, but Kate couldn't pick them out while they were in their gear. "It's quite the show of force. How many departments are participating today?"

"Four, I think." Melinda didn't bother to lock Lizzie before she pulled on her knit gloves. The sun was bright, but there was still a chill in the air.

"Prosper, Eagle River, Swanton and Charles City. There might be some folks from farther away than that, out in the crowd. While hands-on training is crucial, Auggie told me other departments can pick up pointers just by observing."

Kate laughed. "Did he, now? I didn't know he was an expert on firefighting."

"He's an expert on everything, remember?"

There was only one Hartland County cruiser in the sea of first responders' vehicles, and Kate spotted Sheriff Jeff Preston in uniform, chatting with Tony Bevins, Prosper's fire chief.

She wondered how many other law enforcement members were there as well, and guessed they had dressed down to blend in as they sized up the crowd.

Kate and Melinda found Mabel in a small group chatting under a gnarled oak tree.

"How are you holding up?" Kate asked Mabel as she looked around the yard at the growing throng of onlookers. "This is quite the turnout."

Despite Mabel's warm smile, there was a wariness in her eyes. "I just hope the one they want is here."

Kate agreed, but knew it was unlikely someone would be apprehended today. Unless somebody did something really crazy, drew too much attention to themselves in some odd way, they wouldn't stand out in this large crowd. Everyone was bulked up in coats and boots, chatting and greeting friends as they sipped their coffee on a brisk late-fall morning.

Given the jovial mood of the onlookers, this could have been a farm auction, with a lunch stand selling pie and sandwiches and tables full of treasures to sift through.

But the rundown house waiting forlornly on the north

edge of the lawn, with firefighters swarming in and out as they made their preparations, told a different story.

"It's so sad it came to this," Kate said to Mabel as she gestured around them. "The house, the outbuildings, all of it. But I can see they are beyond repair."

"I remember this house in its heyday, long before it started to go downhill. It's a shame, really. A piece of history about to go up in flames." Mabel then tipped her head to the right. "Over there, by that shed? That's Bart and Marge's son and his wife. The daughter said she wasn't up for this, it's too emotional. I told her, I understand completely."

"But it's for a good cause," Melinda reminded Mabel as she gave her a hug. "Maybe twice over, given what we've all been through over the past month or so."

"Thanks, honey." Mabel blinked back a few tears. "I needed that."

"So, are you going to make a speech?" Kate tried to lighten the mood. "I mean, is there going to be some sort of lighting ceremony?"

Mabel barked out a laugh. "Like the Olympics? It's funny you mentioned that, though. Ed and I were asked to say a few words, but we declined. It's not about us, it's about the animals. But Everett, the conservation officer we've been working with, stepped up. He's offered to emcee for us."

Mabel pointed to a cluster of people talking and laughing by one corner of the house. It took Kate a moment, since Everett wasn't in his county work gear, but then she picked him out. "Oh, yeah. I ran into him at the nature preserve a while back. Nice guy. Very smart."

"He's divorced," Mabel said in a stage whisper that made Kate blush.

"*What?*"

"Just thought I'd point that out," Mabel added in a sing-song voice. "We get this arson nonsense resolved, maybe you can move on to other things, huh?"

Melinda had already been absorbed into a cluster of her neighbors, so Kate ambled across the roughly mowed yard to where Grandpa Wayne and some of his friends had congregated.

"No Grandma today?"

"Nope. She'd rather go grocery shopping, I guess. Too barbaric for her. I told her it's for a noble cause, but no dice."

Harvey pointed out an older woman now chatting with Mabel. "My wife didn't want to come, either," he told Kate. "But I reminded her, this is a big day for our family. Once this place is restored to its natural state, I think she'll be glad she was here for the start of it."

Grandpa Wayne gasped when a younger man with a tripod in one hand and a backpack over his other arm stepped out of the crowd. "Well, look at that. Guess they're going to record the whole show."

"This is an invaluable training opportunity for all the crews." Kate heard the pride in Harvey's voice. "I hear they're going to make the most of it. Tony gave us the lowdown the other day."

After the firefighters ensured the old house had been stripped of anything of value, they'd stocked its rooms with a scattering of wooden pallets and straw bales to feed the flames. The plan was to start several fires inside and one on the weathered siding, let them gain traction, then have the crews move in and work those scenes.

Once those exercises were completed, the chiefs would give the go-ahead for a complete burn down. The crews' tactics would then turn toward containing the fire and extinguishing it in a way that didn't put the firefighters or the land around the house in more jeopardy than was necessary.

Kate thought of the arson cases and the accelerants found at the scenes. "How are they going to set the fires?"

Grandpa Wayne laughed. "Diesel fuel, we hear. And, get this: potato chip bags."

Kate stared at him in disbelief.

"No, really!" He looked to Harvey for support, and Mabel's brother nodded in agreement. Grandpa gestured toward the gaping hole that used to house the kitchen door, which had been pulled from its rusted hinges and tossed in the dead grass.

"They take them in there, light them up and toss them on the straw bales. Of course, the fire here on the outside corner? They'll just light that with a big stick, I guess."

While Grandpa and his friends turned their chatter toward the end of harvest, Kate studied the dozens of firefighters hanging around their trucks and recalled what Corey told her about the chiefs' list. A few faces looked familiar, folks she'd spotted around Eagle River or perhaps handed a package to recently. What if the arsonist was here today, but he was in uniform?

That thought was so unnerving that Kate set it aside to give the growing throng another review, now that the burn was about to begin.

Alex hadn't come; or at least, she'd yet to pick him out of the crowd. But there was Stan, huddled with a group of men his age. And she spotted Brody and Chester, looking weary and wary, beyond where the back porch splintered away from the house. Was that Deputy Collins, there in that group across the way? He was out of uniform but, yes, that was him. That must be his wife, Kate decided. Jen had gone to school with Melinda.

And then, Kate spotted another familiar face. Marshal Werner, coffee mug in hand, was chatting with Ed and two other men Kate didn't recognize.

The marshal's presence both comforted Kate and raised her suspicions about what might happen that morning. Without his laptop bag, and sporting a dusty chore coat and a worn ball cap, Gage Werner could be any other man in this crowd. A neighbor, a friend, a well-meaning gawker who was willing to give up a few hours on Saturday morning to witness firsthand what his buddies would be talking about at the office on Monday.

Marshal Werner was the highest-ranking official at this event. But not one person was staring at him, gesturing to their friends about the state investigator standing just a few feet away.

Smart guy, Kate thought. *No wonder you were so eager to take Roberta up on her offer of a hangout at the post office. Only a few people here even know who you are.*

Sheriff Preston and his handful of deputies were well-known throughout the county. It would be difficult for them to hang out anywhere, even in civilian clothes, and not be recognized by someone. That made Kate wonder where else the marshal had been in the past few weeks, dressed down and blending in, getting a feel for the locals and following up on leads.

As far as Kate knew, there wasn't anything solid to go on. But that didn't mean anything. After all, what good was a hot tip if it tipped off someone that they were being scrutinized?

"Looks like they are about to start." Grandpa Wayne could hardly contain his glee as a handful of firefighters, their thick coats emblazoned with their hometowns, pulled hoses from the pumper truck closest to the house.

Kate gave him the side-eye.

"What?" Grandpa snorted. "Don't tell me you're not excited about this."

She could only shrug and take a gulp of her coffee. Despite her concerns, she had to admit this would be fascinating to watch.

The rest of the onlookers seemed to feel the same. As the fire crews made their way around the foundation, and gallons of high-pressure water soaked the ground surrounding the house, gasps of curiosity and murmurs of anticipation swept through the crowd.

Tony soon broke away from the huddle of officials gathered near the closest pumper truck. Cordless microphone in hand, he walked toward the front of the house. Once there, he held up his hands to get everyone's attention.

"Thanks for coming out today. This is going to be a great opportunity for all of us, and we're so grateful to the Bauers for making it happen."

There was a round of rousing applause. Mabel gave a sheepish grin and a shy wave to the onlookers. Ed did the same before he lifted his wool cap in acknowledgement, which brought a chuckle from many of the onlookers.

"I think we can promise you quite a show," Tony told the crowd. "But this isn't a simulation, so there are a few things we all need to keep in mind."

The crowd had to remain beyond the simple rope-and-post fence that had been set up across the south lawn. That was for everyone's safety, but also to leave plenty of staging room for the fire trucks and crews. And while folks were welcome to hang around and observe for as long as they liked, Tony urged everyone to stay alert.

"We have a plan, but we can't promise exactly how this thing's going to come down. That's the danger in what we do, and why this training is so important. Along with that, any significant change in wind direction or speed means you all must be ready to clear out of here, and fast. If we tell you to move, you need to do it."

Nods and affirmations of agreement came from the crowd. "Great," Tony said. "Now, here's what we expect to happen, and when."

Tony launched into a rundown of how the crews would stage and attack the fires. But Kate's mind soon wandered, since Harvey and Grandpa Wayne had already given her the details.

She saw Everett leave the group of officials by the closest pumper truck, and head toward a small cluster of vehicles parked near the barn. The onlookers had lined up their trucks and cars in the south pasture, so Kate assumed these other vehicles belonged to the dignitaries at today's event.

But Mabel said Everett had promised to give a speech. Surely he wasn't leaving?

He must be getting something from his car, Kate thought. She almost looked away, turned her attention back toward Tony. But something kept her focused on Everett.

And then, she saw the truck.

It looked like the one she'd spotted up Brody's lane that afternoon she delivered pies to her neighbors. Reddish orange, but faded. An older model. It wasn't anything special, but unique enough that she remembered it well. She'd assumed it was Brody's truck, that he'd been there checking on his property, looking over the charred remains of his barn.

Kate stared at Everett, and tried to catch her breath. Because he'd just walked up to that very truck, out of the dozen or so vehicles he could have chosen, and opened the driver's side door and reached in for a stocking cap.

With the navy topper pulled down over his ears, Everett started back toward the Wildwood house. He strolled along, a contemplative smile on his face, as if lost in thought. Anyone else aware of the speech Everett was about to make would assume he was running through his talking points one last time.

But a horrified Kate now wondered if he was gloating about the fact he'd gotten away with arson. At least once, and maybe several times over.

And what was about to happen here, in this field just south of Melinda's farm, was eerily similar to all the incidents where local landowners had their properties torched and destroyed.

Decrepit buildings. No occupants. Remote locations. The places where firefighters had battled for hours in dangerous conditions, tried to keep the blazes from spreading to the nearby fields. The fires that had terrorized Kate's community for weeks, kept her up at night.

She stared at the truck again; it had to be the same one. Her hands started to shake, and she gripped her mug tighter so she wouldn't spill hot coffee all over her jeans.

Everett had rejoined the cluster of officials by the pumper truck. He was apparently sharing something amusing with Sheriff Preston, based on the grins on their faces. Everett was just one of the guys, working on a project that would change Hartland County for the better. Someone who'd graciously offered to speak so Ed and Mabel wouldn't have to face the glare of the spotlight.

Kate's initial shock turned to frustration. What could she do, what could she say?

Even if she was right about the truck, about what she saw up that farm lane weeks ago, it wasn't much to go on. The only other detail she had to offer was a guy in a ball cap and hoodie, as she'd been too far away to get a look at his face.

"Are you ready for this?" Harvey broke into her thoughts, and Kate jumped.

"Oh, sure." She took a big gulp of coffee and tried to steady her breathing. For now, she decided, playing dumb was her best chance to get some information out of Harvey.

"Who's that guy there, the one in the navy stocking cap?"

"That's Everett Whitcomb." Harvey gave a nod of admiration that made the coffee sour in Kate's stomach. "The conservation officer who's been helping our family set up the refuge. Great guy. He really knows his stuff. We couldn't have done this without him."

"I'm glad you've had someone so experienced to guide you through it." She had to work at it, but Kate kept her tone light. "It's not an easy job, I'd guess, getting people to put a priority on something like that when they'd rather keep their land as pasture or plant it to crops."

"Well, he knows how to talk to people, get them to see

how important it is." Harvey's complete confidence in Everett made Kate cringe. "He's always cared about conservation, but he told us the full importance of it really hit home a few years ago. See, his family once owned all that land on the southwest edge of Eagle River, where they put in the new high school and middle school and that housing development."

Up by the Wildwoods' former home, Tony rambled toward the end of his remarks. But Kate couldn't focus on anything he was saying.

"Well, some shirttail cousins owned that land by then," Harvey went on. "There was a swath of virgin prairie in the middle of those fields. Rare plants, I guess. Native habitat for the animals. Something his ancestors had the foresight to leave alone even as they farmed the acres around it."

Everett and some other family members fought hard to keep the natural area from being sold, Harvey whispered to Kate. Everett's aging parents even offered to buy those acres outright and turn them over to the county.

But in the end, money was thicker than blood. Developers had offered an astounding price for the land, and they had all the leverage they needed. Eagle River's leaders were eager to build new schools and offer housing that could attract additional residents to their tiny community. The cousins took the cash and retired to Florida.

"It all went under." Harvey's face turned grim as Everett, flashing a confident smile, made his way toward Tony. The crowd cheered as the men shook hands.

"They cut the trees down," Harvey muttered under his breath. "Burned the prairie, brought in the bulldozers. And for what? So they could stuff a few more cookie-cutter houses into that development. What a waste."

That was it, then. Everett's bitterness had morphed into an outsized sense of self-righteousness. Looking through his emotional lens, Kate easily saw how all the arson sites fit both his personal and professional goals.

The houses were vacant, the leftover buildings had little value and were expensive to tear down. Everett had convinced himself he was just helping the process along. If someone like Brody got a little insurance payout in the end, good for them. But most importantly, once the structures were razed and removed, the wildlife and natural vegetation would easily take over.

If the county was called in to provide native plants to rejuvenate these parcels, and offer suggestions on how to attract wildlife, even better. Everett's skills would be in demand as he worked with people like Ed and Mabel to protect nature and establish legacies for future generations.

The very opportunity his own relatives had ripped out of his hands.

"And now," Tony said brightly, "let's hear from Everett Whitcomb, the Hartland County conservation officer who's been such an enthusiastic supporter of this project."

More cheers from the crowd. Kate saw Mabel give Everett a grateful smile as he took the microphone from Tony.

"It's a beautiful day, folks!" Everett's wide grin was quickly reflected back at him from many in the crowd. "But it's more than the weather that has me in such high spirits. This is a milestone moment in the long, proud history of Hartland County, of which the Watson family's ancestors have been a part of for over a hundred years."

Flattery and a big smile, Kate thought. *Works every time.*

Four firefighters stepped forward, gas cans in hand. Three of them went inside the house, and the other started to soak one front corner. In mere seconds, the sharp tang of diesel fuel filled the air.

Kate hoped she was wrong about Everett. It was hard to juxtapose the positive interaction she'd had with him at the nature preserve, and the caring community member on display this morning, with her suspicions about the arsonist in their midst. But Everett's eyes were overly bright and, as he continued his remarks, Kate noticed an undercurrent of rage had crept into his voice. She glanced around. If anyone else had picked up on this subtle change in tone, it didn't show on their faces.

"Too many of these sites have been lost to us over time." Everett held up one hand and squeezed it into an angry fist. "It's time we stand up for nature, do what's right! And it's up to us, all of us, to make it happen."

That final sentiment brought a rousing round of applause. Tony clapped Everett on the back before he reached for the microphone.

Harvey beamed with pride. Grandpa Wayne nodded in agreement. Kate gripped her coffee mug tight and looked away.

"He's so well-spoken," one nearby woman gushed to her friend. "So smart."

"And handsome," the other said. "He should run for public office."

"Let's get this show on the road!" Tony's grin brought more cheers and even a few whistles from the crowd. "We're going to light this thing now, so make sure to remain behind the rope."

Two firefighters went back into the house. Kate caught a glimpse of flames behind them when they returned to the yard, and it took only seconds for the first plumes of thick smoke to follow them out of the open doorway.

Kate was light-headed, and not just from the diesel fumes. Everett had fooled everyone. His fellow county employees, the community, and Kate herself.

People had assumed some troubled person was at fault. A young man with few opportunities in life, or maybe a hotheaded older guy filled with bitterness. Perhaps a scorned woman angry about losing her home, or a firefighter obsessed with flames. Or, at the very least, some outsider who cared as little for the residents of this rural community as they did for the structures they'd destroyed.

But while mean-spirited gossip spread through the county and residents pointed fingers at their neighbors, a respected, well-educated person was hard at work in the dark. Kate thought again of the list Corey had told her about, and suspected Everett had one, too. Just how many abandoned homesteads were on it?

And then she thought of her little farm, and the natural area in her pasture. No, surely he wouldn't have. Her place was occupied, it was nothing like those other sites. But ...

"You OK?" Harvey nudged her with an elbow. "This thing's going to spread fast once it takes hold." Even though he was in his sixties, Mabel's brother was as expectant as a little boy on Christmas morning.

"It's just the smoke." She tried for a casual shrug. "I'm fine."

But Kate was more than unnerved; she felt helpless and trapped. As everyone around her gasped at and applauded the rising flames, what she suspected weighed on her conscience. And there was nothing she could do about it, at least for now.

Except stand there and watch this crazy charade unfold, play her part of the local resident with nothing better to do than hang out in a field and watch a sad, old house go down in flames.

Tony stepped forward again. "We have one more fire to set," he told Everett. "Why don't you do the honors?"

Kate could hardly bear it. Everett eagerly took the scrap of lumber Tony offered him, and held it steady while the fire chief lit the other end.

Everett lifted his makeshift torch for everyone to see, a move that brought more cheers. Once he'd received yet-another round of appreciation from the crowd, he marched over to the old house's front corner and touched his stick to the fuel-soaked wooden siding. Snakes of flame crawled up the wall, followed the weeping trails of diesel fuel that had been splashed on the siding just minutes before, and hungrily consumed the rotten clapboards as they slithered toward the kitchen's roof.

Kate felt like she was stuck in some sort of nightmare. The kind where there was no logic and, no matter how scared you felt, it seemed impossible to wake up and escape. Because here, right in front of her, was a sickening replay of exactly how Everett started the fire at the Flood Creek site.

Yet only a handful of firefighters paid any attention to the flames. The rest remained among their trucks, chugging water and coffee as they waited for the fires to gain in size and strength. It wasn't long before two of the decrepit house's still-intact windows exploded from the heat and pressure building inside, which brought a fresh round of whistles and cheers from the restless crowd.

But not everyone was so jubilant. Tears filled Kate's eyes when she spotted the Wildwoods' son slumped against the ancient oak tree on the side of the driveway, one hand over his face and his wife's arm around his shoulders.

The rundown house was now like a homecoming bonfire on steroids, and the energy of the crowd intensified with the blaze. The flames doubled, then tripled. The air on Kate's face went from cool to warm to nearly hot. People instinctively stepped back, but no one could pull their gaze away from the violent destruction on display.

Including Everett. He'd doused his stick in the bucket of water at his feet, but hadn't retreated to the cluster of local officials by the pumper truck. He studied the flames with an experienced eye; he lingered closer to the house than he should.

And the smirk on his face made Kate's skin crawl.

No one else seemed to notice. And then, she spotted Marshal Werner. While Everett watched the flames, the marshal was watching him.

The worn-down house made a sudden noise, somewhere between a pop and a groan, and hungry flames roared out of the shattered window in its front gable.

"We're full on!" Tony shouted. "Everyone, move in!"

"Look at that!" Harvey whistled. "Never seen the likes of it. Amazing, huh?"

Kate couldn't answer. She turned away and started to walk. She wasn't sure where she was headed, and she didn't care; anywhere that was far from the smoke and the flames and the spectacle. She got a closer look at Everett's truck as she passed the pack of officials' vehicles, and almost broke into a run as she tried to put behind her what she'd seen, what she'd realized just minutes ago.

One of the old sheds loomed before her, and she rounded its corner with relief and leaned against its sloping wall for support. As her mind raced on, Kate stared out over a rolling, golden carpet of harvested fields under a cloudless, brilliantly blue sky.

It was a beautiful day, just like Everett had said. But there was something sinister here at this abandoned farm that made Kate shiver.

Even from this far away, she could hear the cheers of the crowd and smell the smoke. She put her hands on her knees and leaned over, tried to catch her breath and calm her nerves.

The sudden sensation of a hand on her arm made her jump. It was Deputy Collins.

"Kate!" Steve called over the roar of the blaze and the shouts of the firefighters. "What is it? Did you get too much smoke? Can I help?"

"Yes." The tears started to flow, and she couldn't stop them. Because along with the shock and the fear, Kate suddenly felt a wave of relief.

"Yes, you can," she gasped. "Go get the marshal. I need to talk to him."

❋ 23 ❋

Hazel whined with anticipation as Kate guided her to the post office's back entrance.

"I know, you're excited to be on duty today." The vestibule was quiet, but Kate could hear her co-workers chatting and laughing on the other side of the second door. "And from what I hear, you'll be the guest of honor at this very-early-morning party."

A round of applause greeted Kate and Hazel as they came into the back room, and Kate was suddenly filled with joy and gratitude. Everyone was there; including Randy, even though Wednesday was his regular day off.

"There she is!" Roberta cooed to Hazel. "It feels like forever since we've seen you, pretty girl."

"It's only been, what, a few weeks?" But Jack was laughing, and he was next in line to give Hazel a pet. "You scared off a bad guy a while back, didn't you?"

"Kate scared him off, too, I bet," Allison beamed with pride. "But on a different day."

"Oh, I don't think I did." Kate shook her head. "I doubt Everett saw me at the end of Brody's lane, snooping around."

"She's probably right." Jared reached into the box of pastries on the counter and handed Kate a cherry turnover smothered in cream cheese icing. "Everett was too busy doing some snooping of his own. By the way, Eloise sends her regards along with the snacks. She and Henry were happy to feed us firefighters all those mornings, but it was about to wear them out."

"I feel the same." Bev helped herself to a chocolate-glazed donut, then gestured at Jack to pick what he wanted. "Thank goodness it's over."

"Well, it should be," Randy said around a mouthful of blueberry muffin. "That's the word that's going around, and I'm inclined to believe it's true."

* * *

While Deputy Collins stood by to offer moral support, Kate told Marshal Werner what she suspected about Everett. The state investigator had been silent for a moment, then simply thanked her for speaking up and asked her not to share her observations with anyone else for the time being.

A look that Kate couldn't quite read passed between Marshal Werner and Deputy Collins before the state investigator retraced his steps. Steve went next.

But before he turned away, he gave Kate a small smile and told her she'd done the right thing. Oh, and to give him a few minutes before she started toward the fire so they didn't draw attention to themselves.

Kate wasn't sure what she expected to happen next, but nothing did. Deputy Collins rejoined his wife and their friends, and Marshal Werner blended back into the crowd. Everett continued to watch the flames, sip coffee and chat with local officials.

Grandpa Wayne asked Kate if she was all right, of course, but took her at her word when she repeated her excuse about being bothered by the smoke.

With everyone around her mesmerized by the shooting flames and busy debating how long it would take for the house to collapse, no one noticed how quiet Kate had become.

When an emotional Melinda came by a few minutes later and said she was ready to go, that the destruction of her former neighbors' home was more than she could bear, Kate had been eager to leave.

Sheriff Preston called her late that afternoon to take her formal statement. While her observations weren't enough to charge Everett with any crimes, the sheriff said, they could be crucial to moving the arson cases forward. Oh, and by the way, please don't tell anyone else what you saw.

Everyone always said it was impossible to keep a secret in Eagle River. Kate kept hers, but word started to spread Sunday afternoon that Everett had been brought in for questioning regarding the arson cases.

And, following a few hours of interrogation, he'd been let go for lack of evidence. But only after Sheriff Preston and Marshal Werner made it very clear they suspected him of arson, several times over, and he was going to be watched closely from now on.

As fellow public employees, they reminded Everett that their occupations came with generous benefits packages and retirement programs that bested anything offered by the private sector.

It'd be a shame, really, to lose one's job, not to mention your financial security, over something like this. Wasn't it bad enough that gossip was already spreading about his alleged involvement in the arson cases?

Trust would be a problem, going forward. And not just with folks like the Bauers and the Watsons, who'd wanted nothing more than to help their community. They needed to put this terrifying series of events behind them, as did everyone else in the area.

A career change, or at the very least a conservation post in another county, would be a good idea.

While the marshal and the sheriff didn't have what they needed to charge Everett, there were several things that made them suspect the conservation officer. His claims regarding his whereabouts on the nights of the fires were questionable, yet they were difficult to disprove. Since his divorce, Everett had been renting a remote farmhouse over by Swanton, so his nocturnal comings and goings weren't easy for anyone to verify.

He had an alibi for the afternoon Kate spotted his truck up Brody's lane, but it wasn't a very good one. Even so, officials couldn't prove he'd ever been there.

While many landowners had cameras on their rural properties these days, none of the arson sites were under surveillance. With nothing of value remaining, it wasn't worth the expense and hassle to set up security systems on these parcels.

Kate didn't know for sure, but Harvey couldn't have been the only local resident familiar with Everett's family history. That made her wonder if Sheriff Preston and Marshal Werner had Everett on their list of potential suspects for some time, but no good justification for bringing him in for questioning.

She knew the Bauers had declined to speak at the controlled burn. But had Everett really offered to take their place, as Mabel was told, or had somebody casually mentioned to him how important it was for someone to make a few public remarks?

Everett had an oversized ego to match his self-righteousness. Perhaps the sheriff and the state investigator had set a trap for the conservation officer that they knew he couldn't resist.

Crafted a plan to hand Everett a microphone, as well as a flaming torch, in front of a crowd and see what he would do, what he would say, that might hint at his potential guilt.

Kate waited to hear tidbits about that part of the situation, expected there to be hot gossip tied to Everett's starring role in the fiery destruction of the old Wildwood farm. But ... nothing.

She knew Marshall Werner to be a man of few words, and ones that were carefully chosen. The same could be said about Sheriff Preston. And after a few days, Kate decided the wall of silence around that part of the investigation spoke for itself.

* * *

"It's a real shame they couldn't pin those fires on Everett," Randy said bitterly, then soothed his outrage with a hearty bite from his muffin. "You know damn well he set them. All those weeks of terrorizing everyone, the hours spent fighting the flames. What a waste."

Roberta sighed. "Winter will be here before you know it. How many of these poor people will have to wait until spring to get the debris cleared?" Then she pointed at Jack.

"I'm sure I'll never hear the end of this, but I'll admit it: You were right to go up to the Flood Creek house that morning and check it out."

"Hah!" Jack clapped his hands with glee. "Everyone, take note!" Then he shook his head in defeat. "If it hadn't rained the night before, maybe they could have gotten what they needed to nail Everett for what he did."

Jack's hunch that something wasn't right had paid off, at least in one way. The sheriff's deputies and the fire marshal had found a partial fingerprint on the side of the Flood Creek house just hours after Jack called in his discovery.

"Fingerprints are fragile," Kate reminded Jack. "They said the fact that it was down along the foundation, under that evergreen bush, kind of protected it from the rain. But it wasn't clear enough that they could use it."

"Which is a shame," Allison said. "Everett's fingerprints are on file somewhere, like most other public employees." She gestured at her fellow carriers with her coffee cup. "It's tough, though. Because that's the only one they found, anywhere."

Jared's usual grin settled into a scowl. "Everett's not stupid. In fact, he's wily as a fox to pull off what he did. I'd like all those hours and nights back, and so would the rest of the crews." He shrugged in defeat. "I guess he must have worn gloves everywhere else."

"Might have had them on at Flood Creek, too," Bev suggested. "But for whatever reason, he took them off at some point."

"That's the one that never really burned," Jack reminded the group. "He started it, but didn't finish it. I'd give good money to find out exactly what happened that night."

Randy pounded one palm on the metal counter. "And something did, you know it! Otherwise, that old place would've come down, just like the rest."

Kate sipped her coffee and said nothing. Given what she experienced that hair-raising night up at Flood Creek with Hazel and Corey, she found it very interesting that it was the one site where Everett didn't, or couldn't, finish what he started. If that abandoned farm was haunted, as people liked to claim, perhaps Everett encountered something there that chilled him to the bone. Or at least, spooked him enough that he doused his flames and headed home.

While Kate vowed to keep that theory to herself, the fact that she and Hazel had taken part in one of the night watches was now public knowledge. Allison went into the break room, then came out with a small plastic container in her hands. One whose fresh-grilled aroma made Hazel wriggle with excitement.

"And here's a treat for our brave girl." Allison popped the lid on the diced-up hamburger patty and set the dish on the floor. Then she laughed. "Henry wasn't sure how Hazel likes her beef, so he went with medium-well, just to be safe."

"That's fine." Kate beamed as Hazel started in on her snack to a round of appreciative applause. "She's not picky."

Bev put an arm around Kate's shoulder. "Guess all that training paid off, even if she didn't make the cut to be a service dog. I just wish we had more justice to celebrate this morning. But Jeff said unless something else comes up, this is as much as we're going to get."

Not all the samples from the arson sites were back yet, but it didn't really matter. It had been obvious to Marshal Werner and Sheriff Preston that accelerants were used at all the locations, and the fires were deliberately set. There just wasn't enough evidence to tie Everett to the incidents, nothing that would hold up in court. And, as self-important as the conservation officer seemed, and how much he believed in his self-appointed mission, he wasn't about to implicate himself in a series of crimes.

"It's like Mayor Benson said," Kate reminded Bev. "It's easier to convict a murderer than an arsonist. I guess we'll have to settle for peace and quiet as our only outcome."

"And that's worth it, all on its own." Bev finished the rest of her donut and wiped her hands on a paper napkin. "Well, that hit the spot. The mail always goes through, right? I guess I'd better get started on my stacks."

Kate and the other carriers soon did the same. Hazel finished her treat, then lounged at Roberta's feet as the postmaster fired up her computer for the day's tasks.

"You know, I'm going to miss Marshal Werner," Jack admitted. "He sort of livened up the place."

Randy shook his head. "He's a good guy, but I've had enough excitement for a while. Besides, winter's coming. I bet he'll be glad to not have to drive down here all the time when the roads are rough. It's over, and that's what matters."

Kate had Mae's route that day, and her packages and letters were soon in order. Bev insisted she take the last muffin from the box as a to-go treat. After the usual potty breaks, and water and coffee fills, it was time to load Bertha and hit the road.

The sun was bright, even if there was still an etching of frost on the sidewalks and the bare-limbed trees along the back parking lot. Kate enjoyed a deep breath of the crisp air after she settled the mail case in the passenger seat, then turned to where Hazel waited patiently by the post office's back entrance.

"Time to go." She pointed toward Bertha. "You're in charge of the packages, remember?"

Hazel answered with a happy bark and, with no further urging needed from Kate, hopped into the back of the car. Kate organized her drinks, turned on the radio, and took Main Street north out of town.

At the first crossroads, she turned west. All that was ahead of them was a wide ribbon of gravel, flanked by brown grass and weeds and lined by fence rows punctuated by the occasional volunteer tree. Not much to see. But to Kate, on this early-November day when the horizon was distant and the sky so blue, the scene ahead was nothing short of beautiful.

And much later, when the sun settled in the west and the stars began to shine, Kate and her critters would be able to settle in for the night and not have to worry about what might happen in the dark hours to come.

"It's wonderful, isn't it?" Kate glanced in the rearview mirror, and saw Hazel had already settled on the seat, her head on her paws. "Well, our first stop is just down the road. Let's see if Cooper is patrolling his yard this morning. Maybe you can get out and say hello."

WHAT'S NEXT

Read on for an excerpt from "The Lane That Leads to Christmas," Book 3 in the Mailbox Mysteries series. Look for it in late 2023! Visit fremontcreekpress.com and click on the "Connect" tab to sign up for the email list. That's the best way to find out when future books will be available.

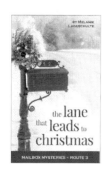

SNEAK PEEK:
THE LANE THAT LEADS TO CHRISTMAS

Late November
Rockwell Township

Kate was northeast of town today, filling in for Jack. Not long after the first snowflakes hit Bertha's windshield, she pulled over in a field drive to make sure that everything was in order for the next section of her route.

The snow wasn't going to amount to much. In fact, it was melting as soon as it touched the ground. It was likely to switch back to a cold rain, which was perfectly fine with Kate, but the few flakes dancing in the air gave her just a bit of holiday spirit. Before she pulled back out on the road, she switched Bertha's radio to a station playing seasonal songs.

This area of the county was mostly gently sloped fields, but there was a sizeable ravine up ahead where a creek crossed under a bridge. The gravel twisted and turned as it left the waterway behind, and Kate could see how this section of road would make for tricky travel in ice and snow.

The mailbox's odd angle caught her eye as soon as she rounded the first bend. The container was old and a little rusted, like so many of those along these rural roads, but still in serviceable condition.

Or at least, it must have been until recently. Its wooden post was now awkwardly askew, and Kate guessed the box had been hit by a car or a truck. A vehicle that had taken the curve too fast, and possibly with an inebriated driver behind the wheel.

The closer Kate came, the worse the situation looked. Someone had tried to secure the mailbox's warped door with a length of twine. It wasn't enough, however, and it was clear to Kate that any mail left in the box would be exposed to the elements. Not only that, but it was now impossible to pull up close enough to leave the mail without having to get out of the car.

This mailbox was too far gone; something had to be done. Kate reached for the clipboard on the passenger's seat and pawed through its stack for the form she needed. The document even had an illustration of a mailbox, and Kate's drawing ability was put to the test to note the specific problems that had to be addressed. Until they were, the carriers couldn't leave mail at this location.

It would be easiest to leave the form in the mailbox, but Kate wasn't going to do that. Roberta believed in personal service and accessibility, and Grandpa Wayne had handled such dilemmas in the same way. Kate felt it was only right to go up to the house and break the bad news in person.

Besides, there was some important mail that needed to be delivered today. A letter that looked like it might be from a collection agency, and another from the county assessor's office.

The farm lane wasn't long, at least. But from what she could see from her car, the place didn't look too promising. The house had been white once, but its paint had flaked and peeled until it was mostly gray. An older-model car rested by a slanted garage.

Kate's knock at the kitchen door was likely to be met with anger and frustration, maybe even tears. She'd been through this before, in Chicago. People wanted their mail, it was their right to have it delivered. But the feds had their rules and regulations, and everyone had to follow them to the letter.

At this struggling farm, that meant a new mailbox. And a new post, which should be set in concrete given its location along this winding road. If another reckless driver didn't take out what was left of the current box, the county snow plow just might finish it off over the winter.

Kate studied the dark skies and the worn-down house, and hesitated for a moment. She was alone, and had no way of knowing who might come to the door. She fished her pepper spray out of her purse, and deposited it in the pocket of her parka. Then she texted Roberta, told her exactly where she was and what she needed to do.

Thanks for letting me know, Roberta texted back. *I want to hear from you within fifteen minutes that you are OK. I'll start calling you if I don't.*

But Kate felt a little better once she was up by the house. The now-dormant flowerbeds had been carefully cleared in the fall, and several sassy chickens strutted about near the back porch. A medium-sized black dog hurried out from behind the barn, its tail wagging a friendly greeting.

"Just because they might be poor, that doesn't mean they're dangerous," she chided herself. The dog nosed her hand for a pet when she got out of the car, and accompanied her to the back porch.

Kate knocked, and waited. Just when she thought no one was home, she heard steps on the other side of the door. A tired-looking woman about her age opened it.

"I see you've met Champ." The woman tried for a smile, but her face was wary. It was obvious that Kate was a mail carrier. But without a parcel in her arms, it wasn't clear why she was up here by the house. They stared at each other for a few seconds, as this woman seemed too tired to ask too many questions.

Kate searched for a good opener; animals were usually a safe topic. "He's such sweet dog. Or, is it a girl?"

"Oh, he's a boy all right." That brought a grin, and a quick pet for Champ. "He likes to dig in my flowerbeds, but I'm willing to overlook it."

"I'm Kate. I see your mailbox ... needs a little help. I'm guessing you're Candace?"

The woman gave a short nod and self-consciously brushed one hand through her light-brown hair.

"I'm so sorry about this," Kate said gently, "but we can't leave anything in the box until it is repaired. You could pick up your mail in town, or ..."

"I tied it closed." Candace's mouth trembled, and it seemed like she was about to cry. "Why isn't that good enough?"

Kate explained the regulations. Candace gave a nod of defeat, then studied Kate more closely. "You look familiar, maybe. Are you from around here?"

"Yes, I went to high school in Eagle River. Kate Duncan. I moved back from Chicago earlier this year."

Candace gave her a surprised look that said, *why would anyone do that?* "Oh, yeah! I think I was a year behind you. Thompson is my maiden name."

All the pieces fell into place. "Yes, now I remember!" Kate grinned. "Haven't seen you in a long time." She stopped herself, however, before blurting out: how are you?

In high school, Candace had been so outgoing, the life of the party. But as Kate glanced around the other woman's narrow shoulders and took in the worn kitchen, with its grumbling refrigerator and scuffed linoleum, she felt a mix of sympathy and guilt.

Kate had been blessed with so many opportunities in life; Candace likely couldn't say the same.

"It's really good to be back in Eagle River," Kate said instead. But the weary expression on Candace's face said that she maybe didn't agree. "Especially with the holidays coming up."

That elicited only a small smile. "They come around faster every year, seems like." Candace shook her head. "I don't know how we'll manage, but ..."

Somewhere inside the house, a baby started to cry.

"Jenny, honey, please see what Martin needs," Candace called over her shoulder. "Give him the rest of the bottle, maybe." She turned back to Kate. "Sorry. Now, what do I need to do?"

Candace had plenty on her plate, that was obvious. A scolding from the federal government was the last thing she needed.

"Give this form a look, when you get a second." Kate casually wrapped it around the ominous-looking letters before she handed the bundle to Candace, as a young girl with curious eyes had just wandered into the kitchen. "It explains everything. And please," she added with a smile, "call the post office if you have any questions. We'd be happy to help."

Candace only nodded, then softly closed the door. Kate turned away and took another look around this forlorn farm yard, and suspected the holidays wouldn't exactly be merry here this year.

"You're a good boy," she told Champ as she gave him another pet, then slipped him a few doggie treats from the pouch she kept in her parka pocket.

All is well, she texted to Roberta as soon as she was back in the car.

But that wasn't quite true, Kate decided.

I'm fine, at least, she added. *But I think these people need more than a mailbox.*

*Look for "The Lane That Leads to Christmas,"
Book 3 in the Mailbox Mysteries series, in late 2023.
Paperbacks, hardcovers and large-print paperbacks
will be available, along with Kindle editions.*

ABOUT THE BOOKS

*Don't miss any of the titles
in these heartwarming rural fiction series*

THE GROWING SEASON SERIES

Melinda is at a crossroads when the "for rent" sign beckons her down a dusty gravel lane. Facing forty, single and downsized from her stellar career at a big-city ad agency, she's struggling to start over when a phone call brings her home to Iowa.

She moves to the country, takes on a rundown farm and its headstrong animals, and lands behind the counter of her family's hardware store in the community of Prosper, whose motto is "The Great Little Town That Didn't." And just like the sprawling garden she tends under the summer sun, Melinda begins to thrive. But when storm clouds arrive on her horizon, can she hold on to the new life she's worked so hard to create?

Filled with memorable characters, from a big-hearted farm dog to the weather-obsessed owner of the local co-op, "Growing Season" celebrates the twists and turns of small-town life. Discover the heartwarming series that's filled with new friends, fresh starts and second chances.

**FOR DETAILS ON ALL THE TITLES
VISIT FREMONTCREEKPRESS.COM**

THE MAILBOX MYSTERIES SERIES

It's been a rough year for Kate Duncan, both on and off the job. Being a mail carrier puts her in close proximity to her customers, with consequences that can't always be foreseen. So when a position opens at her hometown post office, she decides to leave Chicago in her rearview mirror.

Kate and her cat settle into a charming apartment above Eagle River's historic Main Street, but she dreams of a different home to call her own. And as she drives the back roads around Eagle River, Kate begins to take a personal interest in the people on her route.

So when an elderly resident goes missing, she feels compelled to help track him down. It's a quest marked not by miles of gravel, but matters of the heart: friendship, family, and the small connections that add up to a well-lived life.

A TIN TRAIN CHRISTMAS

The toy train was everything two boys could want: colorful, shiny, and the perfect vehicle for their imaginations. But was it meant to be theirs? Revisit Horace's childhood for this special holiday short story inspired by the "Growing Season" series!

Made in the USA
Monee, IL
08 April 2023

31562793R00171